Chris Culver grew up in southern Indiana. He moved to Arkansas when his wife was offered a faculty position at a [s]mall university there, and in between teaching [philoso]phy classes, wrote *The Abbey*, which spent nine [weeks] on the *New York Times* bestseller list. He and his [wife n]ow live near St Louis, Missouri, where Chris is [writi]ng on another Ash Rashid novel.

THE ABBEY
CHRIS CULVER

sphere

SPHERE

First published in the United States as an ebook in 2011
First published in Great Britain as an ebook in 2011
This paperback edition published in 2012 by Sphere

Copyright © 2011 Chris Culver

The moral right of the author has been asserted.

*All characters and events in this publication, other than those
clearly in the public domain, are fictitious and any resemblance
to real persons, living or dead, is purely coincidental.*

A CIP catalogue record for this book
is available from the British Library.

ISBN 978-0-7515-4911-9

Typeset in Adobe Garamond by Palimpsest Book Production Limited,
Falkirk, Stirlingshire
Printed and bound in Great Britain by Clays Ltd, St Ives plc

Papers used by Sphere are from well-managed forests
and other responsible sources.

MIX
Paper from
responsible sources
FSC
www.fsc.org
FSC® C104740

Sphere
An imprint of

Little, Brown Book Group
100 Victoria Embankment
London EC4Y 0DY

An Hachette UK Company

www.littlebrown.co.uk

To my wife – thanks for putting up with me.

Chapter 1

I hated doing next of kin notifications. Most people guessed why I was there as soon as they opened the door. They put on airs of fortitude and strength, but almost all fell apart in front of me. I could see it in their eyes. They looked at me and knew something, too. I'd go home afterwards as if nothing was wrong. I might hug my family a little tighter than usual, but the world would go on for me without much of a hiccup. Most hated me for what I had to do, and I couldn't blame them. My Islamic faith told me that drinking to escape their stares was an abomination in the sight of God, but I didn't care as long as it helped me sleep without dreams.

I pulled my department-issued Ford Crown Victoria to a stop beside the mailbox in front of my sister's house and took a deep breath, stilling myself as a familiar anxiety flooded over me. I knew as soon as I had volunteered for the duty that I was going to have one of those nights I'd need to forget, but it took that moment for it to become real. It tore at my gut like barbed wire.

I opened my car door. My sister and her husband lived in a four-thousand-square-foot historic home that could have comfortably housed my entire extended family. As a resident of the poorer, smaller neighborhood next door, I was glad that it didn't. My brother-in-law Nassir smiled and put his hand on my shoulder when he opened the front door, but stiffened when I didn't return the gesture.

'What's wrong?' he asked.

'We'll talk in a moment,' I said. 'Where's Rana?'

'In the kitchen,' said Nassir, leaving his hand on my shoulder a moment longer. 'Come in.'

I walked in, and Nassir shut the door behind me. The house's first floor was typical of well-kept historic homes. The woodwork was straight and clean with a rich patina that could only come from eighty years of polishing, and the rooms were open and bright. Nassir half-led and half-pushed me down the home's main hallway to the kitchen in back. Rana was in front of a gas stove large enough to have been at home in the kitchen of a Las Vegas strip hotel. The air smelled like garlic and yeast.

'Ash,' she said, smiling at me. 'I thought you and Hannah were going out tonight.'

'We were,' I said. 'I need you both to sit at the table. We need to talk.'

Nassir and Rana did as I asked. In return, I broke their hearts as gently as I could.

Nassir and Rana had taken the news about as well as anyone could expect. They hadn't cried in front of me, but they told me they wanted to be alone. If I went home, though, I'd have to tell my wife why I canceled our wedding anniversary plans. I didn't think I had the strength or stomach for that yet. Instead, I drove to my office. It wasn't my case, but I had enough friends in my department that I had a stack of eight-by-ten photos and notes on my desk when I arrived. They made my stomach turn.

I read through the timeline quickly. The call had come in at six in the evening. The caller reported the presence of a prone female, approximately sixteen to eighteen years old, in the guest home of one of Indianapolis's most wealthy citizens. The first officer on the scene checked her pulse but found nothing. He called in a probable homicide, and that's when the gears started moving. Within half an hour, five forensic technicians were documenting the scene, and Detective Olivia Rhodes was interviewing potential witnesses.

I flipped through the photographs. Each picture was numbered and had a written description. The first few were wide-angled shots of the scene. The photographer had snapped pictures of a kitchen with light maple cabinetry and a living room with a television, lounge chairs, and pool table. A vase of calla lilies rested on the counter beside the stove. They were my niece's favorite flower; my wife and I always sent them to her on her birthday.

Rachel, my niece, was in the center of the room. Her skin was pale, indicating that her blood had already begun to pool beneath her, and her arms were pressed against her sides like a supine soldier at attention. I stared at the picture for a moment, my stomach twisting. She didn't deserve that.

I skimmed through the next few pictures. The photographer had snapped more shots of the kitchen and living room. They were helpful for orienting someone in a crime scene, but not particularly interesting to me. I stopped when the photographs started focusing on my niece. The photographer had started with wider shots of her placement and then continued by photographing her closely from her head to her feet. She had no obvious external injuries and nor could I see puddles of blood around her. That was comforting. Unfortunately, I knew without even reading the crime scene report that her body had been staged.

I turned through the stack of photos until I found one focusing on Rachel's neck. She wore a light-blue Polo shirt with an open collar. I couldn't see ligature marks on her neck, but the bottom button on her collar had been popped off, leaving a pair of strings in its place. The detective in charge might not have thought much of it, but that wasn't like Rachel. She was as meticulous about her clothes as anyone I had ever met. She wouldn't have worn that shirt until she had a new button sewn back on.

I shifted on my seat and flipped through a few more pictures until I saw one focusing on her waist. Rachel wore a denim skirt with buttons instead of a zipper on front. The buttons were misaligned, though, so the skirt would have ridden uncomfortably against her abdomen. She wouldn't have done that to herself.

I continued turning over photographs until I saw one I couldn't explain. It looked like a shot of the carpet. Puzzled, I scanned through the notes that accompanied the photographs until I found the appropriate one. The photographer had tried to capture track marks. I looked at the picture again, straining my eyes until I saw two long strips where the carpet's matte was flattened in one direction. Rachel had been dragged in there with her feet dangling behind her.

I could feel bile rise in the back of my throat.

I stared at that picture for a moment, thankful I hadn't seen it before going to my sister's house. Since I had come right from home, I hadn't been able to tell her much about her daughter's death. That was probably good.

The rest of the pictures focused on something odd, a glass vial full of a brownish-red liquid. The technician's notes said someone had found it on an end table in one of the bedrooms. It was roughly the size of a cigar, and when the technician picked it up to catalog it, the liquid inside coated the glass like cough syrup. There was pink lipstick on the rim that appeared to be a match to Rachel's.

What were you into, honey?

My desk phone rang, startling me. I glanced at my watch. It was after ten, well past my regular hours, so I doubted it was a casual phone call. I picked it up.

'Rashid,' I said. 'What can I do for you?'

'Yeah, Detective Rashid. This is Sergeant Hensley at IMPD downtown. Olivia Rhodes brought in somebody in your niece's case, and I thought I'd give you the heads up.'

I nodded. Hensley was an old school watch sergeant and had been on the force before we had civilian oversight committees or cameras in every room. When he was my age, interrogations had included rubber hoses and phone books. I envied him. Justice may not have been pretty, but shit got done.

'Suspect or witness?' I asked.

Hensley chuckled.

'Fuck if I know,' he said. 'They don't tell me anything. If you want, I could do some poking around.'

I almost snickered. Hensley was as well connected in our department as anyone alive. He probably knew exactly who Olivia brought in and why, probably before she even entered the building. He wanted a handout.

'Don't bother,' I said. 'When'd she bring him in?'

'Just walked by my desk.'

If they had just walked by the front desk, I had at least twenty minutes to get over to IMPD. While I was still officially a detective, I was on a permanent investigative assignment with the Prosecutor's Office, so I shared office space with the prosecutors about a block from the department's downtown bullpen. In another year, I'd hopefully finish law school and be done with the department completely. I still loved the work, but I could only see so many bodies before I became as broken as the victims I investigated.

'Appreciate the call, Sergeant,' I said. 'I'll be over in a few.'

I hung up before Hensley could respond and grabbed my tweed jacket. My shoulder ached dully when I twisted my arm inside. I was thirty-four and generally too young to have arthritis, but I had been shot with a hunting rifle four years earlier while serving a high-risk felony warrant. I was the lucky one; my partner had been shot in the neck and bled out before paramedics could stabilize him.

The concrete outside my building radiated pent-up

heat from earlier that day. My throat was dry and scratchy. One of my favorite bars was just a block away, and for a brief moment, I considered stopping. I decided against it, though. The station wasn't far, and I could probably find someone inside willing to give me a pick-me-up if I needed it.

I reached the building quickly. IMPD's downtown station was at least fifty years old, and it smelled musty. The front lobby was large and clad in white marble polished to a mirror shine by footsteps. A middle-aged couple clung to each other in the waiting room. They were well-dressed and looked nervous. My guess was that they were picking up their delinquent kid for his first DUI. That happened a lot. I'd see them again.

I walked to the front desk. Sergeant Hensley sat behind it, reading *Sports Illustrated*. He dropped his magazine and looked at me with green, rapacious eyes.

'You look like shit, Rashid.'

'Feel like it, too,' I said, reaching over the counter for a sign-in sheet. I scribbled my name and rank. Detective Sergeant Ashraf Rashid. I had been named after my father, although I hadn't ever met him. He had been a history professor at the American University of Cairo, but one of his students shot and killed him before I was born. Apparently that kid's family took grades seriously. The remnants of my family immigrated to the US shortly after that.

I pushed the sign-in sheet toward Hensley and pulled out my wallet. I took out two twenties and put them on top of the counter.

'I think I missed your kid's last birthday. Buy him a football for me.'

Hensley slipped the money in his pocket and smiled.

'I'm sure he'll appreciate this,' he said. 'Detective Rhodes is in interrogation room three with Robert Cutting.'

If Hensley thought that earned him another payoff, he was wrong. I thanked him and headed toward the elevators to the left of the desk.

The homicide bullpen hadn't changed much since I had left it. Unlike most regular office buildings, IMPD didn't have individual offices. At least not for peons like me. It had desks in open rooms. The administration justified the arrangement by arguing that separate offices would impede communication on sensitive investigations. In actuality, I'm pretty sure they were just too cheap to spring for the extra materials when they last renovated the building.

I weaved my way through desks and columns of file folders. The interrogation rooms were designed to be oppressive and to give a suspect the feeling that there was no escape. They were cramped, they had no windows, and the airflow inside them was carefully regulated depending on the interrogator's mood. If a suspect looked around before going in, he'd even see a well-labeled express elevator that went directly to the holding cells on the top four floors of the building.

I walked until I came to interrogation room three. The door was shut, but Detective Olivia Rhodes stood outside, cup of coffee in hand. She nodded at me when I drew close. Olivia was a good detective. I had been in homicide for six years before being transferred to the Prosecutor's Office. I spent one of those years as her partner. From what I had heard earlier, she fought to be assigned to my niece's case. I liked her.

'I thought you might be up,' she said, turning down the hallway. She opened an unmarked door beside the interrogation room and held it for me. 'Come on.'

Police interrogations have come a long way in the twelve years I've been on the force. Our station no longer had the infamous one-way mirror overlooking the inter-rogation room. Instead, we had a sophisticated set of hidden video cameras and microphones around the room. Everything was recorded from the moment a suspect walked inside to the moment he walked out. I had heard those recordings could disappear if the right person got the right incentive, but I had never taken advantage of that. It was nice to know the option was there if I needed it, though.

Olivia turned on a flat-screen monitor attached to the wall. The picture showed a kid in jeans and a blue

T-shirt. He had curly brown hair and one of his arms was handcuffed to the wall, keeping him upright. He stared at the steel table in front of him, apparently unaware that he was being filmed.

'Is this Robert Cutting?' I asked.

'He goes by Robbie,' she said. 'He's your niece's boyfriend. Was your niece's boyfriend, at least. I appreciate you doing the next of kin notification.'

'That's no problem,' I said. 'The kid have a lawyer yet?'

'Meyers,' she said. That figured. John Meyers was one of the best defense attorneys in town. 'He's on his way in.'

'Did the kid ask for him?'

Olivia shrugged.

'Sort of. Nathan Cutting called him, and Robbie agreed to use him. I think we can nail this kid, so I'm not going to push and try to talk to him before Meyers comes in.'

'What do you think you have?' I asked.

'You seen the crime scene photos?' she asked.

I nodded.

'Upper-class victim without signs of trauma or injury,' she said, slipping her hands through her blond hair and securing it in a ponytail. 'I think she overdosed and Robbie tried to cover it up.'

I shook my head.

'Rachel wasn't on drugs,' I said.

'You sure about that?' asked Olivia.

'Yeah. She's got a scholarship to play tennis at Purdue next year, and her high school tests randomly to make sure the kids aren't doping. My sister would have said something if Rachel wasn't clean.'

Olivia bit her lower lip.

'We'll see how things go, then,' she said. 'You hang around here. I'm going to wait downstairs for Meyers to show up and get this started.'

Olivia left shortly after that. I sat and waited, staring at the monitor. Robbie looked thin and awkward. Appearances could be deceiving, but I doubted he was Islamic. That wouldn't sit too well with Rana and Nassir, which might have been part of his appeal to my niece.

I leaned back in my chair, wishing I had thought to grab a cup of coffee on my way in.

Olivia returned about five minutes later with John Meyers in tow. Meyers looked as if he was in his fifties. He wore a lustrous blue suit and carried a soft leather bag over one shoulder. He sat at the table in the inter-rogation room beside his client while Olivia sat across with a file folder in front of her. The microphones inside were sensitive enough that I could hear the clatter of the metal buckles on Meyers' bag strike the steel table.

'Okay, so why don't we get this started,' said Olivia. 'For the record, it's eleven in the evening on August nineteenth, and this is Detective Olivia Rhodes interviewing Robbie Cutting. Sitting in on this interview is Mr Cutting's lawyer, John Meyers. Is that correct?'

Robbie mumbled 'Yes,' but didn't meet Olivia's gaze. I took a closer look at him then. He had bags under his eyes, and he swayed as if he were being buffeted by wind. He looked lost.

'Good,' said Olivia. 'Right now, this is an information-gathering interview. I'm trying to figure out what happened. You're not under arrest, but I can use what you tell me here in court. Just to be clear, you don't have to say anything, and you're free to leave at any time. Do you understand these rights, Mr Cutting?'

Robbie looked up, hope in his eyes.

'Does that mean I can go?'

Meyers reached over and squeezed his client's shoulder.

'We can leave now, but we should answer Detective Rhodes' questions first,' he said. 'The sooner we get the questions out of the way, the sooner you and your parents get your lives back on track. Okay?'

Robbie nodded for Olivia to continue. She smiled at him.

'Tell me about yourself. You're in high school?'

'I'm a senior, but I take mostly college classes.'

Robbie's voice was so soft that even that short answer

13

seemed labored. I shifted, unsure what to make of his apparent anguish.

'Any thought about where you're going to college yet?'

'Purdue. With Rachel.'

Olivia and Robbie went back and forth for a while. His shoulders relaxed and his answers became more verbose the longer Olivia questioned him. She was a good interviewer. She established rapport and common ground before diving into her questions. More than that, she listened sympathetically to Robbie's answers. If I didn't know her better, I would have thought she actually cared about him.

'Okay,' said Olivia after a few minutes of conversation. 'What was your relationship to the victim?'

Robbie looked down.

'She was my girlfriend. I've been with her for about two years.'

I paused for a second. My sister hadn't mentioned Rachel had a steady boyfriend. I doubted she knew, making me wonder what else Rachel had been hiding.

'What can you tell us about her death?' asked Olivia. I leaned forward, resting my elbows on my knees.

'Rachel came over at four this afternoon while my Mom and Dad played golf. She's not very good at math, so I was tutoring her. We did that for a while and then we played a video game.'

That at least sounded like my niece. She played with

14

my family's Nintendo Wii more than my daughter did.

'Okay,' said Olivia, nodding. 'What happened after you guys played a game?'

Robbie looked down again.

'Rachel got sick in the bathroom. I don't know what happened. Then she died.'

'So she puked and then she died. And you have no idea why.'

Robbie didn't answer, so Olivia opened the file folder in front of her and began to pull out pictures. They were probably the originals of which I had copies. She laid them in an array in front of Robbie. His lower lip quivered, and his lawyer put a hand on his shoulder.

'I think we're done here,' said Meyers. 'If you have any need to question my client further, I expect you to call me at my office.'

Meyers stood, but Robbie didn't move.

Olivia pressed one picture under Robbie's gaze. It was a headshot of my niece. Her eyes were closed, and rigor had contracted her face into a grimace.

'I bet she was a pretty girl,' said Olivia. 'At one time.'

'She is pretty,' said Robbie, a tear streaming down his cheek. 'I loved her.'

'This interview is over,' said Meyers, his voice strained. 'Get these cuffs off my client. Unless Robbie is under arrest, we're leaving.'

Robbie still didn't move. Meyers said the interview

15

was over, but it wasn't his call. If his client didn't want to take advice, there was no reason for Olivia to stop.

'Look at her, Robbie,' said Olivia, tapping the picture she had slid toward Robbie. 'If you don't tell us what happened, we're going to cut her open, we're going to photograph her, and then we're going to put her on display. Is that how you want to remember her?'

Robbie didn't say anything, but another tear slid down his cheek. Olivia continued.

'We haven't found the girl's underwear, and I know you redressed her. If you don't tell us what happened, this girl you supposedly loved will be forever known as the bimbo who died with her pants down in your bedroom. Is that what you want?'

I winced. I'm not a prude and nor am I naive. Rachel was seventeen and had apparently been dating the same boy for two years. Of course they were having sex. Rana wouldn't see it like that, though. Hopefully we'd be able to keep that detail out of the papers.

'Don't say anything, Robbie,' said Meyers. 'Let me handle this.'

For a moment, I thought Robbie was going to take his lawyer's advice, but then his lips started moving. No sound came out for a few seconds.

'She wasn't supposed to die,' he said. His voice was so soft I almost didn't hear it above the ambient room noise.

'No, I'm sure she wasn't,' said Olivia, matching Robbie's voice. Meyers rubbed his brow, his eyes closed. Olivia ignored him. 'What happened? Did you have some kind of accident?'

Robbie closed his eyes, his lips moving before he spoke. 'Rachel was a Sanguinarian.'

'I'm sorry?' asked Olivia.

'She drank blood. She drank part of a vial of blood. That's when she started puking. Then she died.'

Robbie didn't say anything after that. I took a deep breath. As a detective, I'd been to more death scenes than I cared to remember, thirty-four of which had turned into criminal homicide investigations. Even with all that experience, this was my first vampire. I doubted Hallmark made cards to commemorate the occasion.

'Okay,' said Olivia. 'Let's start at the beginning and go from there.'

Chapter 2

Olivia and Robbie went back and forth for the next two hours. Robbie admitted redressing and dragging Rachel from the bathroom after she died, but he claimed he wasn't trying to cover anything up. He just didn't want his father to see her naked. Bottom line, he denied killing my niece or supplying her drugs, and I believed him. When a suspect lies, he usually pauses every few seconds or asks his interviewer to repeat questions, giving him time to think. Robbie never did. He was smooth, and he never stumbled. But that left me unsure what to think. Teenage girls don't die without cause.

Even though I was confused, Robbie hadn't wasted our time. He claimed he and Rachel had purchased the blood from a club in Plainfield, a suburb west of town. The blood was supposed to have some sort of anti-coagulant in it that kept it from spoiling. I wasn't a blood expert, so that was possible, but my guess was that it had something else in it, too. Our lab would find out for sure, though.

I was still in the watch room when Olivia dismissed Robbie. She joined me a few minutes later, carrying a cup of coffee in each hand and yawning. She handed me a cup.

'You should head home,' she said. 'It's late.'

I nodded, taking a sip of the coffee and wishing I hadn't as soon as it touched my tongue. It tasted like it had been sitting around for a while.

'Coffee hasn't changed since I was last here,' I said, glancing at the cup. 'I think I might have made this a couple of years ago.'

'Probably close,' said Olivia, sipping hers. 'I've got an autopsy scheduled for tomorrow afternoon. We'll know more then.'

I put my cup on a table. 'Rachel needs to be buried as soon as possible afterwards, preferably right afterwards. It's our custom.'

Olivia nodded. 'I'll tell Dr Rodriguez. We'll do what we can.'

I thanked her before heading to the parking garage. I was in my car at ten after one in the morning and in my driveway fifteen minutes after that. The lights were off in the house, but I saw the flicker of a television in the front room, which meant my wife had probably fallen asleep on the couch waiting for me.

I didn't go inside immediately. Instead, I closed my eyes and allowed myself to sink into my cruiser's seat. It had been a long day. I reached to my glove box and pulled out a pint of bourbon. I took two long pulls. The liquid burned down my throat and into my stomach. I closed my eyes and stayed like that for a few minutes, watching the colors and shapes swirl behind my eyelids, waiting for the liquor to hit me. I took another long drink before capping the bottle and sticking it back in my glove box.

A realtor would say my house had charm; that meant it had plumbing and electric systems that predated Roosevelt's tenure as president. It had nice woodwork, though, and it was big enough for my family. More than that, I was a part-time law student, so the house was all my wife and I could afford until I graduated.

I slipped through the side door that led to our kitchen and immediately went by the hall bathroom. I rinsed with a generic green mouthwash to cover the smell of liquor on my breath before going to the living room. My wife, Hannah, was asleep on the couch. I muted the already low sound on the television and put my hand on her shoulder, gently waking her up.

'Hey,' she said, blinking several times. 'You back for the night?'

'Yep,' I said. 'Is the munchkin asleep?'

Hannah yawned and nodded. Neither of us said anything for a moment.

'You smell like mouthwash,' she said.

I looked away from her.

'It's been a long night,' I said. 'You ready for bed?'

'Yeah,' she said. 'What was the emergency?'

I kept my eyes on the floor.

'We'll talk tomorrow morning,' I said. 'I'm going to say goodnight to Megan, so I'll meet you in bed in a moment.'

I followed my wife halfway down the hall but stopped outside my little girl's room. She was so small that her legs barely made it halfway down her bed, and her brown hair was spread out on her pillow like a halo. A plastic night-light by the door created stuffed-animal-shaped shadows along the wall. She looked like her cousin. I swallowed the lump in my throat, staying in the doorway so I wouldn't wake her up.

The floor creaked as I turned to leave, and Megan's eyes fluttered open.

'*Baba*,' she said, rubbing her eyes. She put her arms out towards me. She was so sleep addled she probably wouldn't remember it in the morning, but I tiptoed in and kissed her forehead as she gave me a hug.

'Hi, pumpkin,' I said, laying her back on the bed. 'Try to go back to sleep.'

'*Ummi* says you were catching bad guys tonight,' she said.

'I was, but I'm home now.'

She yawned.

'I want to catch bad guys, too,' she said.

'Some day, honey,' I said. I pulled her blanket up so it would cover her chest. She folded her arms on top. 'Try to get back to sleep now.'

'If I helped you catch bad guys, would I see you every day?'

I kissed her forehead again.

'I'll try to be home more often, honey.'

'Good,' she said, squirming. 'Can you stay here for a while? I think there are monsters out there.'

'Sure,' I said, sitting beside her bed and knowing full well that there were monsters out there. 'I'll be right here.'

I intended to sit with Megan until she fell asleep, but I must have fallen asleep myself because Hannah woke me up at around seven the next morning. Megan was still out, so we let her sleep and went to the kitchen. Hannah poured me a cup of coffee and sat across from me at the breakfast table. Since we had a moment, I told her about Rachel. Hannah took it stoically; it was her way. While we were talking about what to tell Megan, she walked in the room. We did our best to explain what had happened. She didn't understand, but she would eventually.

Hannah called my sister at shortly before eight and started making arrangements. When a Muslim dies, a couple of things have to happen. The deceased has to be ritually washed at least three times. Rana, Hannah, and some of the older women in our community would do that. They'd also comb her hair and put perfume on her. After that, they'd cover Rachel with three white sheets, and we'd bury her on her side facing Mecca. Since we don't embalm our dead, everything had to happen as soon as possible.

Once Hannah got off the phone, I called my boss and said I wouldn't be in that day. She knew the situation, so she didn't question it.

It was a little after the prescribed time, but Hannah, Megan, and I had dawn prayers as a family, but I wasn't really into it. I rarely was. I called Olivia an hour later on the phone in my home office. I heard a low murmur in the background when she picked up, and I could make out the occasional clink of glass against glass as dishes banged together.

'Olivia, it's Ash,' I said. 'Sounds like you're in a soup kitchen.'

'The Acropolis,' she said. That explained the noise. The Acropolis was a Greek diner near the County Courthouse downtown. It served pancakes as big as hubcaps and was a popular spot for lawyers and cops alike. 'You had breakfast yet?'

'No, but I can't eat there anyway,' I said. 'They fry their pancakes and bacon on the same griddle. How'd things go after I left?'

Olivia grunted, or made an approximate feminine version of a grunt.

'Not as well as I had hoped,' she said. I leaned back in my heavy oak chair. It creaked in that satisfying way only antiques can. 'We took a drug dog through Robbie Cutting's house, but we couldn't find a damn thing.'

That was disheartening. Our drug dogs were pretty good. A guy I know on the K9 unit took one to a local high school a couple of weeks back. His dog was able to find marijuana seeds wedged in the back seat of a kid's car. The kid had smoked the pot weeks earlier, but he still got caught. If there had been drugs at Robbie's house, the dog would have found them.

'What are you up to now?' I asked.

'I plan to finish my hash browns if you let me,' she said. 'After that, I'm going home to take a nap because I've been up all night. I got Rachel's autopsy bumped to noon, so she'll be released to your family by two or three.'

'Thank you,' I said. 'My sister will appreciate that. You think this case will go anywhere?'

Olivia grunted again.

'I don't know if it's even a criminal homicide,' she said. 'I'll find out more and let you know.'

'Please do,' I said. 'Kids don't just die. I want to find out what happened.'

'Me, too,' said Olivia. Before hanging up, she told me to tell Rana and Nassir that she would do her best for their daughter. I told her I would.

Hannah, Megan, and I spent the rest of the day with my sister and her husband. Nearly every family from our mosque came by. It was a long day, but true to Olivia's word, the Coroner's office released Rachel to us by two. She was prepped and ready to be buried by four. By five, the ceremony was over and my wife and I were driving home, too shell-shocked by the whole experience to talk.

The next day was Sunday, and I was back at work. Since I was with the Prosecutor's Office, most of my assignments were about as entertaining as watching CSPAN. That day was no exception. My boss asked me to babysit a pair of crackheads who were scheduled to testify against their dealer on Monday morning. My job was to keep them sober and out of jail. Unfortunately, that meant I had to watch cartoons with them for eight hours straight in a low-budget hotel by the airport. By the time my shift ended, my mind was jellified.

On my way home, I went by a sports bar and had a beer with a bourbon chaser. I probably would have had a few more if my wife wasn't expecting me. Olivia called as I finished my drinks.

'Ash,' she said. She paused. 'Are you in a bar?'

Somebody leaned against the counter beside me and bellowed for a Budweiser.

'Yeah,' I said, clearing my throat. 'I'm in a bar.'

Olivia paused again.

'I didn't think Muslims could drink.'

'If God didn't want me to drink, he wouldn't let children die,' I said, laying a ten on the bar and motioning at it to the bartender. He nodded, and I stepped through the crowd. Technically, Olivia was right. Alcohol is forbidden for non-medicinal purposes. I figured that since I was self-medicating, though, my use was justified. Two men were smoking outside the bar's front entrance, so I went to my car and shut the door. 'What's going on?'

'I thought I'd call to give you a heads up about a few things,' she said. 'I haven't got autopsy results from your niece yet, but we're operating under the assumption that her death is a criminal homicide. I'm going to talk to some of her friends at school tomorrow, and I want you to be there. I think they'd be more willing to talk to you than to me.'

''Cause I'm a man?' I asked, unsure what she was getting at.

'Because you're a Muslim,' she said. 'And I figure most of her friends are, too.'

'I wouldn't worry about that too much. Rachel was

26

about as pious as I am, and I'm at a bar,' I said. 'I doubt she has many Islamic friends, but if you still want a second body there, I can get the morning off.'

Olivia paused for a moment, presumably rethinking her invitation.

'No, I'll still take you,' she said, finally. 'How about if I swing by your place at nine?'

'That's fine. I've got class at one, but that should give us time.'

Olivia agreed that we'd be done by one and hung up. I drove home. Hannah usually kisses me as soon as I walk through the door, so I told her that I had onions with lunch so she wouldn't. I rinsed with mouthwash in the bathroom and then called Rana and Nassir from my office.

It was one day after their daughter was buried, but they were holding up well. Indianapolis doesn't have a large Islamic community, but we're close. Two families from the mosque had brought over dinner, and I suspected Rana and Nassir already had a freezer full of casseroles. I asked if they wanted me to come over, but they said they were fine.

My family had dusk prayers and then we ate dinner. After that, we watched Animal Planet until Megan went to bed. Since I had a class the next day, I studied for about an hour. Realistically, I needed another two hours to be fully prepared, but after the past few days, I was dead to the world. I'd have to wing it. Hannah and I went to bed at about ten.

The next morning came early when a pair of sticky hands shook me awake. I don't know how my daughter always had sticky hands, but somehow she managed it.

'*Baba, Baba!*'

My eyes fluttered open to see Megan's straight brown hair and brown eyes. The blinds were still drawn, but it was dark enough outside that I knew it was before sunrise. I glanced at the alarm clock. A little after six. My daughter beamed at me, as if proud to wake her father up before any sane man should ever rise.

'*Ummi* made breakfast.'

'Did she?' I asked. I reached over and tickled her shoulders through her Winnie-the-Pooh pajamas. She squealed in delight and ran back to the kitchen screaming, '*Baba*'s up. *Baba*'s up.'

I swung my legs off the bed and shook my head, hoping to clear it of any residual sleep-induced fog. The house was still cool, so I threw a robe over my pajamas before making my way to the kitchen. Hannah was standing in front of the stove, a spatula in one hand and the handle of a skillet in the other. Like me, she wore a bathrobe, but unlike me, she had already showered. Her hair was matted and wet against her neck.

'Morning, dear,' I said, yawning and pouring myself

28

a mug of coffee. Hannah had a gift with coffee, but not in a good way. The liquid I poured into my cup was so black it could probably bend spacetime like a black hole. I smelled it, trying to hide my wince and hoping it hadn't singed my nose hair. Hannah's black death six a.m. roast. If it doesn't wake you up, you're probably already dead.

I poured a generous serving of half-and-half into mine and sipped. I don't know how, but my wife drank her cup straight.

'I'm sorry, honey,' she said. 'I told Megan to get dressed. I didn't know she'd wake you up.'

'That's okay,' I said, grabbing a piece of toast from the pile beside the stove. 'I've got a meeting this morning anyway.'

Hannah turned her attention to the stove.

'Breakfast will be done soon,' she said, scrambling what looked like half-a-dozen eggs. 'Can you make sure the kid gets dressed? I've got a long shift today, so we have to leave by seven.'

My wife's long shifts were ten hours in a pediatric emergency room downtown. Her schedule allowed her to spend a majority of the week at home with Megan, but I didn't envy her.

'Sure,' I said.

I helped Megan pick out a pair of jeans and yellow T-shirt with Curious George on it while Hannah finished making breakfast. It was a nice morning. Simple, quiet; I wish we had more like it. We ate breakfast and had morning prayers together. Megan counted everything on our breakfast table while we ate, although she started over every time she got to fifteen because that was the biggest number she knew. She and Hannah were out the door at just before seven, giving me more than enough time to get dressed and watch the news.

There had been another murder the night before, bringing the total to nineteen for the month. That was almost three times our average murder rate. The Chief of Detectives chalked it up to the heat when he gave press conferences, but I don't think anyone seriously believed that. At least not anyone who knew enough to form an opinion that mattered. Something else was going on, but we hadn't figured it out yet.

I turned the news off before a perky weather girl could tell me that the hellish heat wave would continue. While I had a moment, I called my sister and brother-in-law to see if they needed anything. They didn't, although we made plans to see each other that evening.

True to Olivia's word, she pulled up to my house at about ten to nine. She wore a thin beige blazer and a pair of jeans. I thought I could see the outline of a holster beneath her jacket, but didn't want to comment in case she thought I was staring at her chest. I slid onto the blue vinyl seat and pulled the door shut. It creaked, making it sound as if I had shut the exterior door of an airplane.

'Morning,' I said, sinking into the vinyl and positioning my briefcase between my legs. 'You have a nice weekend?'

She shrugged and put the car in gear.

'Not really,' she said. 'I was hoping I could have closed this case.'

I knew the feeling. Olivia's car was unmarked, but the antenna array on the trunk wasn't subtle. Everyone within eyesight knew we were in a police vehicle and adjusted his or her driving accordingly. I saw more blinker lights used in five minutes with Olivia than I would have seen in a week driving my wife's Volkswagen.

We arrived at my niece's school about twenty minutes later. Reportedly, it was one of the city's best private high schools, as it should have been with thirty-thousand-dollar yearly tuition. My sister said it was worth it, but I had my doubts. Of course, it didn't really matter anyway because Hannah and I would have to sell ourselves into slavery to afford it. That's how it goes, though. As a public employee, I was accustomed to second or third best. The Principal met us outside. His forehead glistened, and his pink Oxford shirt stuck to his chest and arms with sweat.

'Principal Eikmeier, I'm Detective Olivia Rhodes. We

spoke on the phone,' said Olivia. She gestured at me. 'And this is Detective Sergeant Ash Rashid.'

I shook the Principal's hand and immediately stuck my own back in my pocket to wipe off the sweat. I hoped he didn't notice.

'We're ready to go,' he said. 'One of our guidance counselors made a list of Rachel's friends. They don't know you're here yet, but we can round them up quickly.'

'Get everybody together,' said Olivia. 'I want to address them as a group.'

Eikmeier led us in. The main hallway was wide and long with branching hallways to the left and right. Crimson lockers lined the walls and a line of glass trophy cases led to the gym in the rear of the school. Eikmeier led us to a staff-only conference room on a side hallway. The overhead lights tinted everything in the room a faint blue, and the walls were covered in motivational posters.

I pulled out a black leather chair from the conference room table and glanced at Olivia.

'I want to interview the kids individually,' she said. 'I'll take the lead, and you look scary. Tap my leg if you want to ask a question, and I'll take a step back. That sound good to you?'

I took a quick look around the room.

'That sounds fine,' I said. 'You ever interviewed kids at school before? Some of the rules are different.'

Olivia started to say something, but someone knocked on the door before she could. An Asian girl poked her head inside. Olivia directed her to have a seat across from us while we waited for the other students to arrive. There were ten of them. Most were girls, and none was over eighteen.

I passed around a sheet of paper and asked each student to write his or her name, address, and phone number on it. Chances were that we'd never have to call any of them into court, but we wanted to be covered. Olivia started speaking when everyone was seated.

'I'm Detective Olivia Rhodes with IMPD. My partner is Detective Sergeant Ash Rashid with the Prosecutor's Office. By now, I'm sure you've heard about Rachel Haddad, and I know some of you are probably pretty upset. We understand that, and we're sympathetic. Our department is doing its best to find out what happened to her, and since you were her friends, we wanted to speak to you. Just to be clear, you are not in trouble, and we're not looking to get you into trouble. Unless you tell me you've got a body buried in the backyard, what you say here stays here. Okay?'

There was a general murmur of agreement. Olivia continued.

'We're going to ask each of you a series of questions while the others are in the hallway. Since you're minors, Principal Eikmeier or your Guidance Counselor can

33

remain in the room with us. That's up to you. Bear in mind, though, that school officials have different priorities than we do. If you say you were involved in something that violates school policy, chances are that Detective Rashid and I won't care, but Principal Eikmeier might. You can make your own decision. Right now, go back in the hallway, and we'll call you individually.'

The students filed into the hallway. I turned to Olivia when they were gone.

'I hope that bit about school policy doesn't come back on us. Those students are entitled to have someone here with them if they want.'

'It's still their choice,' she said. 'They wouldn't say a thing if Principal Eikmeier was in here, and you know that. Call the first one on the list. Let's get this started.'

I didn't argue with her. Instead, I grabbed the list the students had filled out and read the first name. The handwriting was angular and slanted to the left. I'm not an expert, but it looked masculine.

'Our first guest is Heywood Yablowme,' I said. 'You want to get him, or do you want me to?'

Olivia's eyes narrowed slightly.

'I hate kids,' she said, rubbing her temples. 'Find out who he is and talk some sense into him. I'll start with someone else.'

'Sure,' I said, standing up. I opened the door and stepped into the hallway. The students were lined up with their backs to the wall while Principal Eikmeier sat across from them on a wheeled office chair. He started to get up, but I motioned for him to stay seated. I counted three boys and seven girls. Two of the boys were in front of the line talking to each other, but the third was in back and looked lost in thought. I ignored him and motioned the first two toward me.

'Which of you is left-handed?'

They both smirked. I tilted my head to the side and raised my eyebrows, but that just caused them to snicker. I was about to turn around and get the list from Olivia when a brunette girl next to the two boys stepped forward.

'Don is left-handed,' she said. 'The one with black hair.'

Don shot her a withering, malevolent stare. He was tall with spiked black hair. He didn't look like he could handle himself well against a grown adult, but he could probably hurt a teenage girl. I stepped in front of him and smiled. He stepped back.

'Is she right?' I asked.

He shrugged.

'So what?'

'That means you and I need to talk in private.'

Before Principal Eikmeier could stop me, I put my hand between his shoulder blades and gently led him down the hall. The kid came willingly, but the smirk never left his mouth. We rounded a corner, and I led him into a boy's restroom so we could talk without interruption. It smelled like cigarettes and urine. The walls were covered in an institutional green tile, and the floors were some sort of gray stone. The ceiling was black in spots, probably from years of clandestine smokers, and none of the toilet stalls had doors. At least I knew we were alone.

'You are so totally screwed, taco vendor,' Don said. 'You can't drag me away like that. My dad's lawyers are going to be all over this.'

I turned and twisted the deadbolt on the bathroom door. The bolt hit home with a clang.

'I'm an Arab, dipshit,' I said. 'And your Dad's lawyers aren't in here.'

Don's smirk slowly disappeared. He backed up to the far side of the room, pressing himself flat against the wall.

'What are you doing? Is this like a terrorist thing?'

'No,' I said, walking to one of the porcelain sinks.

I unbuttoned my shirt cuffs and pushed up the sleeves of my jacket an inch or two. I threw water on my face as if I were preparing myself for prayers. I glanced at the kid again. His breathing looked shallow, and his face was white.

'This isn't funny,' he said, pressing his back to the tiled wall. 'You can't lock me up here. I know my rights.'

36

I shook water off my hands before drying them with paper towels.

'You're right. I can't keep you here, but I didn't lock the door for you. I locked the door to keep Principal Eikmeier out. You can go any time you want.'

Don took a step forward but stopped before reaching the door.

'You're going to hit me or something, aren't you?'

I leaned my hip against the sink and crossed my arms.

'You've got my word. I won't touch you,' I said, shrugging my shoulders. 'But you ought to stay.'

He bunched his eyebrows up and took a hesitant step back.

'Why?'

'Because if you stay and talk to me, Detective Rhodes won't arrest you for providing false information to the police, Heywood.'

'Are you serious?' he asked. I raised my eyebrows but didn't say anything. He threw his hands up. 'Come on. That thing with the sign-in sheet was a joke. I hardly even knew Rachel. I sat beside her in homeroom and American History. That's it.'

I took my notebook out of my pocket. Olivia asked me to talk some sense into the kid, but I couldn't help if he was talkative.

'If you sat beside her, you must have talked to her some. She ever have problems with anybody?'

'We didn't talk about those sorts of things. We made fun of the teacher. We talked about TV. Stuff like that.'

'Who would she have talked with?'

He gave me a list of five names. He called them her freaky friends. There were three girls and two boys, one of whom was Robbie.

'Before you go, can I give you a word of advice, Don? If a law enforcement official asks you a question, answer it. Don't be a jerk. If you do, I will send you to jail, and your cell mates will pass you around like a bong at a Grateful Dead reunion concert. Do you understand me?'

Don started forward.

'I get it,' he said. 'And I won't do it again. Can I go now?'

'Yeah. Go.'

We left the restroom after that, although we went in different directions when we got into the hallway. When I got back to the conference room, Olivia had already begun to interview students. The Asian girl I had seen earlier was at the table, but she and Olivia stopped talking when I entered.

'Excuse me, Detective Rhodes,' I said, nodding to Olivia. I turned my attention to the girl. 'What's your name, Miss?'

'Joy Li.'

I looked at the list Heywood had given me for confirmation but came up empty.

'Okay. You can go back to class, Joy. Thanks for your help.'

Olivia coughed, but didn't say anything until the girl gathered her backpack and left the room.

'I thought we had a plan. I talk to the students while you sit there and look intimidating.'

I handed her my notebook with the five names on it.

'These are Rachel's actual friends. They're the ones we need to focus on.'

Olivia scanned the names.

'I think a couple of them are out here. Your conversation with Heywood went well, I see.'

I shrugged.

'You have to know how to connect with a kid,' I said. 'It's all about building trust. Sometimes it takes a parent's practiced hand.'

Olivia shook her head and stood up.

'I'll see if Principal Eikmeier can round up everyone we need.'

Chapter 3

We started with a girl named Alicia Weinstein. She looked vaguely familiar, so I might have met her at a birthday party or some other milestone in Rachel's life years earlier. I didn't remember her eyes, though. They were calculating and probing, making me feel like a horse being evaluated by a gambler before a big race. I shifted on my seat uncomfortably and glanced at Olivia.

Olivia warmed her up with small talk for a few minutes. She and Rachel lived near each other and had played on the same soccer team when they were younger. She said she was seventeen, and judging by her designer clothes, I doubted she had to work her way through school. My guess was that her family had enough money to have a lawyer on permanent retainer. Hopefully that wouldn't be a problem.

Before she started the interview, Olivia gave the same introductory speech she had given to the group of students before. Alicia took it in the same glassy-eyed fashion they had.

'So we're here to talk about Rachel, obviously,' said Olivia. 'As I mentioned earlier, we're trying to find out what happened to her. You can help us by filling in some details about her life. What can you tell us about her?'

I thought it was a good question. Young, inexperienced investigators often jump right in without letting the witness establish his own rhythm. Asking an open-ended question let Alicia dictate how the conversation went early on. It would give her the feeling of control.

'Rachel was the nicest person I knew. Everyone loved her, so this was a surprise. Maybe it shouldn't have been, but it was. I don't know. Forget I said that.'

Olivia and I both sat up straighter and glanced at each other. The comment was off. Under most circumstances, it takes prodding for a suspect to make an admission like that.

'Why shouldn't it have been a surprise?' asked Olivia. Alicia looked down.

'I shouldn't say anything. It's not my place.'

'She was your friend. It is your place,' said Olivia. 'We need to find out what happened so no one else gets hurt.'

'Rachel had problems,' said Alicia. She paused for a moment and breathed deeply as if talking were difficult. Olivia offered to get her a bottle of water, but Alicia declined, took a couple of deep breaths and started again. 'Rachel had problems with drugs. We all knew about it, but we didn't know what to do. Nobody thought anything like this would happen.'

'What was she on?' I asked, hoping my incredulity didn't show through my voice.

'The usual stuff,' said Alicia. 'I saw her smoke pot once, and I knew she drank at parties, but everybody does that. I heard she started doing more serious stuff lately.'

'What do you mean by serious?' asked Olivia, glancing at me.

Alicia took a moment to respond.

'They were just rumors,' she said. 'But I heard she tried cocaine at a college party last month. People said she did some other stuff, too.'

I squeezed my hands under the table hard enough that I could feel my nails bite into my skin.

'Have you heard rumors that Rachel was doing drugs on a regular basis?' asked Olivia, reaching beneath the table and tapping my knee. I unclenched my jaw and forced my shoulders to relax.

'I don't know,' said Alicia, shaking her head. Her eyebrows were scrunched, and her eyes were glassy and wet. She started and stopped talking twice. Finally she said: 'We were worried about her. She wouldn't talk to us about it, though.'

'Do you know where she would have kept her stash?' I asked. 'We need to find it so no one else gets hurt.'

Alicia paused again and closed her eyes as if thinking. She eventually took a deep breath as if she had made a tortuous decision.

'Check her locker. She used to keep stuff in a perfume box on the top shelf. She might have put something there.'

Olivia continued asking questions, but nothing pertinent came from it. Alicia denied knowing where Rachel got her drugs or how often she took them. Before she dismissed the girl, Olivia said she had one more question.

'Do you know someone named Azrael or have you ever visited a nightclub called The Abbey?'

Alicia didn't blink or even pause to respond.

'Vampires aren't real. A lot of us read books and talk about them, but that's it. It's a way to express ourselves and be creative. That's what we like about them.'

'I didn't ask you about vampires,' said Olivia, smiling. 'So it's interesting that you bring them up.'

'I thought . . .' Alicia faltered mid-sentence, her face pale. It was the first honest response we got out of her. It took her a moment to compose herself. 'I've heard of the club. You have to be twenty-one to get in, though, so I've never been.'

I reached into my pocket, took out my cell phone,

and snapped a picture quickly. Alicia's eyes were closed, but it'd do. I turned my phone around and showed her the screen.

'If I show this picture around, they're not going to recognize you, right?' I asked.

'Right,' said Alicia, not taking her eyes from my phone. Her breathing was shallow. Olivia put her hand on my knee before I could press the point further.

'I'm going to let you get back to class,' said Olivia, reaching into her purse. She pulled out a business card and handed it to Alicia. 'If you change your mind about anything you've said here, my number's on the card.'

Alicia grabbed her backpack and left the room. Olivia turned towards me, her head tilted to the side.

'How much of it do you think she was lying about?' she asked.

I shrugged.

'Most, maybe all,' I said. 'My niece didn't do drugs, and my sister has test results that prove it. Alicia is hiding something.'

Olivia looked off into space for a moment, her eyes unfocused. 'The question is what.'

Before I could answer that, another girl came in. She gave us nearly the same story as Alicia, and rather than waste our limited time with a third and fourth interview, we decided to check out Rachel's locker. While I wandered in the school's main hallway, Olivia ran to her car for her crime scene kit. It looked like a standard-issue fishing tackle box, but it held latex gloves, evidence bags, tags and search forms. It had everything she'd need to search for and store evidence.

Classes were still in session, so Olivia and I were able to work relatively unimpeded. Principal Eikmeier opened the locker for us. Its interior was about five feet tall and had two shelves for textbooks as well as a hook for a coat. Rachel had personalized it by pasting pictures of her friends on the walls and door. Most of the kids in the pictures were vaguely familiar, even if I didn't know their names. One girl was in more pictures than others, though. She had curly red hair and pale skin. I was sure that I had seen her somewhere, but Principal Eikmeier didn't recognize her. She must have been at a different school.

True to Alicia's word, we found an Elizabeth Arden perfume box on the locker's top shelf. Olivia pulled a camera out of her evidence kit and snapped a shot of the box and its placement before putting on gloves. She was almost delicate as she pulled the box from the locker, gently touching only its edges to minimize contact.

'There's something in here,' she said, tilting the box to the side. 'Get a couple of pictures of this, Ash.'

I grabbed Olivia's camera and took pictures of everything she did. Olivia popped the top. There was a plastic bag inside that contained small clumps of what looked like a hard, white cheese as well as a clear glass tube with a bulb on one end. I had never worked narcotics, but it wasn't hard to recognize an unused crack pipe and what was probably ten bucks worth of crack. I snapped a picture of both.

'What is it?' asked Principal Eikmeier. 'Are those drugs?'

'Maybe,' said Olivia, placing the lid back on the box. She slipped the entire container into a Ziploc bag and started filling out an evidence tag. 'I'm labeling it as a white, rocky substance and a glass pipe.'

Drugs played a role in about half the cases I had investigated while a detective, and that box's placement wasn't right. It was too convenient. Serious drug users hide their stuff well. Rachel wasn't an idiot. If she were a user, she'd be more careful.

'Principal Eikmeier, can you give us a moment?' I asked.

He looked at his watch. 'A minute, but that's it. The students will be changing classes soon.'

As he walked off, I looked at the locker from top to bottom again, trying to find anything else out of place. I knelt to take a look at the stack of books on the bottom shelf, and that's when I knew that we had a problem. Olivia's eyebrows were raised expectantly when I glanced up.

'There are two math books in here,' I said. '*Elementary Trigonometry* and *Advanced Calculus*.'

Olivia shrugged. 'Rachel could have taken Trig one year and then Calculus the next.'

I shook my head and stood upright. 'You went to high school out of state. Students in Indiana rent their textbooks and then return them at the end of the year. There are multiple people with access to this locker.'

Olivia paused, thinking. 'We'll brush the box and pipe for prints and see what we can come up with,' she said finally. 'If they don't match Rachel, we'll go from there.'

I nodded, shifting on my feet. As I did that, Olivia pulled the gloves off her hands.

'Did you get the autopsy results yet?' I asked.

Olivia's eyes narrowed questioningly. 'Preliminary results, but no tox screen if that's what you're asking about.'

I ran my hand across my face.

'No, that's not what I'm asking,' I said. 'Did the Coroner say anything about her fingers?'

Olivia's eyes had a distant look. 'I don't think so.'

That was what I needed to hear.

'If Rachel had been doing crack, her fingers would have been calloused and burned. The Coroner would say so. This isn't right, and you know it. If Rachel had drugs in her locker, the drug dogs would smell them immediately. More than that, her principal doesn't even need probable cause to search her locker, just a reasonable suspicion that she broke some sort of rule. Only a moron would hide drugs here.'

Olivia nodded again, thinking.

'You think this is a setup?' she asked.

I leaned against the locker and shook my head.

'I don't know, but something isn't right.'

'We'll look into it,' she said. Before she could finish, the school's bell rang and a wave of students crashed out of nearby classrooms. Olivia leaned close enough to me that I thought she was going to kiss me. 'We'll bring Alicia in and see what she has to say about it at our station. Right now, though, we need to get out of here. I've got a meeting downtown this afternoon. I'll take you by your law school on my way.'

I glanced at my watch. My class started in twenty-five minutes. I didn't like leaving things unfinished, but we were out of time. We put a uniformed officer assigned to truancy prevention in charge of Rachel's locker until crime scene technicians could arrive and empty it completely. I left with more uncertainties bouncing around my head than when we had arrived. Rachel's death was beginning to look like anything but an accident.

Chapter 4

Work crews were resurfacing the roads downtown, making the area difficult to navigate. Olivia had to drop me off two blocks from my law school, which meant I had to sprint to the building. I made it to my classroom out of breath and sweating, but with three minutes to spare. The professor wasn't in yet, which was good. He had a tendency to pick on those arriving late.

I stepped into the room and took a quick look around. A classroom in a law school isn't like classrooms in most schools; it's more like an amphitheater with tiered seating so everyone can see the horrible spectacle in front. I scanned the room for open seats. As late as I was, the only one available was in the first row. It was so close to the professor's podium that I'd probably feel spittle as he rained vitriol on those unfortunate souls who displeased him that morning.

I walked to the empty seat, nodding hello to a few

familiar faces as I passed, and sat down in an uncomfortable black plastic chair. I spread my class materials on the table in front of me and smiled hello to the guy sitting beside me. I didn't know his first name, but the professors called him Mr Mason. He had a hooked nose, and his sport coat and slacks looked like something ripped off a mannequin at Brooks Brothers. In law school vernacular, he was a gunner. Most students don't aspire to the title, but Mason reveled in it. He always had something to say whether it was pertinent to that day's discussion or not, and he was almost always the first person to shoot his hand in the air if someone gave an incorrect answer. In short, he was an asshole. The rumor was that his father was a senior partner in a major firm in Chicago, though, so he could afford to be an asshole.

Mason smirked in response to my smile.

Nice to see you, too, douche bag.

The atmospheric change when Professor Ruiz walked into the room a moment later was palpable. Conversations halted mid-sentence, postures improved, and all shuffling of notes ceased. For a small, stooped man in a navy-blue cardigan, Professor Ruiz was damn intimidating. He was sort of a pint-sized Mr Rogers from Hell. Theoretically, I knew he had a heart, but I was pretty sure it pumped some vile black liquid instead of blood.

He walked to the clear plastic podium in front of the room. Sixty pairs of eyeballs followed; sixty prayers, my own included, floated to heaven. God would answer fifty-nine of those prayers and throw one unfortunate soul to the fire. I hoped it was Mason. Ruiz spread out his notebook and looked up.

'Okay, let's get this started. Detective Rashid, tell me about Baber v. Hospital Corporation of America.'

Shit.

Being a police officer made a lot of law school classes interesting, especially criminal law. Unfortunately, it made health law a bitch because my professor held the police in less than high esteem. On the first day of class, he had railed for forty-five minutes about the erosion of civil liberties by law enforcement officials. It was impressive work for a class that had little to do with either civil liberties or law enforcement.

I flipped through my outline. It was thinner than usual. With everything that had happened that weekend, I hadn't been able to focus on class. I glanced at Mason's casebook. It had so many highlighted passages that it might as well have been a coloring book.

'The case involved an intoxicated patient who walked into the ER,' I said, flipping through my notes. 'He had stomach pain, I think—'

'Wrong. Is there someone who can fill Detective Rashid in here?'

Mason shot his hand in the air, and Ruiz called on him. 'An intoxicated patient walked into the ER, but she wasn't having stomach pain. She was agitated and restless. While there, the patient fell and hit her head . . .'

Mason continued reciting the facts of the case as clearly as if he had witnessed the events himself. Professor Ruiz smiled approvingly. There was a group discussion for a moment as others in the class advanced additional facts relevant to the case, but I wasn't paying that much attention. Instead, I was imagining an errant bus running both Ruiz and Mason over. That was satisfying. I finally found my notes and already had most of the facts written down.

'Back to the point on hand, what was the holding on this particular case, Mr Rashid? Or should I ask Mr Mason directly?'

A legal holding was the court's determination of the matter of law in a particular case. It's one of the most important parts of a decent legal brief, so I paid it special attention in my outline.

'The Court held that because hospitals have varying capabilities, there is no national medical malpractice standard for ERs.'

At least I knew something.

'Oh good. They still teach reading in the police academy. And how does that relate to EMTALA?'

I clenched my jaw as I flipped pages in my outline. Some of the students around me shifted uncomfortably.

'What a surprise. You don't know. Can someone who's actually read the material fill us in?'

Heat rushed to my face, but my momentary embarrassment only lasted a moment before a cell phone rang, interrupting Ruiz before he could call on Mason again. My shoulders loosened. I closed my eyes and breathed deeply. Bringing a working cell phone into Ruiz's classroom was like smoking a cigarette in a fireworks factory. Whoever was stupid enough to do it deserved whatever happened to him. At least the pressure would be off me for the moment.

The phone rang a second and then a third time. I rarely carried my phone when I was going to class, and even when I did, I always turned it off beforehand. At least almost always. It didn't occur to me to look in my briefcase until I felt a classroom full of eyes bearing down on me.

Damn it.

My briefcase was a good-looking bag, the sort of thing a business executive would carry. Hannah had given it to me when I went back to school. Despite its aesthetic appeal, it wasn't practical. The metal latches were hard to open, and I could only fit two or three books in it at once. I bent down and fumbled it open. The phone rang a few more times and went to voicemail before I could turn it off. I silenced it with the power button without looking at it. My stomach twisted in knots, and I balled my fists as I straightened.

'I'm sorry for the interruption, sir.'

'And I'm sorry we allowed a clearly unqualified applicant into this law school based on some supposed community service.'

My nails bit into my palms. I shook my head and started gathering my notebooks.

'Did I pick up your daughter for solicitation or something? Or are you an asshole to everybody?'

I didn't think there was going to be any oxygen left in the room after the collective intake.

That's probably going to hurt my grade.

Before Ruiz could recover, I shoved my belongings into my briefcase. I didn't even look over my shoulder as I left. I had probably just tanked my legal career, but that would take time to sink in.

I walked to the school's multi-story glass atrium, my head held high. I probably should have felt nervous or even a bit guilty. Both were appropriate responses to my situation. I didn't feel either, though. Instead, I felt like a conquering hero returning after a long absence. If nothing else, I'd be remembered for a few years. Few law school graduates could boast that.

I plopped onto a black leather chair that would have looked at home in an Ikea catalog and placed my briefcase on one of the glass coffee tables near the center of the room. Classes were still in session and the room was nearly empty, so I didn't feel terribly guilty about pulling out my cell phone.

One new message from Olivia.

I leaned back in the chair and put my feet on the table. We weren't supposed to do that, but I didn't think it mattered too much. As soon as the Dean of Students heard about my outburst, I wouldn't be a student there, anyway. I dialed my voicemail and put the phone to my ear.

'I need you at the Cuttings' house ASAP. They're on North Meridian. Call dispatch to pick you up. Lights and sirens.'

The Cuttings' front yard was the size of a small city park and was surrounded on all sides by a chest-high, iron fence. The police cruiser I was riding in pulled through the front gate slowly, giving me a chance to look around. The Cuttings had formal rose gardens in their front lawn and numerous vine-covered arches over the driveway. My driver followed the road around a sharp left, and as he did that, I caught my first glimpse of the Cuttings' home. It was an Italianate mansion with at least five chimneys, a symbol of Nathan Cutting's success and excess. My niece had died in the guesthouse catty-corner to it.

My driver parked between an unmarked police cruiser and ambulance in front of the main house. Before stepping out of the vehicle, I asked him to stick around for a few minutes until I could figure out what was going on. Two paramedics leaned against the ambulance beside me. One smoked while the other simply stood there. No one seemed to be in a hurry.

My guess was that Nathan Cutting was dead. I didn't think he was very old, but he had probably experienced enough stress over the past few days that a heart attack was a very real possibility.

The front door was open, so I stepped into the home's foyer. The floor was dark hardwood. A pair of curving symmetrical staircases led to a second floor landing in front of me, while a crystal chandelier that would have looked at home in Versailles scattered the light that came through the front windows. I followed the sound of voices to the home's kitchen. There were a number of people inside, including Olivia and John Meyers, the Cuttings' attorney.

The focus was on a couple at the kitchen table. Nathan and Maria Cutting, I presumed. Since Nathan was alive, I had no idea why I was there. He was short, squat, and completely bald, while his wife was thin with wavy brunette hair. Their eyes were bloodshot, and they held hands on the table.

I glanced at Olivia and motioned toward the entryway with my head. She followed me as I walked out.

'What's going on?' I asked, leaning into her and speaking softly.

'Robbie Cutting is dead.'

'Murdered?' I asked, my eyebrows scrunched.

'Suicide,' said a loud, baritone voice I didn't recognize. One of the men I had seen in the kitchen stepped into the foyer. I'm not a pushover, but the guy stepping towards me was built like a refrigerator and probably had fifty pounds on me. He wore a cheap brown jacket, slacks, and a mustard-stained tie.

I glanced at Olivia. She motioned towards the walking refrigerator with her head.

'This is Lieutenant Mike Bowers. He's in charge of homicide now.'

The name was familiar. I hadn't met Bowers before, but he was well known in law enforcement circles. I had heard he was a good investigator. The rumor mill reported that when he was my age, he infiltrated the Aryan Brotherhood and single-handedly dismantled a violent narcotics trafficking ring. I had also heard that his wife was less than discreet about her marital indiscretions while he was under.

'Is there something I can do for you, Detective Rashid?'

'I'm following up on my niece's case,' I said. 'Is that a problem?'

Bowers' eyes looked me up and down before he gestured his head towards the front door.

'Outside,' he said.

I followed the two of them to the front porch. It was hot and muggy out of the air-conditioning. I pulled the front door shut behind me so the Cuttings and their lawyer couldn't hear us talking. When I turned around, Bowers was staring at me. I looked from him to my old partner and back.

'Can someone tell me what's going on now?' I asked.

Olivia looked as if she were going to say something, but Bowers stepped in before she could. The two paramedics leaning against the ambulance perked up.

'Here's the deal,' said Bowers. 'Robbie Cutting died this morning, and he took responsibility for your niece's death in his suicide note. He said he drugged her so she'd sleep with him. I'm sorry for your family's loss, but this is a satisfactory outcome as far as I'm concerned. I'm closing the investigation.'

I stared at him, allowing the information to ruminate inside my head.

'Robbie and Rachel had been dating for two years,' I said. 'She's a good kid, but I don't think he'd need drugs to have sex with her.'

Bowers shrugged.

'No matter how he seemed, Robbie admitted drugging her,' said Bowers. 'She's a Muslim, and correct me if I'm wrong, but that means she can't have sex until she's married. Robbie apparently got tired of waiting.'

I raised my eyebrows.

'Islam does say sex is for marriage, but it also says pigs are unclean and I can't eat them. That doesn't stop me from loving bacon, Lieutenant,' I said. 'Rachel was with him for years. They're teenagers; they don't change. There's a reason people in my culture get married young.'

Bowers rolled his eyes, his face growing redder the longer he spoke.

'The kid's note says he slipped her drugs, and her preliminary toxicology report says there was enough cocaine in her system to kill a horse. Case closed, Detective.'

I took a step back and put my hands up defensively.

'I don't doubt what you're saying, Lieutenant,' I said. 'But I still think it's a little early to close this. You didn't even find drugs at the scene.'

Bowers shifted and muttered something inaudible.

'You're defending the guy who killed your niece. You do realize how absurd that is, don't you?'

'I'm not defending anybody. There are things to investigate here. If Robbie drugged her, why didn't you find anything at the scene?'

Bowers glanced to Olivia.

'You want to take that one?' he asked.

My old partner stepped forward. She glanced at Bowers before turning towards me.

'We're guessing that the drugs were in that vial of liquid we found.'

'You're guessing?' I asked, my eyebrows raised.

Olivia cleared her throat.

'It's been misplaced,' she said, glancing at Bowers. 'We picked up three homicides that night. It was probably filed with the wrong case. It'll turn up.'

'That's an optimistic assessment,' said Bowers, glaring at my old partner. He turned towards me. 'You don't work for me, so I'll make this quick. I don't know what kind of scam you're running, but my department does not misplace evidence. If I find you had any part in making that vial disappear, I'll go for your badge. Is that clear?'

I could feel my temper bubbling to the surface.

'I don't know what sort of information you've got, but my only connection to this case is my niece. I haven't touched a thing.'

Bowers cocked his head to the right.

'Make sure you keep it that way, Detective,' he said. 'Now if you'll excuse me, I have real work to do.'

Bowers pushed past me and walked toward one of the awaiting police cruisers. When his shoulder hit mine, it felt as if I had run into a brick wall. I rocked back on my heels and clenched my jaw but said nothing. The paramedics near the ambulance went back to loitering and pretending not to notice us.

'What's that all about?' I asked as Bowers' cruiser backed out of its spot.

'The Lieutenant's been trying to get me transferred since he took over homicide,' said Olivia, looking up and squinting in the afternoon sun. 'He doesn't like women, and I think he sees this as another chance to get rid of one.'

'And he's willing to blow an investigation to do that?'

Olivia shrugged. 'If it looks like my fault, yeah.'

I shook my head.

'Okay, fill me in for a moment so I can understand. What happened to Robbie Cutting?'

Olivia looked away from me.

'From what I could tell, Bowers was right. He killed himself. He took a piece of hardwood flooring left over from a renovation in the main house, sharpened it into a point and then jammed it through his bed so it would stand up. Then he jumped on it.'

'Suicide by self-impalement? That's ridiculous.'

'It sounds ridiculous, but that's what it looks like,' she said. 'Robbie left a note. It said that he was a vampire and the only way to kill himself was by stabbing him through the heart.'

I closed my eyes and rubbed the bridge of my nose, hoping to stave off an impending headache.

'The note is probative, but not sufficient to close the case. What else do we have?'

Olivia grimaced. 'Lieutenant Bowers thinks it's enough. He's an administrator. His job is to close cases. Until the Coroner's office says Robbie's death is a criminal homicide, it's going nowhere.'

What she didn't need to say is that by the time the Coroner's office made that ruling, every trace of physical evidence would be gone, memories would have started fading and stories would be solidified. I ran my fingers through my hair.

'Did Robbie seem suicidal to you when we talked to him the other night?'

'I don't think so, but I'm not qualified to make that judgment,' she said. 'And neither are you.'

I leaned back on my heels.

'There's more going on here than we know,' I said. 'Someone I love is dead, we're missing evidence, and everyone connected to the case is lying their asses off to us. No matter how much of a bureaucrat Bowers is, he can't ignore this.'

'He can, and he did,' said Olivia. 'We don't have unlimited resources. Bowers thinks he's making the right call.'

'You don't believe that, do you?'

Olivia squinted at me and shook her head. She closed her eyes before speaking.

'I think it's time to back off unless something else shows up. I'm not going to risk my job by going behind my lieutenant's back.'

'He's not my lieutenant,' I said.

'He's not, but he'll burn you if you get in his way. Back-dooring him on this case is not a good idea.'

I slipped my hand to the back of my neck. Being a detective was more than a job for me. It was a calling deeply rooted in my identity. I may not have been a very good Muslim, but my religion called me to seek and foster justice. It's a divine edict as stringent as any command in any faith. Nobody gets a pass, least of all somebody who hurt my niece.

'Why would Bowers want this case closed?' I asked.

Olivia shrugged.

'Aside from solving the manpower shortage in our department?'

'If the problem was manpower, he could graft detectives from other departments,' I said. 'We've got two former homicide guys in our bullpen alone. He's got something else going on.'

'You're being paranoid, Ash,' said Olivia.

'I'm paid to be paranoid,' I said. 'I'll keep you out of it, but I'm not done with this case.'

Olivia sighed.

'Don't do anything stupid,' she said.

'I'll do my best.'

Chapter 5

It was mid-afternoon when the patrolman dropped me off at my house. I had missed noon prayers, but I wasn't in the mood to pray. I grabbed the bottle of bourbon from my car's glove compartment and poured the remaining three fingers into a juice glass in the kitchen. I leaned against the counter, my mind racing.

Bowers may have been an administrator, but he had spent most of his life as an investigator. There were too many open questions and too many inconsistencies in the story to close Robbie's death investigation. He would have known that. I didn't know who was involved or what the goal was, but he was running a play on somebody.

I downed the drink quickly and shoved the bottle into the trash can, burying it beneath rubbish. I felt better after that, and I allowed my mind to wander. Robbie had purchased the vial of blood at a club in Plainfield.

If no one else was going to look at it, I needed to. I googled the address on my computer and was in my car shortly after that.

I drove for about forty-five minutes. Maybe that wasn't the smartest thing to do after a drink, but I arrived safely anyway. The nightclub was called The Abbey, but I didn't know if that was a clever reference to Carfax Abbey, one of the properties Count Dracula bought in Bram Stoker's famous book, or to the fact that the club was located in a converted country church that could have been a monastery.

I parked in an expansive gravel lot beside the building and stepped out. The church overlooked a valley planted with soybeans that undulated in the wind like green waves, and the air smelled fresh and sweet. There were woods behind the building. The club was the only commercial enterprise in sight.

I walked to the steps in front of the building. Like many old churches in central Indiana, it was covered in pitted, grayish-green limestone, a plentiful resource quarried from the nearby hills. It was a shame the former congregation had sold the place. If the cross on top of the steeple hadn't been inverted, they could have made a fortune holding weddings.

The front door was propped open, and I caught a whiff of bleach as I walked towards it. There were at least two people inside, and they both spoke the rapid

Spanish of native speakers. With any luck, there'd be a manager on duty supervising them who could tell me a bit more about the club.

I pounded on the door to let the staff know I was there and walked into what would have been the church's narthex. It looked like the waiting room of a bordello. A long purple sash ran the length of the ceiling, and purple velvet couches lined the walls. Despite the garish decorations, I could still see remnants of the church's previous tenants. Someone had carved a cross into the limestone above the front door and a stained-glass window filtered the sunlight into a deep crimson.

The hardwood floor groaned as I walked, and the Spanish chattering ceased.

'Hello?' I called. I pushed aside a pair of velvet drapes that demarcated the narthex from the sanctuary and stepped deeper into the club. The Abbey's main room was maybe ten-thousand square feet and had an expansive dance floor, raised stage for a band, and a bar on the left side. A pair of Hispanic women mopped while a middle-aged guy with black hair scurried behind the bar. I waved at the cleaning staff but neither woman stirred.

'What do you want?'

The barkeep stopped working and leaned against the concrete bar, scowling. He was thin and had an angular face with wavy black hair. He looked like a forty-year-old Mick Jagger if the Rolling Stones hadn't taken off. I flashed my badge at him, purposefully holding my arm up long enough that Mick would see the firearm inside my jacket.

'Are you the usual bartender here?' I asked, clipping my badge back to my belt.

'Depends on how you define usual.'

I supposed that was literally true. I leaned against the bar while Mick knelt down and grabbed a case of Bud Light from beneath. He took a six inch butterfly knife out of his back pocket and sliced into the cardboard like a butcher. I shifted on my feet and eased my hand to my side so my gun was within easy reach if I needed it.

'Like I said, what do you want?' asked Mick, putting his knife back in his pocket. I looked over my shoulder. The two Hispanic women still hadn't moved.

'Tell them I'm not with INS, would you?' I asked, pointing over my shoulder with my thumb. 'They seem a little spooked.'

He nodded and yelled in Spanish. I could have done it myself, but I wanted to see what he'd do. His reaction was mildly comforting, actually. If he was good enough to his cleaning staff to let them know they weren't in trouble, maybe we wouldn't have to end in a shootout.

While he yelled, I pulled out my wallet and thumbed through the pictures inside until I came across one my sister had sent me a year earlier. It was a headshot Rachel's school had taken for the yearbook. It was a good picture. I took it out and pressed it across the bar toward him.

'Have you seen this girl in here?' I asked.

Mick studied the picture before sliding it back to me. 'Not our type of clientèle.'

'You guys probably do like them a little more lively,' I said, sliding the picture back toward him. 'She's my niece and she's dead. Does that jog any memory loose?'

Mick grimaced and picked up a pair of beer bottles in each hand before putting them in a cooler behind the bar.

'I'm sorry she's dead,' he said. 'But I wouldn't serve her if she gave me her passport, driver's license, and birth certificate. Like I said. She's not our type of clientèle. We don't serve kids.'

I took out my cell phone and flipped through its built-in memory until I came across the shot I had taken of Alisha Weinstein earlier that day. My phone's screen was small, but it was large enough to make out her features. I held it to the bartender.

'How about her?'

Mick took a look and his eyes widened with recognition.

'She's in every now and then,' he said. 'Never pays for her own drinks.'

I slipped the phone back in my pocket. 'Care to reevaluate your statement about serving kids, then?'

Mick stopped what he was doing and leaned against the bar. He closed his eyes and shook his head.

'She's a minor?'

I nodded, and Mick swore under his breath.

'She's got to have ID to get in,' he said, putting up his hands defensively. 'If they get past security, I serve them. I assume they're twenty-one.'

'I'd say you should beef up security.'

'I'm starting to agree with you there.' He rested his elbows on the bar and leaned forward. 'You haven't arrested me yet, so what do you want? Free drinks? A payoff? What?'

'I'm here for information,' I said, pulling out a barstool. I sat down and folded my hands in front of me. 'I want to know what sort of place this is and who comes here.'

Mick looked at his cleaning staff for a moment and then reached for a bottle of a green cleaner. He sprayed the bar top around my arms and started wiping in a clockwise motion. The cleaner smelled like pine.

'We're a club, like every other club in town. Our visitors are usually in their twenties and thirties. Men, women, straight, gay. We don't discriminate. We get it all and then some.'

It sounded like a rehearsed speech. I smiled but didn't let it reach my eyes.

'Most nightclubs don't have inverted crosses on their steeples.'

'Our clients are creative people,' said Mick, shrugging. He reached beneath the bar and came up with two bottles of cheap vodka in each hand. 'They don't like a standard club experience.'

'Your clients pretend to be vampires, from what I gather. Creative isn't the first adjective that comes to mind.'

I thought I saw Mick smile, but it was gone as quickly as it appeared. He reached into his back pocket again, withdrew his butterfly knife, and sliced through the plastic spout built into each bottle.

'Our clients come here because they want to be someone different for a night. That's what we give them. The decorations are theatrics.'

'You have any problems with drugs here?'

Mick put down his knife and rested his elbows against the bar.

'If we see anything suspicious, we call the police. This is a legitimate operation.'

I raised an eyebrow, not entirely sure that I believed him.

'You know somebody named Azrael?' I asked, remembering Olivia using the name earlier that day.

'He's a regular. Uses one of our VIP rooms,' said Mick, indicating a balcony overlooking the room with his chin. At one time, it had probably been overflow seating for Easter Sunday services. 'He's not into drugs.'

'You know that for a fact?'

Mick shrugged.

'Not a fact,' he said. 'But I've never heard he's pushing.'

'How hard are you listening?' I asked.

'Fuck you,' said Mick, turning and reaching under the bar. I couldn't see his hands for a moment. I wasn't comfortable with that, so I grabbed the front of his shirt and yanked him forward. The fabric ripped at the collar, and he stood up straight, his hands in the air. 'Easy, easy. Who do you think you are, fucking Wyatt Earp?'

I let go of Mick's shirt, and he made an elaborate show of straightening his collar and slicking back his hair. His shirt had been stretched so far that I could see a faded black tattoo on his chest. The lines were so crooked and blotchy that I couldn't see what it was supposed to represent. It was sloppy work, even for a prison tattoo.

'Someone I care about is dead, so I'm not in the mood to put up with shit. Tell me what you know, or I'll arrest you for serving alcohol to minors. How do you feel about going back to prison?'

Mick adjusted his collar, hiding the tattoo on his neck.

'Tell me what you want.'

'I'm glad we're on the same page,' I said. 'Is there any way I can get in touch with Azrael?'

'We don't keep a roster with our clients' information, if that's what you're asking,' said Mick.

71

'How does he pay for his drinks?' I asked, crossing my arms.

'Cash.'

I waited for Mick to continue, but he didn't.

'Who pays for Alicia Weinstein's drinks?'

'The blond girl?' he asked.

I nodded.

'A lot of men,' he said. 'A lot.'

'Are you implying something?' I asked, my eyebrows narrowed.

'Take a look around, Detective,' he said, sweeping his arm across the bar. 'This place has a lot of dark corners, a lot of couches, a lot of places to do things unseen. She was with a lot of men.'

I scratched the back of my neck, letting that sink in. Maybe she had worked for her designer clothes after all.

'Anything else you can tell me about her?'

'I serve drinks to the freak show. I don't join in.'

I pointed to the picture of my niece on the bar.

'Somebody connected to this club killed my niece. If I find out you're running anything illegal through here or that you're lying to me now, you're not going to make it to jail.'

Mick swallowed.

'Yeah, I got ya.'

I closed my eyes and was about to turn away, but stopped.

'Word of advice, lose the knife. You might have other detectives stop by, and they're not all as forgiving as me.'

'Thanks,' said Mick, his lips thin.

'Don't mention it.'

I left the club the same way I had gone in, already taking out my cell phone. Mick might have professed ignorance of what went on in the club, but someone had to know something.

I punched in a text message to Jimmy Russo, a confidential informant I used to run when I worked homicide. He was a mid-level street dealer with his ear on the ground. If someone was moving drugs through The Abbey in any kind of volume, Jimmy would know about it. I asked him if he could meet me that afternoon near Monument Circle.

After that, I hopped in my car and headed downtown towards a bar I knew that served two-ounce shots. I had a couple of drinks as I waited for Jimmy's response. When he still hadn't returned my message an hour later, I left feeling more than a little buzzed. I bought a newspaper from a vending machine and sat on a bench in the Indiana Artsgarden, a seven-story glass-and-steel atrium suspended above the intersection of two busy downtown streets. I read a few articles, but mostly I watched the cars pass by.

My cell started beeping twenty minutes later. The drinks were wearing off a little by then, and I could walk without my head feeling as if I were swimming. Jimmy agreed to my meeting and said he was five minutes out. I dropped my paper and took the stairs to street level.

Monument Circle is a circular piece of real estate in the center of town with an elaborately carved memorial to Indiana soldiers in the center. At one time that memorial would have towered above everything in town, but now it was dwarfed by the forty-story bank buildings that had sprung up around it. The area smelled faintly of sulfur, a gift from our aging sewage system, and there was a big enough crowd that I could hide if need be.

I crossed Meridian Street in front of Christ Church Cathedral and took a look around. Jimmy was leaning against a brass plaque describing the monument. He wore a white Oxford shirt, gray slacks, and a pair of aviator sunglasses. If I hadn't known better, I would have thought he was one of the fresh-from-college, white-collar bankers that worked in nearby buildings. He nodded at me when he saw me.

'You look good, Jimmy,' I said, putting my hand forward for him to shake when I was a few feet away. Jimmy pretended not to notice, so I dropped it to my side. 'It's been a long time.'

'That it has, my man,' he said. 'It's James, now.'

'Moving up in the world, huh?'

He snickered.

'James is always moving up,' he said, casting his gaze around the crowd. 'Let's take a walk.'

I followed him. A group of kids stood beside the monument while their teacher told them about World War II and Indiana's role in the supply chain that fed and armed our soldiers. James looked at the crowd before his shoulders relaxed again.

'Now what can James do for you, Detective?'

'I need some information about a club in Plainfield.'

Jimmy or James or whatever he was called stopped and tilted his head.

'Plainfield? The 'burbs are a little out of my regular rotation.'

'Club's called The Abbey,' I said. 'The guy there I'm interested in is named Azrael.'

He shrugged. 'I ain't heard of it or him.'

'Azrael may think he's a vampire,' I said. 'Or at least he may pretend to be. I think he's moving something through the club.'

James stopped then and tilted his head. He took off his glasses, allowing me to see his hands for the first time. He had bandages on his thumb, index, and middle fingers. He shifted his weight from foot to foot and looked uneasy. In the past, James had always been forthcoming with what he knew, and if he didn't know something, he could almost always find out. Something had him spooked.

'Now I already said James doesn't know anything, so why are you still talking?'

'If I find something, your name will stay out of it,' I said. 'No one will know we talked.'

James turned and continued walking. We left Monument Circle and started walking south on Meridian Street. When I was growing up, that might not have been the smartest move, but the city had gentrified and cleaned itself up in the past twenty years. Downtown was now trendy and had some of the nicer bars, restaurants, and stores in the region. James finally stopped and sat at an empty table in front of a microbrewery. He rested his hands in front of him. The bandages over his fingers were tinged with red.

'My office can take care of you if you're having a problem,' I said.

'James doesn't have any problems with anybody, Detective.'

I leaned back in my chair and stretched, deciding to take a different tack.

'What happened to your fingers, James?'

He looked down and immediately pulled his hands off the table.

'Nothing.'

I leaned forward.

'James, we've always been straight with each other,

and I'm starting to get pissed. I'm on a case, and my time is limited,' I said. 'I think you know something and you're scared, so I'll make you a deal. If you tell me what I want to know, I won't arrest you for trying to sell me an ounce of cocaine.'

'I didn't try to sell you nothin'.'

'Who do you think the Prosecutor's going to believe? Me or you? Especially when I search you and find drugs in your pockets.'

'Fuck you, man,' he said. I thought he was going to leave, but he stayed at the table, apparently thinking. His forehead was furrowed, and I could see the carotid arteries on his neck pulse fast.

'What happened to your hands?' I asked, softening my voice.

James stared at me for a moment, but then he laid his hand flat on the table and peeled back the bandage over his index finger. It was purple and swollen; the fingernail was completely gone. I looked up, my mouth open. 'Who did this?'

James swallowed.

'I don't want none of this,' he said, securing the bandage over his fingers again. 'Whatever you're doing, keep me out.'

'If you tell me what happened, I might be able to make sure it won't happen again,' I said. 'You're my CI. I'll take care of you.'

James looked away. 'You've been out of the game for a while. Things change.'

'Some things stay the same, though. Someone's giving you a problem. You tell me who it is, I'll give them a problem.'

James ran his unbandaged hand across his scalp. I saw his throat dip as he swallowed.

'Fuck, man,' he said. He was almost shaking. 'I tried to make a buy. That's it. It went bad. What else you want to know?'

'Who'd you make a buy from?'

James reached into a pocket and pulled out a cigarette. He lit up and leaned back.

'I don't know their names. Heard they've got good shit. Almost pure and fucking cheap. I put out some feelers and got jumped. Took my girl and me and tied us to chairs. They wanted to know how I heard of 'em. I told 'em just rumors, but they wanted to know who's been talking.'

I gestured for him to go on, but he didn't say anything.

'What did you tell them?'

'I told 'em that fucking everybody's been talking,' he said, throwing his hands up. 'They pulled off my goddamn fingernails with pliers anyway. Didn't even say nothing. Just did it and left.'

That was a little rougher than usual, even for the drug trade.

'What'd they look like?'

James snuffed his cigarette out on an ashtray on the table.

'I didn't see no faces. They wore ski masks,' he said, trembling by that point. 'I need a new job, man. These cats are for real.'

I took a deep breath.

'Who set it up?'

James looked off into the distance.

'Fucking fat bastard named Rollo,' he said. 'Ain't heard from him since.'

Rollo wasn't familiar, but I could look him up if need be.

'You got any family outside Indianapolis?' I asked.

James nodded.

'I think you should visit them for a little while,' I said. 'I might stir up some trouble in the next few days.'

I figured I was sober enough after my meeting to go into work and check my messages, so I stopped by my office. Someone had put a manila file folder and stack of yellow Post-it notes on my desk. The first note told me to call Susan Mercer, my boss. The second was in the same handwriting and suggested that I wear something fire retardant because she sounded pissed. Of course, Susan was always pissed, so that wasn't anything new.

I ignored the notes for a moment and flipped through the contents of the manila folder. It was a report from my niece's preliminary autopsy. I scanned through it until I found the opinion. The assistant coroner, Dr Hector Rodriguez, pegged the time of death at five to six in the evening and said the immediate cause of death was a probable overdose leading to heart failure. That didn't tell me much new, but the typed note at the end of the report did.

From a friend. Be careful.

At least Olivia hadn't abandoned me completely. I tucked the folder into the top drawer of my desk and locked it. I called Susan's office next. She answered quickly and requested I meet her in her office to discuss Rachel and Robbie. I could already feel the headache starting to brew in my skull. I swore under my breath and told her I'd be up in a few minutes.

Rather than get up immediately, I stayed at my desk, considering what would happen if I simply went home. The pros didn't outweigh the cons, though. I sighed, wadded both notes and threw them in the trash before getting a cup of coffee at our communal coffee maker. It was scorched and stale. That was about how my day had been going.

I tossed my coffee down a nearby drinking fountain and headed to the elevator for a short ride upstairs. Susan's office was on the fourteenth floor. Unlike me, she had an actual office with walls and a door. Officially, she was the Assistant Prosecutor, the second most powerful law enforcement official in the city. Unofficially, she ran the office while her elected boss explored the possibility of running for governor. He was a schmuck; she was a hard-ass prosecutor who gave defense attorneys the shakes. We usually got along fairly well.

Her secretary let me into her office. It was roughly fifteen-by-fifteen and had a large picture window over-looking a pedestrian park. Bookshelves covered the walls, and files were stacked chest-high on her desk. Susan was on the phone, but she motioned me in with her free hand. I plucked a file from the chair in front of her desk and sat down, waiting for her to finish the call. She did about five minutes later and faced me for a moment without saying anything.

'How are you, Ash?' she asked.

'Fine,' I said. 'Unless you've heard otherwise.'

She opened a folder on her desk. I couldn't see its contents.

'I just got a call from Lieutenant Mike Bowers in homicide. He said you were at Nathan and Maria Cutting's house this afternoon.'

'Detective Rhodes asked me to come over. Robbie Cutting died. He was the suspect in my niece's death.'

Susan nodded. 'That's what I've heard. How are you handling things?'

'I'm handling them,' I said. 'I appreciate the concern, but I'm fine.'

'Lieutenant Bowers suggested I give you some time off. I tend to agree with him.'

Of course Bowers would want me off. He was up to something. I looked out the window. Susan had a nice view; I guess her eighty-hour work week had some perks.

'You can do what you want, but I'm fine.'

She nodded again.

'If I gave you a blood alcohol test right now, what would it tell me?' she asked.

'I'm fine, Susan,' I said. 'You don't need to worry about me.'

She waited for another moment as if expecting me to continue. Eventually, she took the hint that I wasn't.

'I'm taking you off the rotation for the rest of the week. Paid leave. Take a break. You need it.'

'You're ordering me to take a vacation?' I asked.

'Yeah,' she said. 'Take your kid to the park, go out to dinner with your wife. Do whatever married people do to relax. I don't want to see you until next Monday. Is that understood?'

'I don't have a choice in this?' I asked.

'No,' said Susan, already reading the file in front of her. 'Have a nice break.'

Subtlety was not Susan's strong suit.

I left the building and went to a nearby bar that

catered to cops. I wanted to drive home afterwards, so I didn't have much. Just a beer and some pretzels to soak up some of the liquor already in my stomach.

When I got home, I rinsed off in the shower. I stayed in there for maybe twenty minutes. As the water cascaded over me, my mind flashed to cases I'd rather forget. It did that when I drank sometimes. Liquor usually helped me forget, but occasionally it helped me remember. It was a bitch like that. After my shower, I swished with mouthwash and went to the backyard.

My backyard was my slice of heaven. Hannah and I lived in an old part of the city, and our house had been built when lots were measured in acres rather than in square feet. We had a covered patio big enough for parties, a swing set for my daughter, and a pair of ancient oak trees that shaded the entire place. I settled into the hammock slung between two patio posts and swayed gently in the afternoon breeze. As soon as I closed my eyes, I was out.

I rarely remember my dreams, and that day was no exception. I woke up sweating and feeling as if a weight were pressing against my chest. That happened sometimes. I probably had a nightmare, and I probably deserved it. I rolled out of my hammock and made a cup of tea in the kitchen.

Hannah and Megan came home while my tea steeped,

and we had dusk prayers as a family. Megan was still too young to be required to partake in our formal prayer life, but she usually joined us on her own. When Hannah and I first had her, we decided that we wouldn't force our religion on Megan; it would be her choice. After everything that had happened to Rachel, though, I was beginning to doubt the wisdom of that plan.

After evening prayers, we went to my sister's house for dinner. There was an empty seat at the table where my niece would have sat. That was hard for Megan to understand, but I felt like it was important that we were there. Hannah offered to do the dishes after dinner, giving me the chance to talk to Rana and Nassir alone. I didn't want to talk to them about Rachel, but since I was the only investigator still looking into her death, I had to.

We settled into chairs on their covered front porch. I didn't know what to say for a few minutes, so I stared across the street. I could smell horse shit; evidently my sister was still on her organic gardening kick. Eventually, I cleared my throat and glanced at Rana and Nassir. Rana smiled weakly in response.

'You look like you want to say something,' she said.

'Robbie Cutting died today,' I said, still nodding. 'He was Rachel's boyfriend.'

Nassir stood and spit onto the hedges in front of the porch. He rested his hands on the rail, his back towards me.

'We heard this afternoon,' he said.

'Did you know him?' I asked.

'No,' he said, turning around, his arms crossed. 'Rachel never told us about him.'

I leaned back in the chair, waiting for the angry glare to leave Nassir's face. It never did.

'Do you think there were other things she was hiding from you?' I asked.

'Rana and I have answered enough questions today,' he said, putting his hands flat towards me. 'We don't need more.'

My sister reached over and put her hand on her husband's side. She looked to him before looking back at me.

'Why are you asking about Rachel?' she asked.

'I've taken over her case. I want to find out what happened to her before someone else gets hurt.'

Nassir and Rana looked at each other. He exhaled heavily through his nose and looked away. Rana looked back at me, uncertainty etched across her face.

'A man from the police department visited us this afternoon,' she said, her eyebrows pressed together and her forehead furrowed. 'He said the case was closed, that Robbie admitted killing Rachel.'

Thank you, Mike Bowers.

'That might be true, but we don't know for sure,' I said. 'We have to be positive so no one else gets hurt.'

Nassir's throat bobbed. Redness formed around his eyes.

'Do you believe what they said about my daughter?' he asked, his voice cracking. 'That she slept with this boy, that they did drugs?'

I ran my hand across my face, thinking my answer through.

'I loved Rachel,' I said, leaning forward and resting my elbows on my knees. 'She didn't deserve what happened to her. That's all I know.'

I don't know if that was the right thing to say or not, but Nassir started pacing slowly, the muscles of his jaw protruding as he clenched his teeth. His nostrils flared with every exhalation. Rana stared at him for a moment, but then turned towards me.

'I'll answer your questions,' she said. 'Promise me you won't hurt Rachel. Her memory, I mean. And if you find something bad, we don't want to know about it.'

A big part of me wanted to shut up right there. Interviewing someone after they lose a loved one is worse than pouring salt on old wounds; it's like dipping them in hydrochloric acid. For what it was worth, I promised that I'd do my best. I paused for a moment, gathering my thoughts and looking at my feet so I wouldn't have to meet Rana or Nassir's eyes.

'How were things at home lately?' I asked a moment later. 'With Rachel.'

My sister shrugged.

'She was growing up,' she said. 'You know how that is.'

'That means a lot of different things for a lot of different people,' I said. 'What do you mean?'

Rana looked at Nassir for a moment. He didn't return the gaze.

'She was a teenager,' she said. 'She wanted to go to her friends' houses, she wanted to stay out later, she wanted us to stay out of her room. Things like that.'

'Did she ever get in trouble?' I asked. 'At home or at school?'

Rana paused.

'She broke curfew,' she said. 'And she got a speeding ticket last year.'

I nodded, hoping Rana would continue. She didn't.

'Is there anything else?' I asked.

Nassir stopped pacing and leaned against the porch railing, shaking his head. Rana looked at her shoes.

'I was in her room two months ago,' she said. 'I found a bag of something when I was putting clothes in her drawers. It was marijuana.'

Nassir's shoulders dropped. Rana looked at him and then down at her feet.

'I'm sorry I didn't tell you,' she said. 'I thought it'd be better if you didn't know.'

'You should have told me,' he said, his voice low and soft. 'We could have done something together.'

'I didn't tell you because I knew how you'd react,' said Rana. 'You'd want to send her away so she'd marry some boy she's never even met. That's not what she wanted.'

'At least she'd be alive,' he snapped. Nassir stopped speaking for a moment. Eventually, he shook his head. His voice was softer when he spoke again. It almost cracked. 'She was a child, Rana. She didn't know what she wanted. We could have protected her.'

'She needed guidance, not our protection,' said Rana. 'We couldn't hide her behind a veil. That isn't right.'

Neither spoke again for a moment. I felt like a voyeur intruding upon someone else's private life. I started to stand, but Rana put her hand on my knee, stopping me. She looked at Nassir.

'I'd like to talk to Ashraf by myself,' she said. 'Is that okay?'

Nassir hesitated, but then walked toward the front door. Before opening it, he looked back.

'You should have told me, Rana. No matter what. You should have told me.'

'I know I should have,' said Rana. 'Now please go inside.'

Nassir dropped his head and did as Rana asked, leaving the two of us alone. My sister was a strong woman. She got that from my mother. My family had never faced the sort of discrimination African Americans faced in the deep South, but we weren't welcomed with open arms by our community, either. Despite having a doctorate in English Literature from Cambridge, my mother couldn't even get a job teaching High School Composition. To make ends meet, she worked two full-time jobs, one at a dry cleaners and the other at a janitorial service. Rana raised me while my mother was at work. It wasn't how either of our childhoods should have been.

'Are you okay?' I asked.

'I will be,' she said. 'Now please, ask your questions, and I'll tell you what I can.'

I took a notebook from my pocket and opened it to the first clean page. I took a deep breath before speaking.

'You found marijuana in her room,' I said eventually. 'Did you ever find anything other than that?'

'No,' she said. 'She said it wasn't even hers. Some girl at school had given it to her to hide. The drug tests the school gave her always came back clean, so I believed her.'

'How about her friends? Did they ever get in trouble?'

Rana looked down. 'I don't know who her friends are anymore. That boy Robbie. She never even told us about him.'

'Do you know Alicia Weinstein?' I asked.

Rana looked wistfully at a Tudor-style home across the street.

'We used to be neighbors. She and Rachel played

together every day when they were young, but her family moved a few years ago.'

'Do you know if the kids kept in touch?'

'They weren't close any more,' she said. 'At least not like they were. I guess they still saw each other at school, but Alicia hasn't come over here in years.'

'How about a girl with curly red hair?' I asked. 'Rachel had pictures of her in her locker.'

'Her name is Caitlin Long,' said Rana. 'She and Rachel played tennis together. They were going to share a dorm in college. They even had the color scheme for their room picked out.'

I leaned forward and took a business card from my wallet. I handed it to Rana.

'Can you give her this?' I asked. 'I'd like to talk to her.'

Rana took my card and nodded as I thought my next question through.

'This is going to sound strange, but I am coming from somewhere with this,' I said. 'Did Rachel ever talk about vampires? Or a dance club in Plainfield? Or even someone named Azrael?'

Rana looked away from me.

'She read those books, the ones Imam Habib talked about.'

Imam Habib was the leader of our mosque and had warned some of the young girls in our community against

90

the Twilight series. I hadn't read the books, but Hannah had. She liked them, but novels about vampires were definitely not Islam-approved.

'Was there anything more to it than books?'

Rana wrung her hands together, a pained expression on her face.

'You have to understand. I wanted her to fit in,' she said. 'You don't know how hard it is to be a teenage girl in this country, to see your classmates stare at you for being different. I do. I wanted her to find herself and be happy.'

'What did she do?' I asked. Rana paused before speaking.

'She and her friends wore black, they watched bad horror movies. It was nothing. If I had thought she was in trouble, I would have stepped in.'

'And you never got the sense that there was more to it than just black clothes?'

She looked away.

'Looking back, maybe. I don't know,' she said. She looked at me. 'Some of Rachel's friends changed. Alicia was such a nice girl when she was growing up. She always smiled at me, always said hello. I saw her when I picked up Rachel at school a few months ago. She smiled and said hello, but it was superficial. It made me feel uncomfortable.'

Having interviewed Alicia, I knew the feeling Rana was describing.

'Do you hear any rumors about the girls or anything like that?' I asked.

Rana looked away.

'I try not to keep up with gossip,' she said. 'Most of the women at Rachel's school prefer to ignore me at PTA meetings, anyway.'

Rana and I talked for a few more minutes, but I didn't learn anything new about the case. After promising me whatever help she could give me, Rana went back inside, leaving me on the porch alone with my thoughts.

I stayed there for a moment, leafing through my notes and filling in parts I had left blank. The case was frustrating. If Rachel's death was an accident, why would someone try to cover it up by hiding drugs in her locker and lying to the police? And if it wasn't an accident, what would anyone gain by killing a teenager? It didn't make sense.

I closed my notebook and sat up straight, trying and failing to fit together pieces in my obscure and macabre puzzle. The lights flicked off as I put my notebook in my pocket. I doubted Rana would turn the lights off on me, so it was probably Megan. Hannah and I had taught her to shut off lights when she left a room, and she was pretty good about it. She had probably used the hallway bathroom and shut everything off on her way. I turned to go back inside when I noticed something across the street move in my peripheral vision. I stopped as my eyes adjusted to the darkness. What had been shadows became shapes and what had been shapes became images.

Someone was watching me.

As if noticing my stare, the figure turned and darted through a chest-high hemlock hedge, disappearing completely. Without thinking, I jogged down the front steps and across my sister's lawn. I stopped on the side walk and looked up and down the street. The night was silent and dark. I couldn't see anyone. A chill that had very little to do with the temperature traveled up and down my spine.

That was a little creepy.

I went back to the house and rounded up my family. I didn't tell Rana why, but I reminded her to put on her security system as soon as we left. She and Nassir would be fine. They were in a wealthy area, so officers from the local precinct patrolled it pretty heavily. If someone tried to break in, he'd be arrested before getting past the front door. I doubted the mystery stalker was after Nassir or Rana, though. He had been watching me – and with two people already dead, that was worrying.

Chapter 6

Hannah and Megan went grocery shopping the next morning, giving me the house to myself for an hour or so. I went to my home office and spun around in my chair. The case wasn't just about Rachel anymore; it was about Robbie Cutting, too, and I needed to find out what I could about him. I fired up my computer, and when it finished loading, I opened a web browser. The Cuttings were among the wealthiest people in town; hopefully they were wealthy enough to need a security system with surveillance cameras.

I googled John Meyers' firm and had a secretary on the phone within two minutes. She put me on hold while she conferred with her boss. I grabbed a cup of coffee from the kitchen as I waited. I could hear the thrum of a busy office in the background when Meyers picked up.

'This is John Meyers,' he said. 'What can I do for you, Detective?'

'Thanks for taking my call,' I said, walking from my kitchen to my office. 'I'm investigating a case related to Robbie Cutting's death, and I wanted to call and see if the Cuttings had security cameras at their house.'

Meyers was silent for a moment, presumably thinking.

'I was told that all investigations into Rachel Haddad and Robbie Cutting were closed.'

'Mostly,' I said. 'The homicide investigations are closed for now, but we've got a couple of loose ends to tie up. Rachel supposedly died of a drug overdose, and we haven't found any drugs yet. We're trying to find out what's going on.'

'And surveillance footage would help you how?' asked Meyers.

I thought through my answer for a second, but I couldn't come up with anything offhand.

'I'm not at liberty to discuss operational specifics at this time,' I said.

'Then I'm sorry, but the only way you'll see that footage is with a court order, Detective.'

Shit.

I exhaled slowly, thinking.

'Lieutenant Bowers and I disagree about certain things,' I said. 'I want to see the tape to make sure Robbie Cutting was alone when he died.'

Meyers clucked his tongue.

'So this is about Robbie's death,' said Meyers. 'Is this an official request?'

'No,' I said.

'Suppose I tell you to get a warrant, then.'

'Then your clients will likely never find out what happened to their son,' I said. My voice was sharper than I intended, and I could hear Meyers breathe heavily. 'I'm sorry, but that's how it is. This case is closed. I'm your clients' only shot at finding out what happened.'

'Give me a moment to confer with the Cuttings. I'll call you back.'

Meyers hung up before I could say anything else. I squeezed the phone for a moment, but eventually I forced myself to relax. I really wanted a drink, which was a good sign that I didn't need one.

I took the phone to the living room to wait. It was early enough that the morning news was still on, but they didn't report anything terribly interesting. There were no reported murders the night previous; that was probably a relief to the boys and girls in homicide. Despite the respite, a group of churches on the city's near-north side planned a peace rally downtown to protest the recent surge in violence. Nothing would come of it, but it was nice to hear that neighborhoods were pulling together.

My phone rang about fifteen minutes later. I picked it up and put it to my ear.

'They'll meet you,' said Meyers. 'One this afternoon. Don't be late.'

I scratched my forehead with my thumb.

'Think we could make it a little earlier? The sooner I get the information I need, the sooner I can solve this case.'

'Be pleased with what you have, Detective,' said Meyers. 'This isn't my idea. And Mrs Cutting's blessing or not, if you screw us on this, I'll screw you twice as hard. That's a promise.'

That was a disturbing image.

I thanked him for his time and hung up. I had anticipated spending the day on Robbie and Rachel's case, but I had other things I could do, too. I cleaned myself up in the bathroom and had morning prayer in the living room. After that, I got dressed and hopped in my car. IMPD's narcotics squad played by slightly different rules than the rest of our department. They almost never went on TV, they rarely attended morning briefings, and they didn't even occupy the same building as the rest of us. Instead, they stayed in an old warehouse a couple of blocks away in order to maintain their anonymity. They were a professional unit, though, and did good work.

I parked in the city government parking lot and

hiked the three blocks to their building. By design, the place looked abandoned. I walked to its only door, a solid, slate-gray piece of steel, and hit the buzzer on the keypad beside it. The door popped open about three minutes later, and I flashed my badge at a short Hispanic man in a Hawaiian shirt and jeans. He let me in.

While the exterior of the building looked derelict, the inside was a buzzing, modern office with advanced video and sound labs to process surveillance evidence. My escort stopped in the front hallway and raised his eyebrows expectantly.

'You seen Detective Lee this morning?' I asked.

'He's the wino in sound booth one. You know how to get there?'

I nodded and headed in the direction of the sound booth. Since I had never worked narcotics, I didn't know a lot of its detectives, and I was stopped twice to explain who I was. Both times I had to hold up my badge and explain that I was on my way to see David Lee in sound booth one. Lee met me in the hallway before I was stopped a third time. He was a small man with a thin goatee and jet-black hair. He wore an old brown suit that was as wrinkled as anything I had ever seen, and I could see dark makeup beneath his eyes. He looked as if he had gone through a rough couple of years, which I assumed was intentional.

'Heard you were looking for me, Ash,' he said, putting out his hand for me to shake. 'Been a long time.'

'The Prosecutor's Office keeps me pretty busy,' I said. 'Witnesses don't babysit themselves.'

He snickered.

'What can I do for you?'

'I'm looking for information,' I said. Lee nodded and motioned down the hallway with his head. I followed as we walked towards his actual desk. 'One of my confidential informants got jumped the other day. Somebody pulled off some of his fingernails with pliers.'

Lee whistled.

'He put his dick in the wrong hole or something?'

'I don't think so,' I said. 'James told me he was trying to make a buy, and it went bad. He's a good source, so I want to take care of him and make sure it doesn't happen again.'

We entered the bullpen. Like nearly everyone in IMPD, the narcotics squad shared a large open room rather than individual offices. They had cubicles, though, and Lee's had pictures of suspected drug pushers thumbtacked into the walls. I pulled a rolling desk chair from a nearby cubicle and sat beside Lee's desk. He leaned back and put his hands behind his head.

'I haven't heard about anybody with a fingernail fetish,' he said. 'Your CI get a name?'

I shook my head no.

'He didn't even know who he was supposed to meet, but the buy was set up by a guy named Rollo.'

Lee looked interested. 'Real name is Rolando Diaz,' he said, leaning forward. He moved his computer's mouse and typed in a password to turn off the screensaver before calling up one of the department's felon databases. He typed in the name and sat back as it searched. 'He's basically a middleman. Sets up a lot of deals so upper management doesn't have to meet with the guys on the street.'

That jibed with what I had heard from James.

'Think he'd burn a dealer if given the order?'

Lee shrugged.

'Rollo's not a choir boy, but I don't think he's pulling off too many fingernails.'

'You know who he works for?' I asked.

'He was with the Cubans, but the Russians pushed them out a year or two back. He's probably moved on. Is your source worth some work?'

'He's done good work for me.'

Lee ran his hand across his goatee, presumably thinking. He was smart enough to avoid asking what sort of work James had done for me, and I sure as hell wasn't going to say. Bottom line, James did things for the department few other people could. He knew that sometimes people had to be taken off the street and was willing to help us do that. IMPD owed James as far as I was concerned.

'We can roll on Rollo this morning,' said Lee. 'Haven't rousted him for a few weeks.'

'You got an address?' I asked.

Lee tapped his monitor.

'Yep,' he said. 'You up for it?'

'Hell yes.'

We took Lee's department-issued car, a black '63 Chevy Impala polished to a mirror shine. It stood out downtown, but it was right at home in the neighborhood where we were heading. We drove north for about ten minutes, the streets gradually becoming more residential the further we drove. Eventually, we were surrounded by apartments and small bungalows on all sides. Most of the buildings had at least one window broken, and the streets were riddled with unfilled potholes.

Lee parked beside a five-story apartment building that looked like it had at one time been a school. Its brick was brownish-red, and the sidewalk in front was cracked and crumbling. I stepped out of the car and pulled my jacket tight across me, hiding the firearm inside. Lee pulled what looked like a forty-five from a belt holster and chambered a round.

'This is it,' he said, holstering his firearm. 'You strapped?'

I nodded and Lee walked toward the building's steel door. The handle was broken, so the door never locked.

So much for resident safety. Rollo lived on the fourth floor at the end of a hallway. The carpet was threadbare and I could see the concrete subfloor through cigarette burns. It smelled like piss. Lee nodded toward the last door on the right. The brown paint covering it was chipped, leaving flakes on the carpet beneath.

We didn't need to discuss what would happen. We both had done it enough times that it was old hat. I put my hand over the peep hole while Lee positioned himself in front with his firearm extended. I counted down from three to one with my free hand, and Lee kicked the door beneath the lock. The door swung inward hard and fast. Lee vaulted inside, sweeping the room with his firearm. I did likewise and almost choked on the stink.

Rollo lived in a one-room shithole apartment. I saw a Murphy bed built into the wall on the left and a small kitchenette with miniature stove and fridge to the right. Empty boxes of macaroni and cheese as well as cigarette butts littered the floor. Flies buzzed everywhere.

'Shit,' said Lee, sliding his firearm into his belt holster. I stepped forward and saw the source of the smell. Rollo was dead. He sat on a chair across from the door, his head leaning back and a slit on his neck from ear to ear like a huge grin. A waterfall of brown dried blood stained his shirt.

I covered my mouth with my hand and strode forward.

Whoever had killed him damn near decapitated him because I could see the vertebrae of his neck. I cursorily looked around but couldn't find weapons or shell casings. It didn't even look like he had put up a fight.

'This is going to ruin my day,' said Lee, already taking out his cell phone. He told the dispatcher to send uniformed officers for crowd control and a detective from homicide. While Lee was on the phone, I checked out the kitchen. Rollo was a man who liked to keep in touch, evidently, because he had a cardboard box full of cheap prepaid cell phones still in their packaging on the counter. It looked like Rollo bought them by the case.

I checked to make sure Lee wasn't looking and picked up the only phone out of its packaging. The call record had one entry, a local number. I memorized it and wiped off the phone with my shirt sleeve before putting it back on the counter. About two minutes later, Lee hung up and looked at me.

'You might want to get a hold of your CI. We're probably going to need him.'

Lee was right. Even if James wasn't involved with Rollo's death, somebody would want to talk to him. I walked to the hallway, adding the phone number I had found on Rollo's phone to my address book as I went. Once that was done, I called James and waited through two rings for someone to pick up.

'Detective Rashid?'

The voice was familiar, but I couldn't narrow it down except to say that it wasn't James.

'Yeah, this is Ash Rashid,' I said. 'I'm looking for James Russo. Who is this?'

'Mike Bowers. And if you want to talk to Russo, you're going to need a psychic because I'm staring at his goddamn corpse.'

Chapter 7

Lee and I got our story straight in the hallway before any officers arrived. Islam usually forbids lying, but there are exceptions. If Hannah asked me if her meatloaf was good, I could lie and say I love it as long as my intention was to avoid hurting her. I could also lie in times of warfare. While I didn't have a background in Islamic law, I figured police work is as close to warfare as I could get without enlisting.

Lee and I waited for about five minutes for the first officers to arrive. Both were young, and neither was of color. That wasn't a good combination for successful policing in that neighborhood. We gave them the basic story we had concocted, and they looked at the scene for a moment. One of the guys looked as if he were going to puke when he saw the body, but he held it together.

It took another half hour for the rest of the troops to

show up. An old colleague of mine from homicide took our statements. Even if he didn't believe our story completely, he wouldn't jam us up; he knew that if we had dropped Rollo, we must have had a damn good reason. He released Lee as soon as he gave his statement but told me to stick around and talk to Lieutenant Bowers. Bowers wasn't my CO, so I could have left. I didn't, though. Instead, I took a moment to watch the crime scene technicians comb through Rollo's apartment.

Indianapolis has pretty good techs. The problem was that they weren't going to solve the case without better information. They focused their efforts on the shattered door frame, presumably thinking the killer got in that way. I doubted he did, though. He would have had to pick the lock, slit Rollo's throat while he was sleeping and get out without leaving a trace. There weren't many people who could do that.

I looked back in the room for a moment. The window behind Rollo's chair was open. I hadn't noticed that before, although it must have been open when Lee and I got in there. That was another viable entrance. With Rollo's chair pressed against the window, the killer would just have to reach in, slice the fat bastard's throat, and get the fuck out. Thirty seconds tops. Of course, it'd take a hell of an athlete to do that from four stories up.

I ran my hand across my chin, considering. I had two

options, and both pointed to a professional hit. Seemed a little extreme to take out someone like Rollo. Most of the time when people like him are killed, the evidence is splattered all over the walls and into neighboring apartments. Spray and pray with an AK47 isn't pretty, but it is effective. The forensics team would have had their work cut out for them even if Lee and I hadn't done anything to stymie their efforts.

Bowers showed up about twenty minutes later. He had changed clothes since the last time I had seen him, but the bags under his eyes had grown. With as many homicides as the city had in the past few days, I doubted he had gotten much sleep. He stared at me, not saying anything at first. Eventually, he motioned to follow him down the hall and away from the hubbub of the crime scene. The urine smell dissipated some, but the overhead lights flickered periodically.

'What can I do for you, Lieutenant?' I asked.

'How do you know James Russo?'

'He's a CI. Nailed him for possession while I was on patrol eight years ago and kept in touch.'

Bowers shifted on his feet, his eyes boring into me.

'Then explain to me why he doesn't have a file downtown. How are you paying him?'

'He never wanted money.'

And that was true, at least. James hadn't ever wanted money; he was an information hound. I periodically told him who got pinched and where on minor drug charges. It was valuable information for a dealer looking to expand his territory, so I always figured he sold it somewhere.

'What'd you guys talk about at your last visit?' asked Bowers.

A door opened down the hall, and an elderly woman stuck her head out but quickly went back inside when she saw us.

'Nothing special. I wanted to see how he was. Hadn't talked to him for a while.'

'And how was he?' he asked.

'You saw his fingers,' I said.

'Yeah, I did,' he said. 'Russo's a goddamn lowlife. We found enough pot on him that we could have charged him with possession with intent to sell if he were alive. You could probably guess that, though. What you probably can't guess is that he made three phone calls yesterday. Just three. You, his grandma, and Rolando Diaz. Now you're here, and Rolando's dead. I want to know what's going on, and I want to know right now.'

I sighed.

'If I knew, I'd tell you.'

'Would you?' asked Bowers, stepping in close enough that I could feel his breath on my face. I took a step back.

'You've got my statement, so unless I'm under arrest, I'm leaving,' I said. I glanced back at Rollo's apartment.

'And a word of advice. Rollo was taken out by a professional. Unless you want bodies piling up, I'd start trying to figure out who he pissed off instead of watching me.'

Bowers looked as if he were going to say something, but he pushed past me and stormed down the hall. While he shouted at evidence technicians, I took the stairs to ground level and had a uniformed officer drive me downtown. He dropped me off near Circle Center Mall. It was too early for the bars to be open, so I went by a café that served brunch and ordered an egg-white omelette with a Bloody Mary on the side. I felt a little better after that.

After eating, I parked myself on a bench and buried my face in my hands. Jimmy Russo. I had known him since he was fifteen. He was a good kid even if he had made mistakes. I stayed there for a few minutes before looking at my watch. It was eleven and I had another two hours before my meeting at the Cuttings' house. I thumbed through the address book on my cell phone until I came to the number of one of our techs who worked with telecom systems. She answered before the phone finished a single ring.

'Sarah, it's Detective Rashid. You got a minute?'

'Yeah, what's up?' she said, her voice raspy from years of abuse. Sarah was the lead singer in an all-female heavy metal band. I'm not a connoisseur of heavy metal music, but supposedly they were good. She played their demo disc for me once. Maybe I'm old, but I didn't get it. I'm not a fan of hearing women scream until they're hoarse, I guess.

'I've got a cell phone number,' I said. 'I wondered if you could trace it for me.'

'Shoot,' she said. I flipped through my phone's address book until I found the entry I had made outside Rollo's apartment. I read the number aloud, and I heard Sarah's keyboard click as she typed. 'It's a prepaid cell on Virgin Wireless's network. No name is assigned to the account.'

That was about what I had expected after seeing the stack of phones in Rollo's apartment.

'Is there anything else you can tell me about it?'

'If we had a warrant. Do you?'

'Can you do anything without a warrant?'

Sarah didn't say anything for a moment.

'Is this for a case?' she asked. 'Or are we spying on your wife?'

'It's a case,' I said.

'Good. You'd be surprised how many people want to find out where their wives go during the day,' she said. 'Give me about five minutes, and I'll make a call and get back to you. I might be able to set something up.'

'I appreciate it.'

Sarah hung up, and I walked the four blocks to my car. It wasn't even noon yet, but it was already hot enough outside that I almost expected my shoes to start melting on the sidewalk. I opened all four doors and let the interior air out for a few minutes before getting in. Sarah called back while I sat in the front seat with my legs hanging outside.

'Did you find anything out?' I asked.

'Sort of,' she said. 'That number you gave me belongs to a phone that's only made two outgoing calls, both in the last twenty-four hours, and both were sent from a tower right outside Plainfield. It's been off for more than twelve hours now.'

What Sarah didn't need to say was that the phone had probably been tossed, so tracking it further would have been a waste. I sighed and wiped sweat off my forehead before thanking her for her time and hanging up. I was starting to hate Plainfield even more than I did most suburbs.

The gate in front of the Cuttings' property was closed when I drove up, but it opened as soon as I turned off the road. Must have been on a pressure sensor. John Meyers met me outside the front door of the main house. He wore a charcoal-gray pinstripe suit, and his silver hair was thick and neat. I shook his hand.

'Thank you for letting me do this,' I said.

Meyers turned towards the front door.

'Thank Maria Cutting,' he said. 'I've already told you that I was against the idea.'

We walked inside, and Meyers led me to a plain white door near the main entryway. It opened into a narrow staircase with rough gray walls and a concrete floor. I followed him for about a dozen yards to a steel door with SECURITY stenciled on the outside. The interior looked like the production booth of a television station with four flat-screen monitors attached to the wall and a control panel with dials and buttons beneath. A balding middle-aged man swiveled on a rolling desk chair and faced me.

'Detective Rashid?' he asked, extending his hand towards me. I shook it. 'Tom Garrity, Garrity Industrial Tech.'

'Good to meet you,' I said, looking at the monitors. 'This is quite a system.'

'One of the most extensive we've ever put into a residential environment,' Tom said. 'Mr Cutting takes his family's safety very seriously.'

If he had taken my niece's safety that seriously, I might not have been there.

'What sort of cameras do you have on the guest house?' I asked.

'None inside, of course,' said Tom, typing on a laptop beside the control panel. Two of the four computer monitors went dark, while the image on the other two shifted to what at first appeared to be static pictures of the guest house. 'These are live feeds from outside, though.'

I squinted and looked closer. As I did, I noticed the shadows shifting as the breeze rustled nearby trees. The picture was so clear that it was almost like looking through a window.

'Is there any way we can back this up to about an hour before Robbie's death?'

Tom nodded and turned a thick, round knob. The picture shifted too quickly to see what was going on until Tom glanced back up at me.

'What you're looking at right now are still images exactly sixty minutes before Robbie Cutting passed away. We can alter the playing speed if you want.'

'Play it regular speed first, and we'll see what happens.'

Tom hit another button, and we watched for about two minutes. Nothing moved.

'Can we try speeding it up?' I asked. Tom fiddled with another knob. The image was largely static still, but the time stamp in the corner shifted rapidly.

'Whoa,' said Tom, straightening about five minutes later and hitting the pause button. I hadn't seen anything and glanced towards Meyers. He shrugged.

'What's so exciting?' I asked.

Without saying anything, Tom pointed to a pair of smudges near the top of the screen on the left monitor.

'Shadows,' he said. He twisted a knob on the control panel, and the color drained from the images. The shadows shifted from gray to black. They were small,

113

but Tom was right. I could make out what looked like a head and torso on one image and maybe the top of a head on the other. Tom played the video at regular speed. My heartbeat ticked up a notch as the two figures walked from one side of the screen to the other.

'Where are these figures going?' asked Meyers.

'Looks like behind the guest house,' said Tom.

I looked at Meyers.

'Is there a back door?' I asked.

He focused his gaze above the monitors, seeming to think for a moment. 'No, but there is a window leading to the bathroom.'

I turned towards Tom.

'Is there any way we can get another shot of these figures? Maybe from a different camera?'

He grimaced. 'We've got pretty good coverage of the main house, but there are dead zones around the yard.'

I bit my lower lip. 'When'd you put the system in?'

'We upgraded the cameras last year, but the basic system was designed four years ago.'

Four years was a long time with a teenager in the house. Robbie and his friends had probably discovered where those dead zones were years earlier so they could break in and throw parties unseen. It's possible that he wasn't alone when he died. That didn't necessarily mean he was murdered, but it was significant.

'Can you get me a copy of this video?' I asked. 'I want some of our technicians to look at it.'

'It's digital,' said Tom. 'I can email it to you as an attachment.'

'Fine,' I said, reaching for my wallet. I took out a business card and wrote my email address on the back before handing it over. I looked at Meyers. 'This may get complicated.'

Chapter 8

I walked back to my car after the meeting, gathering my thoughts. I'd only had one drink that day, and my buzz was gone, leaving a dull, longing ache in its place. I both wanted and didn't want another. I licked my lips. They were dry and chapped. I didn't drink when I was young, not even in college. I started four years ago to help me forget a little boy who had been mauled by a pit bull before dying of exposure. Tyrone Smith. His mother had abandoned him in the middle of the park in the middle of the night in the middle of winter so she could entertain her drug-dealer boyfriend without hearing the kid. He died with tears frozen on his cheeks, presumably crying out for the very woman who had dumped him with the garbage in a city park.

My partner and I arrested her a day later. It wasn't the first time I had seen her, either. I had met her when Tyrone was an infant and that same boyfriend had beaten her up. Their apartment was unfit for a child. There were empty liquor bottles on the counters, empty food containers on the floor, and cockroaches everywhere. I could have called child services. I should have. I didn't, though, because his mother promised me she'd file a restraining order against her boyfriend and call the police if she saw him again. I even gave her the address of a women's shelter that would have taken them both in. I'm sure she forgot about it as soon as I left.

I gave Tyrone's mother a second chance, and in doing so I learned an important lesson. No one deserves a second chance. People don't change; they just get older. A little boy died because I was too naive to believe that. I drink to forget that mistake and many more like it. My religion told me I was damning my soul to hell, but as far as I was concerned, I deserved it.

Before leaving the Cuttings' property, I called Mrs Phelps, one of my neighbors, and asked if she could pick up Megan at daycare and watch her for the next hour or two. Mrs Phelps' husband had been a detective before he died and I had the feeling she already knew what a long day at the office entailed.

I drove for about fifteen minutes and parallel-parked in front of the first bar I could find. It was a dive that had the audacity to call itself a tavern. It was late afternoon, and the place was filling up with men and women coming home from work. I had three drinks and some peanuts before going home. It was enough to give me a buzz and still allow me to function.

I drove home without incident, although that was more testament to the wide berth other drivers gave my unmarked cruiser than my driving ability. I parked in my driveway and jogged to the bathroom inside to rinse with mouthwash before walking to Mrs Phelps' house to pick up my daughter. I could hear them in the backyard, so I followed the house around back. Megan was drawing flowers on the concrete patio while Mrs Phelps sat on a lawn chair in the shade of her covered porch. The muscles in my shoulders relaxed as soon as I saw Megan. I've got a lot of good things in my life. A caring family, friends, a steady job. Without a doubt, Megan was my favorite, though. She ran towards me, so I swept down and hugged her.

'Hi, sweetheart,' I said in a singsong voice I reserved only for her. 'Did you have fun today?'

She nodded her head vigorously. 'We made pictures in art, and then some boy pushed me on a swing, and then we took a nap. And that was all before lunch.'

'That sounds like a very nice day,' I said, turning my gaze to Mrs Phelps. 'Thank you for watching her. Work's keeping me busy right now.'

'It's no trouble,' said Mrs Phelps. 'She's a good girl.'

Megan grinned in agreement before turning and waving at her babysitter.

'Thank you for the lemonade.'

'Any time, honey,' said the older woman.

I thanked Mrs Phelps again before taking Megan's hand and leading her back to our house. She drew pictures at the breakfast table while I started dinner. Hannah came home after six, and we had dusk prayer in the living room. I had a hard time staying focused on the prayer. Some of that might have been because of the drinks I had earlier, but not all. My thoughts kept straying to Mike Bowers. He hadn't even asked the Cuttings about surveillance cameras. A detective with as much experience as he had didn't make those kinds of mistakes.

I was rolling the prayer mats when I felt a hand on my shoulder.

'You okay, honey?' asked Hannah. 'You haven't said much since I got home.'

I shook my head, forcing it to clear.

'Yeah, sorry,' I said. 'I had a long day. My head is elsewhere.'

'You can talk to me about it,' she said, nodding her head earnestly. 'You can talk to me about anything.'

I felt cords tighten around my heart. I smiled weakly and looked down. Hannah would listen if I started talking; she'd sit there quietly with her hand on my knee as long as I needed. It might even feel good at first, at least for me. I've seen and heard so many things I want to forget that they've become part of who I am. If I told Hannah about them, she'd listen, and then I'd see the lights go out in her eyes when she found out who I really was. I've left parts of my soul blackened and dead at more crime scenes than I care to remember. She didn't need to share that; it was my burden to bear.

I cleared my throat.

'We should have dinner,' I said. 'I don't want it to get cold.'

I spent the rest of that night with my family. Megan colored after dinner while Hannah and I watched a couple of home improvement shows. After Megan went to bed, we switched to a bad movie on one of our premium channels about intelligent sharks that escape their holding tanks and eat the scientists studying them. Hannah said it would have been better if the sharks ate lawyers instead. As a former law student, I wasn't sure how to take that.

I got up the next day intending to spend the morning studying the surveillance video from the Cuttings' house with one of IMPD's technicians. It didn't work out like that. Tom Garrity from Garrity Industrial Tech had sent me the video, but his wasn't the only email in my inbox. I had another from Susan Mercer, and this time, she really did sound pissed. She wanted me to call her as soon as I could.

Since I was technically on vacation, I could have ignored the email. The problem was that I wanted to join the Prosecutor's Office if I finished law school, and Susan was on the hiring committee. Hell, she practically was the hiring committee, so pissing her off wouldn't be the smartest career move. I looked at the clock on my computer. It was ten after eight, so she ought to have been in. I called her secretary and waited to be put through to Susan's office.

'Detective Rashid,' she said. 'It's nice to hear from you. How's your vacation?'

Susan's voice was flowery and light. She really was pissed.

'Uhm, it's fine,' I said. 'Very relaxing.'

She scoffed. 'Funny, that's not what I hear. I want you here ASAP. There are some people who need to talk to you.'

'These people have names?' I asked.

'Yeah. Get over here at nine and you'll find out.'

Susan slammed the phone hard enough that it almost made my ears ring. That conversation didn't bode well for me.

Hannah had taken Megan to an eight o'clock swimming lesson that morning, so I had the house to myself. I hopped in the shower and then had a quick breakfast of toast and coffee before heading out.

Susan's floor was buzzing that morning, as it usually

121

was on a weekday. Most of the senior prosecutors had their own private offices, but the junior staff members shared a bullpen like detectives. Since few judges schedule court before nine, there were enough people milling about that it looked like a well dressed and orderly Christmas party.

I slipped through the crowds and walked to the communal coffee machine. The coffee was significantly better than what IMPD had; I guess that was a perk of the job. I poured a cup and started towards Susan's office. People glanced at me and whispered. A few with whom I had worked even mouthed 'good luck.' That really didn't bode well for me.

Rather than let me into her office directly, Susan's secretary led me to the floor's only conference room. On most mornings, it would have been occupied by lawyers holding depositions or pretrial conferences. Not that morning, though. The blinds were drawn, so I couldn't see inside. I put my hand on the door handle, but stopped before pulling it open.

'You know what I'm in for?' I asked Susan's secretary.

'A mess,' she said. 'Good luck.'

I thanked her and pulled the door open. The room had floor-to-ceiling windows overlooking the Federal Courthouse and the busy streets below. I blinked in the early morning light, taking stock of my surroundings. The conference table had seats for ten people, but only three were taken. I was meeting with Susan, Lieutenant Mike Bowers, and Jack Whittler, Indianapolis's elected prosecutor, the big guy with the million-dollar election campaign and Yale law degree. My stomach twisted.

'What can I do for you?' I asked, pulling the door shut behind me. 'I'm on vacation.'

'Sit down, Detective Rashid,' said Whittler, gesturing towards a seat across from him. 'I've been told some things, and I want to hear your side of it.'

I pulled out a rolling black leather chair and sat down before looking around the room. Whittler was the only person who didn't glare at me.

'Okay,' I said, looking at each face in turn. 'Can someone tell me what's going on?'

Susan started to say something, but Whittler held his hand up, stopping her.

'I hear you're a busy man on your vacation,' he said. He opened a folder and pressed it across the table towards me. It contained crime scene photos from Rollo's apartment. 'What were you doing there?'

I shrugged, trying to appear nonchalant. 'Someone from my mosque complained about drugs in her neighborhood. I asked Detective Lee to check it out with me.'

Whittler nodded.

'Do you do a lot of policing on your vacations?' he asked.

'Not usually,' I said, looking at Susan. 'But then again, most of my vacations are voluntary.'

Whittler glanced at her and then back at me. 'Is there any reason someone from your mosque would contact you instead of calling the police?'

That was an easy one to answer, at least.

'Yeah,' I said, nodding. 'In the past year, we've been vandalized six times, been broken into twice, and set on fire once. Imam Habib called the police each time, but nobody's ever investigated. We have at least one incident a month where somebody tries to disrupt Friday prayers, and most of us don't even bother trying to fly any more because we get randomly searched every time. I think people in my community have pretty good reason not to trust the police.'

Whittler shifted uncomfortably. 'Is there anything we can do to improve relations with your community?' he asked.

'Oh, Jesus,' said Bowers before I could say anything. 'You actually believe that sob story? Detective Rashid knew James Russo and Rolando Diaz, and now they're both fucking dead. That's why we're here. Rashid knows something. Meanwhile, I've got eight open homicides and jack shit to work them with because assholes—'

'That's enough, Detective,' said Susan, her voice sharp and loud. Bowers put his hands up defensively.

'Sorry,' he said. 'Haven't slept in a couple of days.'

Susan glared at him for another moment before turning to me. 'What can you tell us about James Russo? You talked to him. You admit that, right?'

There wasn't any point lying. I'm sure they had the phone records.

'I met James to ask him about my niece. Rachel died of a drug overdose, and James knows more about the local drug trade than anybody I know.'

Susan reached for the folder.

'Your niece's case is closed, Ash,' she said, glancing at Lieutenant Bowers. 'We have an acceptable resolution.'

I snorted. 'Because her boyfriend's dead?'

'Because her boyfriend killed himself and took responsibility for Rachel's death in his suicide note,' said Bowers, scowling. 'We've gone over this already. I'm truly sorry for your loss, but her case is closed.'

'Is Robbie Cutting's case closed, too?' I asked.

'Yes,' said Bowers. 'Suicide, as I told you at the scene.'

'Did you even bother looking at the surveillance footage from the Cuttings' house?' I asked.

Bowers snickered. 'He left a fucking note, Rashid,' he said. 'This is ridiculous.'

Susan held up her hand to shut him up, but didn't take her eyes from me.

'What surveillance?' she asked.

'The Cuttings have surveillance cameras all over their

property. The video shows shadows walking across the yard before Robbie was killed. He might not have been alone.'

'Does the video show these "shadows" breaking into the house?' asked Bowers.

I shook my head.

'Quite the case breaker, then,' he said. 'You found a video of the goddamn gardener at work, and now you're wasting my time with it. Great fucking job.'

Susan glared at him again.

'Shut up,' she said before turning back to me. 'You're on vacation. If I hear you're working this case again, I will write you up for insubordination. Is that clear?'

'Yes, ma'am.'

'Good. Now give everything you have on Robbie Cutting and Rachel Haddad to Lieutenant Bowers. He'll handle it. If he thinks the cases should be reopened, he will.'

Like hell he will.

I looked at Bowers. 'It's not all here, but I'll box it up and have it sent over.'

'I'll be waiting on pins and needles.' Bowers' lips were flat.

We glared at each other for a few moments, but eventually Susan kicked us both out so she could have a conversation with Jack Whittler. I ground my teeth and pulled myself out of the chair. It took a real force of will to avoid slamming the door in Mike Bowers' face on my way out. Rather than go by my office directly, I went to one of the big hotels downtown for breakfast. I had eggs with green peppers and onions, wheat toast, and a Bloody Mary with a vodka chaser. It was a nice breakfast.

Forty-five minutes later, I went back to my office, copied everything I had on Rachel and Robbie, and put it into a large, interdepartmental envelope addressed to Bowers. I took my copy with me and drove home, my head buzzing. I was distracted, so I had a little difficulty keeping my car in the lines on the interstate. It was nothing worse than the other commuters putting on makeup, shaving, or talking on their cell phones, though.

Hannah's Volkswagen was in the driveway when I got home. I parked beside it, but stayed in the car to think. I hadn't really lost my job, but it sure felt like it. I didn't know what to say to Hannah. Admitting I was home because my supervisor kicked me off a case probably wouldn't go over very well, especially with my breakfast still on my breath. I closed my eyes and drummed my fingers on the steering wheel until I heard something tap lightly on my window. Megan waved at me. I smiled and waved back before opening my door.

'Hi, *Baba*,' she said. '*Ummi* wants to know why you're home.'

'I couldn't get enough of you,' I said, reaching down

and putting my hand on my daughter's upper back and leading her through the kitchen door. My wife sat at the breakfast table, a cup of coffee in hand and a piece of toast on a plate in front of her.

'Did you forget something?' she asked.

'No, I'm home for the day. We closed some cases, so I'm taking a few days off.'

She smiled and looked genuinely relieved.

'Good. You needed a break. I made coffee if you want some.'

I grunted affirmative and poured myself a cup, hoping it would mask the liquor on my breath. Hannah and I took Megan to the park that morning. I pushed Megan on the swing, and we took a walk through the adjoining nature preserve. My phone rang while we walked through an archway formed by pruned lilac bushes. The blooms were gone, but Megan said it was like a storybook.

I left Hannah and Megan near the archway and looked at the screen on my phone. John Meyers. Odd. I hit the answer button and put it to my ear.

'This is Detective Rashid. What can I do for you, Counselor?'

'Morning, Detective,' said Meyers. 'I'm calling on behalf of Maria Cutting. She believes she might have found something pertinent to your investigation in her son's bedroom.'

I glanced back at my wife and daughter. Megan waved

happily at me while Hannah asked if anything was wrong. I shook my head no.

'I appreciate the call, but you'll have to talk to Lieutenant Mike Bowers with homicide about that. He's heading up that investigation for now.'

'I've already contacted the lieutenant, and he seemed less than enthusiastic to receive the call. I thought you might be a little more interested.'

'What did she find?'

'There was a bloodstain on the carpet in Robbie's bedroom, so Mrs Cutting had that pulled up this morning. While doing that, she found a safe embedded between floor joists. We haven't opened it yet, but we're operating under the assumption that it was Robbie's.'

I thought that through for a moment. That could have held the kid's drug supply, if he had one. Or it could have held a box of condoms and a bottle of rum. Or it could even have been empty. No matter what was in it, it wasn't worth my job.

'I'm sorry, but I can't help you. I have orders. If you feel that the case has been handled poorly, you can file a complaint, and it will be investigated in time. You can also hire a private investigator; I'm sure you have one on staff.'

Meyers sighed.

'That's what I told Maria you'd say,' he said, sighing again. 'Okay, thanks for your time.'

I wished Meyers luck and hung up, my stomach and mind turning. Teenagers hide things from their parents. When I was in high school, I hid a copy of Salman Rushdie's *The Satanic Verses* beneath my mattress. I thought it was cool because my Mom forbade me from reading it. Robbie Cutting's vices were probably a little rougher than heretical literature, but I doubted there'd be anything earthshaking in there, either. Even still, Bowers should have looked into it. I would have, at least.

I rejoined my family and we finished our walk in relative silence, my brain buzzing with thoughts and possibilities. I felt dead sober by the time we finished, so I drove home. As I parked on my driveway, I noticed a yellow note waving on my front door. Probably a flier trying to convince me to help elect some moral retard to public office. We got those a lot. I parked the Volkswagen beside my cruiser and checked out the note while Hannah unhooked Megan's car seat.

It was from Mrs Phelps. She had signed for flowers for us and said she'd be home most of the afternoon. That was weird; I hadn't ordered flowers, and I couldn't think of any special occasions lately. I crumpled the note, turned the corner of our house as Hannah pulled Megan out of the car, and shouted that I'd be back in a moment.

I knocked on Mrs Phelps' door and talked to her for

a few minutes. She had signed for a dozen yellow and white daisies in an oversized yellow coffee mug. I thanked her and headed back towards my house, pulling the card from its spindly plastic holder as I did.

'I have my eye on you. – A'

Must have been delivered to the wrong address.

I turned the card around so I could see if it had any other identifying marks. I read the address and felt my legs stiffen. The flowers were addressed to my daughter. I opened the card again, rereading the message. *I have my eye on you.* If they had been addressed to Hannah, I could attribute it to a simple mistake. I had bought her flowers online several times in the past, so the local florists had her name and address. No one would have had Megan's, though. My fingers trembled. Someone was watching my daughter.

I slipped the note into my pocket and walked back to my house. Hannah and Megan were in the kitchen when I got back. I put the flowers on the counter beside the stove and sat down to think.

'Those look nice,' said Hannah, picking up the mug and turning it around, presumably looking for a card. She put it down and looked at me. 'Who are they from?'

I cleared my throat, hoping my voice wouldn't crack.

'A shop in Plainfield. I think it was a delivery mistake. I'm going to make some calls and make sure somebody gets her daisies.'

Hannah nodded. 'Okay. I think I'm going to change and pull some weeds in the backyard.'

'That sounds good,' I said, already turning and heading towards my office. I plopped down in my chair and called Olivia Rhodes on my cell phone. She picked up on the third ring and cleared her throat.

'Ash, what's up?'

Olivia's voice sounded gravelly. I looked at my watch; it was a little after one in the afternoon.

'I get you up from a nap?'

'Yeah, power nap in Pamela's room.'

Pamela's room was a storage room in the basement of Olivia's station house. It had a pair of cots in it, a bunch of empty filing cabinets, and one poster of Pamela Anderson in a Baywatch red swimsuit. Detectives used it when they were working a case and needed a break but couldn't go home. Olivia must have been exhausted. She once told me she'd never use Pamela's because too many hairy asses had touched those cots during illicit midnight trysts.

'Sorry to wake you up, but I've got a problem.'

I told her about my stalker at Rana and Nassir's house the night before, my meeting with Susan Mercer, and now the flowers someone had sent Megan. Olivia's voice was clearer when she spoke.

'That's creepy. You run this by your CO yet?'

'She's not going to want to hear it,' I said. 'I'm going

to see what I can turn up before I turn this over to anyone else.'

Olivia didn't say anything for a second.

'You considered backing off?'

'No. If I show them my back, I'll find a knife in it eventually. I'm going to find out who's threatening Megan and make sure they can't do that again.'

Olivia paused, then said, 'Are you sure that's a good idea?'

'It's a fucking terrible idea, but it's my only option,' I said, my voice rising in volume and timbre. 'Look, I'm calling to give you a warning. If they're after me, they'll be after you, too. Watch your back.'

'Thank you, then,' she said. 'Be careful, okay? I hate funerals.'

I promised her that I would before hanging up and walking to the kitchen. Hannah was drying dishes at the sink while Megan played with a doll in the backyard.

'I've got some errands to run this afternoon,' I said. 'But what do you say to a matinée while I'm gone? That movie about the princess with the long hair is in theaters now, I think.'

Hannah put down the pan she had been scrubbing, her eyebrows raised.

'Why do you want us out of the house?'

I didn't say anything for a moment. I had learned

early on in my marriage not to hold things back from my wife. She was too smart, and I wasn't very good at keeping secrets.

'Those flowers were sent to Megan. I want to find out who sent them.'

Hannah stood straighter.

'And why would anyone send our daughter flowers?' she asked.

'Someone wanted me to know that they could get to her,' I said. 'It was just a threat, so we shouldn't be too worried.'

Hannah crossed her arms across her chest and leaned her hip into the counter.

'Why should we not be worried?'

'Because a threat means whoever sent the flowers wants something. That gives me time to find out who he is.'

'And what should we do in the meantime? Sit around like nothing's wrong?'

I sighed. 'No. Everything will be fine. I'll have some officers come by the house. Don't worry; I'll find this guy and take care of him.'

It looked like Hannah was going to say something, but she held back and closed her eyes.

'No one better hurt our daughter,' she said a moment later.

'Nothing will happen.'

Hannah turned back to the dishes.

'Fine. Do whatever you're going to do. We'll see that movie while you're gone.'

I stayed put for a moment, trying to come up with something comforting to say. I failed on all accounts, so I reached over and squeezed her shoulder. Hannah squeezed my hand with her own. It was soapy and wet, but it was comforting. I dried my hands on my pants and headed to my cruiser. Someone was about to find out that threatening my family was a very bad idea.

Chapter 9

I drove quickly. Within thirty minutes, I was in suburbia and within forty, I was in the parking lot of a modern gray stone building with a vine-covered cedar pergola out front.

I got out of my car and pulled open the building's front door a moment later. The interior felt cold, like a meat packing plant, and it smelled earthy, but clean. I walked past the displays of plants to find a waist-high counter with a cash register on it. A teenager reading a psychology textbook sat behind the counter. A row of binders and framed pictures of wedding flowers rested on a desk beside him.

I cleared my throat. The kid barely looked up from his book before reaching for a thick binder and throwing it on the counter in front of me.

'Pick out what you want and fill out an order form.'

I furrowed my brow. 'Excuse me?'

The kid didn't even bother to look up that time. 'Open the binder, find the flowers you want, and then fill out the form in the back. It's not that hard.'

I leaned over the front desk and grabbed the kid's book. He jumped as I ripped it out of his hands but didn't stop me. I dropped it on top of the binder and smiled.

'You looked a little distracted. I thought that might help.'

The kid stopped blinking at me and closed his mouth. He leaned back. 'Whatever, man. What do you want?'

'Someone sent my daughter flowers, and I'd like to find out who.'

The kid scoffed and reached for his book. 'Probably somebody she's bumping uglies with. We don't give out that kind of information.'

I breathed out of my nose and gripped the edge of the counter hard enough that my fingers turned white. I wanted to rip the book out of his hands and beat him with it. Instead, I leaned over the counter. The kid instinctively leaned back, probably so I couldn't grab anything else out of his hands.

'My daughter is *four years old*, jackass. Care to reevaluate your position?'

'Not really,' said the kid, flipping through the textbook to find his spot. That was it for me. I reached over the counter and grabbed his book again. The page he was olding ripped down the middle. The kid looked ocked for a second, but when he composed himself, face got red and he vaulted upright. I smacked him on the ear hard enough that I could feel the book's cover bend and flex. He staggered into a table behind him, holding his head with one hand and gesticulating wildly with the other. 'What the fuck, man?'

Instead of answering him, I reached over the counter again and yanked the telephone cord out of the wall so he couldn't dial 911. The kid stood upright, his hands flat against the table and his breath shallow.

'I didn't mean anything by it,' he said. 'I'll look up whatever you want me to look up.'

'Good,' I said, dropping the textbook. It thumped against the desk before falling on the floor behind the counter. I could see the clerk's throat dip as he swallowed. 'I want you to find out who sent flowers to Megan Rashid this afternoon.'

He nodded slowly. 'Cool. Give me a second.'

He turned to go through the door behind the counter, but I grabbed his sleeve before he could.

'Give me your cell phone first,' I said. 'Hate for you to get distracted back there and call somebody while you should be helping me.'

He looked from me to the front door, as if gauging whether he could get past me. I leaned against the counter, and my jacket flared out around me, allowing the clerk to see my firearm. My nylon holster dug into my shoulder. I hated it when it did that. After being shot, my shoulder always ached. My physician said the discomfort would eventually fade, but he had never felt a steel-jacketed forty-five caliber bullet rip through the muscle and sinew of his shoulder. The discomfort never went away.

The clerk swallowed again and handed me his iPhone before disappearing through the door that led to the back room. I put the phone on the counter beside his textbook.

The kid came back a moment later with the order form in his hands. He slid it in front of me and backed off quickly, his hands in front of him defensively.

'Relax, kid,' I said. I reached to my belt and unhooked my badge. I held it up. 'I'm a good guy.'

The clerk's shoulders relaxed but not completely. I clipped the badge back to my belt and skimmed the order slip. The buyer was John Smith at 123 Anystreet, Anytown, Ohio.

'How were these flowers paid for?'

The kid swallowed. 'It's on the bottom of the form.'

I slipped my eyes down to the correct line and felt a tightening in my gut.

'You accepted cash from John Smith at 123 Anystreet, Anytown, Ohio? Does that sound like a legitimate name and address to you?'

He shrugged, his face going pale.

'We're a flower shop. We don't run background checks.'

'Even still, at least get a fucking credit card imprint. This was a threat to my daughter.'

I closed my eyes and counted to ten, calming myself.

'Okay,' I said, nodding. 'Who took the order?'

'Me.'

'Do you remember what your customer looked like?'

'I don't know,' he said, shifting on his feet. 'It was a couple of days ago.'

I breathed deeply and clutched the counter hard, trying to keep myself from exploding. 'Think hard.'

'Come on,' he said, shaking his head. He started to speak a few times but then stopped and restarted. 'He was old. Like, maybe thirty or thirty-five.'

'What else do you remember about him? Was he tall? Short? Did he have tattoos or anything like that?'

'He had a tattoo on his neck, and he wore a frilly shirt like he was a pirate. I thought he was weird.'

'Are you sure the tattoo was on his neck?'

'Yeah. I know a neck when I see it.'

I ignored the barb and took my notebook from my inside jacket pocket. 'What was it a tattoo of?'

The kid shrugged. 'Some sort of weird design. It looked like a spiderweb.'

I jotted it down.

'Was he white, black, or what?'

'He was like Chinese or something.'

'Anything else you remember about him?'

'I don't know. It was a few days ago.'

I asked him a few more questions, but that was all I got out of him. When I finished, I closed my notepad and slipped it back in my jacket pocket. The trip hadn't been a complete waste, at least. I thought I had enough for an ID. I looked up and leaned forward so my face was about a foot from the clerk's.

'If my kid gets flowers from your store again, I'll put your head through the front window. Do you understand me?'

He nodded, his face pale. I turned and walked out of the store, flexing my fingers. I inhaled deeply and opened my car door as I tried to put my thoughts in order. I couldn't be sure, but I had a pretty good idea who had sent those flowers. Now I had to figure out why.

I took out my cell phone and thumbed through its memory until I found John Meyers' phone number. After blowing him off earlier, I hoped he'd still take my call. The phone rang twice before he picked up. I spoke before he could.

'Hi, this is Detective Ash Rashid with IMPD. There have been some new developments in Robbie Cutting's case, and I wondered if I could take a look at the safe Mrs Cutting found.'

I heard Meyers cluck his tongue a few times.

'I'm in court this afternoon, but I think I can arrange that,' he said. 'I'll have Maria call you when she's ready.'

'That's fine,' I said, climbing into my car and turning the key. 'I'm in Plainfield right now, but I can be in Indianapolis shortly.'

'We'll be in touch.'

Meyers hung up, and I turned on my car and headed to the first drug store I could find. I bought a pint of Maker's Mark and put it in my glove compartment. I like bourbon and Maker's Mark is one of my favorites. It comes in a square bottle, so it doesn't roll around in my glove compartment. A big part of me wanted to drink the entire pint right there, but I still had work to do. More than that, drinking in the middle of a parking lot was almost a surefire way to be arrested for a DUI. I closed my glove compartment and left the lot.

Mrs Cutting called as I pulled onto the interstate. She agreed to a meeting at her place in twenty minutes. I threw my cell phone on the empty seat beside me after hanging up. As soon as I flipped on my car's siren and lights, traffic parted in front of me as if I were leading a Presidential Motorcade.

Twenty minutes later, I parked beside the Cuttings' guest house and got out of my car. It was stiflingly hot, and I could feel beads of perspiration slide down my back. I opened my cruiser's trunk to get my evidence kit. Olivia's evidence collection kit was neat and orderly in a fishing tackle box; I'm not that fastidious. Mine was in a cardboard box that had once held paperbacks my wife bought on the internet. I grabbed it and walked to the open front door.

I hadn't been in the guest house before, but I recognized it from the crime scene photos. The home was open-concept and had a small entryway that led to a kitchen and living-room area. Under normal circumstances, I would have taken off my shoes to avoid tracking in mud or other contaminating particles, but the situation being what it was, I wasn't too worried about collecting legally admissible evidence. I didn't expect my investigation to end in a courthouse.

'Hello?' I called, pausing near the kitchen. Maria Cutting shuffled out of a hallway on the left side of the room. She wore a green tank top and jeans that were tight around her hips. I hadn't noticed it before, but she was more than a little attractive despite the puffy gray patches under her eyes. She looked at me, her lips thin and straight.

'Detective,' she said.

'Thank you for seeing me, Mrs Cutting,' I said, crossing the room towards her. 'Your attorney says you have something to show me.'

She nodded and led me down the hallway from which she had come. The guest house's master bedroom had a vaulted ceiling and a large picture window overlooking a formal rose garden. The furniture was gone, and most of the carpet had been pulled up, exposing the plywood subfloor. Mrs Cutting stopped in the center of the room, her eyes transfixed by a red stain on what remained of the carpet. I looked at my feet, preferring my shoes to the intimacy of her grief.

'If you'd like, I can give you the name of a cleaning service that specializes in situations like this,' I said. 'You don't need to take care of the room by yourself.'

'Yes, I do,' she said, her voice hoarse. 'Robbie was my son. This is my responsibility.'

Stepping into the room without explicit permission felt wrong somehow, almost as if I were invading a religious shrine, so I stayed in the doorway. Eventually, Mrs Cutting looked back up at me. Her eyes were momentarily confused, as if she were surprised I was there, but then she regained her focus and waved me over. My feet drummed hollowly against the plywood floor, and I could see a tear slide from the corner of one of her eyes to her cheek.

'It's on the floor in the far corner of the room,' she said, pointing to a spot about ten feet away. 'Please, look at it and leave me alone.'

I thanked her, knowing that anything else I had to say would have been inappropriate. I shuffled across the room towards the far window. As Mrs Cutting had said, there was a green safe lodged between floor joists. It looked like Robbie had peeled back the carpet and cut through the subfloor with a saw. The metal was thin, and it flexed beneath my fingers. On closer inspection, it looked more like a cash box with a combination dial than a safe. I looked back at Mrs Cutting, but she had turned her back to me.

I reached into my evidence kit. I didn't usually collect evidence myself, but part of my job was to be prepared at all times. I had the usual things – latex gloves, bags, and evidence tags. But I also had a number of hand tools, including a thick flat head screwdriver. I jammed my screwdriver in the seam between the safe's door and side and wrenched it to the right. The metal flexed and gave way, exposing a sliver of the interior. I placed the tip of my screwdriver into that slot and pulled again, prying the door open as if I had a crowbar.

I looked inside, and for a moment, it felt like someone had put my guts through an old-fashioned clothes wringer. I hadn't expected much in the safe. Instead, I found a snub-nosed, thirty-eight caliber revolver and some sort of Styrofoam container. I glanced at Mrs Cutting. She was watching me now, but I didn't think she could see the handgun from where she stood.

'Do I want to know what's in there?' she asked.

I licked my lips before answering. 'Probably not,' I said. 'Would you like me to tell you anyway?'

She looked down at her shoes. 'I don't know.'

'Tell you what, then,' I said. 'I'll hang on to it, and you think about it. If you want to know more, you can give me a call.'

Mrs Cutting closed her eyes, and for a moment, it looked as if she were going to start crying. She covered her mouth with the flat of her palm and eventually nodded to me before stepping into the hallway. Once she was gone, I reached into the safe and pulled out the handgun. That gun would have been useless in court, but it told me something important. Robbie Cutting knew someone was trying to hurt him. I wished he had told us.

I turned the gun around and stared down its sights. The piece was old and not particularly well cared for, and I could tell right away that Robbie hadn't fired it. Its barrel and chamber were so far out of alignment that any rounds put through it would have stuck in the chamber and blown up like a pipe bomb. I swallowed and dropped the revolver into my evidence collection kit beside some brown paper bags before reaching back into the safe for the Styrofoam cube wedged in the back.

The cube was maybe five inches on a side and held together by brown packing tape. I cut the tape on one side with a box cutter from my kit and tilted the package open like a jewelry box. Someone had bored six circular slots into the Styrofoam, five of which were occupied by stoppered test tubes of what looked like blood. The sixth slot was empty. I stared at it for a moment. Like the gun, the cube was no longer admissible in court since I wasn't on a case, but I could use it. I dropped it in my evidence kit and shut the safe's door.

I grabbed my box and started to leave but stopped in the doorway and said a short prayer. Robbie was eighteen years old when he died. It was a waste. On my way out, I met Mrs Cutting in the living room and thanked her for her time. Her movements were stilted, but she put her arms around my neck in an awkward attempt at a hug. I patted her back. She looked as if she were going to say something when I pulled back, but I think she realized mid-thought that there wasn't much to say.

Chapter 10

I put my evidence kit in my trunk and pulled up to the gate in front of the Cuttings' house. I looked left and right. The street was empty except for a gray Ford Taurus on the side of the road to my left. That figured. The Cuttings lived in an old covenant community with its own private security force, garbage collectors, and snow-plows. IMPD was called in for violent crimes and other felonies, but the neighborhood's private security took care of noise complaints and other minor incidents. They also kept the riffraff under watch.

I pulled onto the street and glanced in my rear-view mirror. As expected, the Taurus followed about a hundred yards behind me. I could see two men inside. They were a good distance away, but from what I could tell, they looked too young to be retired from the force. They were probably off-duty officers picking up a few bucks for a few hours of easy work. It was a common arrangement. I ignored them and drove through the neighborhood without incident. They followed me for a moment when I turned out, but I lost them in traffic shortly after that, presumably when they turned around to find some other brown person to harass.

Since it was my night to make dinner, I stopped by the grocery on my way home and picked up a rotisserie chicken, coleslaw, and mustard potato salad. The sun was setting on my way out of the store, but the blacktop radiated heat from earlier in the day. I climbed into my cruiser and glanced in the rear-view mirror as I put my packages on the passenger seat. There was a gray Ford Taurus with two men inside a few aisles away. It could have been a coincidence, but I doubted it. They were still following me.

I left the parking lot and took a circuitous route home, including a stop at Starbucks for a cup of coffee, to see if my tail would follow. I lost track of them occasionally, but I eventually managed to spot them again each time. Whoever they were, they were pretty good at being evasive. If I hadn't gotten lucky at the grocery store and spotted their vehicle, I wouldn't have even known they were there. About twenty minutes later, I pulled into my driveway. Thankfully, Hannah and Megan were still out, so at least I didn't have to worry about them for the moment. The Taurus drove past as I opened my door, its occupants never looking in my direction.

I took the food I had purchased to the house and put it in the refrigerator. My street had long, sloping hills and ran straight for about two miles in each direction, allowing multiple vantage points of my house. If the Taurus's occupants were smart, they'd pull off at the church up the street. The building would afford easy cover, and with cars parking near it constantly, an anonymous Taurus wouldn't stick out like it would elsewhere in the neighborhood.

I checked to make sure I had a full clip in my firearm before going to my backyard. My department didn't have a written protocol about what to do in situations like this, but if they did, I imagine the suggested first step would be to call backup. There were at least two problems with that, though. If cars started piling up in my driveway, my tail would know something was up. They'd split before we could find out who they were or who sent them. The second problem was that my call would go over a police radio, which I assumed my pursuers were bright enough to have. If I wanted information rather than to scare them off, I was on my own.

The sky was streaked with oranges and reds by the time I stepped onto my back lawn, and the evening insect symphony was beginning to warm up. It looked like it was going to be a nice night. The skies were clear, and the temperature was relatively balmy. I'd prefer overcast for what I planned to do, but early evening glare would work for me, too.

I walked to my cedar fence and used the center support beam as a step, heaving myself over the top and into the alley behind my house. I was too old to be jumping over fences, though. I rolled my ankle on the landing, but I was okay. I straightened and rotated my foot. It hurt, but not enough to slow me down. My high school soccer coach would have told me to walk it off.

I walked six blocks, roughly half a mile, in the direction the Taurus drove as it passed my house. My neighborhood had been built in a grid pattern with side streets that ran perpendicular to the main road every block. I hung a left at one. I couldn't see the Taurus, but the church was a block in front of me. It was an imposing building with rough stone walls and stained glass windows. It had plenty of shadowed nooks in which to hide. Hopefully my tail was in the lot, and equally important, hopefully they weren't expecting me to flank them.

I walked straight ahead at a leisurely pace, being careful to avoid drawing undue attention to myself. The Taurus was on the edge of the front parking lot about a hundred yards to the left of where I stood. There were a dozen or so cars as well as the church's small front lawn between us. I considered my surroundings for a moment and then walked straight ahead to the church's rear. I could hear music inside. Wednesday night services, maybe. The noise masked my footsteps some, and the shadows hid me fairly well.

I pulled out my firearm and chambered a round before edging around the corner of the church and onto its main lot. The Taurus was straight ahead, maybe twenty-five yards away. The driver's window was cracked open, and he dangled a cigarette through the opening. I pushed off from the building and sprinted forward, my Glock held in front of me. The driver saw me running, but he didn't have a chance to do much more than flinch. His partner never saw me coming. I smashed the rear driver-side window with the butt of my gun. Glass shattered inward onto the rear seat, sprinkling like rain against a red camping cooler. Both men jumped.

'Hands on the dash now.'

Neither man moved for a moment.

'What the fuck, Rashid?' said the driver, pounding his hands against the steering wheel. 'This is my wife's car.'

The voice was vaguely familiar, but I couldn't place where I had heard it.

'Get your hands on the dash or I will end you right now,' I said, pressing my firearm through the now broken window. I held it against the driver's head. He stiffened.

'Relax, Ash,' said the passenger, stretching his hands

152

in front of him to reach the dashboard. 'We're on the job.'

I recognized that voice. Detective Greg Doran from Special Investigations. I shifted on my feet and controlled my breathing.

'What are you guys doing following me?'

Doran turned around and faced me.

'Why don't you put the piece away and we'll talk like adults?'

I considered for a moment, but then did as he requested and slipped my firearm back in my jacket. Both men got out of the car after that, but the driver seemed more interested in his back window than anything else. Doran leaned against the rear bumper.

'Now that we're all comfortable,' I said, casting my gaze from one to the other detective. 'Why is a detail following me and who authorized it?'

'You're paying for my window,' said the detective I didn't know. 'I hope you know that.'

I glanced at him.

'Go fuck yourself,' I said. The guy looked as if he were going to bull rush me, but Doran put his hand up, stopping him. I mouthed 'thank you' and then looked from one to the other. 'Now can you answer my question? Why are you watching me?'

Doran crossed his arms, his eyes unblinking as he stared back at me.

'Why were you at Nathan Cutting's house?' he asked.

The question took me back for a second, but I caught myself quickly.

'Visiting a friend,' I said. 'Does it matter?'

Doran shrugged slightly. 'You tell me. People you visit keep ending up dead. There aren't that many dots to connect.'

'I was checking something out.'

'You're on vacation,' said the detective I didn't know. I looked at him and then back to Doran.

'Who is this douchebag?' I asked.

'Detective Smith,' he said, his face expressionless. 'Now answer my question. What were you doing at the house?'

I snickered and looked down. 'If you guys have any more questions, you can direct them to my union lawyer. You can also tell Lieutenant Bowers that he ought to send better detectives if he wants to follow me next time.'

I smiled at them both and headed back towards my house via the main street. Doran and Smith's Taurus passed me about a block down. The driver, I imagine it was Smith, gave me the finger; I waved in return. By the time I got back to my house, Hannah and Megan were back. My wife was in the kitchen slicing the chicken I had purchased while Megan was watching a cartoon on the Disney channel.

We ate dinner on the back patio as evening faded to night. Hannah was disappointed when I said I had

154

another errand to run, but she seemed more than a little relieved when I told her detectives would likely be watching the house for the next few days. I figured it didn't matter if those detectives were investigating me; they'd still protect my family if need be. Hannah and Megan went back inside after dinner, but I stayed on the porch and took out my cell phone. I dialed Olivia's cell and waited for her to pick up. I left a simple message when she didn't.

'It's Ash. I found something at the Cuttings'. Call me back when you can.'

I hung up the phone and sipped on a glass of iced tea left from dinner. Olivia called me back about five minutes later. I heard the swoosh of a freeway in the background, making it difficult to understand her.

'I've only got a minute, but what'd you find?'

'A gun. Kid hid it in a safe in his floor,' I said, turning the volume on my phone higher. 'He knew someone was after him.'

It sounded as if Olivia said something else, but it was muffled by the rush of traffic.

'Is there any way you can go somewhere a little less noisy?' I asked. I don't know if Olivia said anything in response, but I heard a car door opening and closing. The freeway noise dissipated. 'Where are you?'

'In the parking lot at work,' she said. 'You stirred up a lot of shit today.'

'By catching the tail Bowers put on me or making him look like an idiot in front of the prosecutor?'

Olivia snickered, but there was little merriment in it.

'You need to learn to quit when you're ahead, Ash,' she said. 'Watch your back.'

I nodded even though she wasn't there to see it. 'You think he'll keep the surveillance on my house?'

'Yes,' she said. 'Only this time, you're not going to see them.'

That was fine with me. As long as they were watching my house, Hannah and Megan were relatively safe.

'Forget about Bowers for now. Robbie Cutting was murdered, and I'm guessing he knew who did it.'

Olivia paused for a moment, presumably thinking it through.

'Okay, I'll play along. Suppose he was murdered. Let's also suppose you find out who did it. What are you going to do?'

I glanced at my house. I could see Hannah through the kitchen window. She looked up and smiled at me. I returned it as well as I could, unsure how I should answer Olivia.

About six years back, my first partner in homicide and I caught a case involving a security guard at a university downtown. Two girls on campus had gone missing, and we figured the guard was good for it even if we couldn't pin it on him. If we had waited to nail the case down, the girls were almost guaranteed to be dead before we could find them. My partner and I didn't like that option, so we broke into the guy's house while he was at work. Unfortunately, we were right about the guy, but wrong about the timing. The girls were both dead in his basement. Worse than that, since we broke in early, the evidence was fruit of the poisonous tree. We couldn't use it in court because we found it while conducting an illegal search.

It had been a nasty case, and nobody liked the outcome, especially me. I ended up borrowing a stack of photos from an old sex crimes case and hiding them along with marijuana in the guy's car. A drug dog sniffed him out at the post office, and he was arrested and convicted for possessing child pornography. Somebody slit his throat in the shower on his second day in prison.

I've never questioned if I did something wrong that day with the pictures or with the search. Given the chance, I'd do both again and sleep fine for the rest of my life. The system needs people like me to work. Right, wrong, justice, injustice. The concepts sound good in a sermon or in a speech, but things are more complicated in real life. In real life, you've got to get your hands a little dirty, and occasionally you've got to stick them in so much shit you'll wonder if the stink will ever come out. I knew that, and I accepted it. At the same time, there was a big step between planting evidence on a suspect I know is guilty and taking that suspect out myself. I didn't know if I had a right to do that.

Olivia must have sensed my hesitancy because she asked if I had hung up.

'I'm here,' I said. 'I don't know what I'll do.'

'You're going to have to figure it out quick, Ash, and I'm not going to help you. You want my advice, though? Get rid of anything you found at the Cuttings' house, quit this investigation of yours, and spend time with your family. Stop stirring up shit before somebody gets seriously hurt.'

'Is that what you'd do?' I asked.

'Yes.'

I guess Olivia wasn't the person I thought she was.

'I'll give your advice consideration,' I said. 'Take care.'

I hung up after that and leaned back in my chair. Losing Olivia was a loss, but not a big one. I had hoped she'd be able to go with me that night as a small show of force, but I could do it without her. She was a good detective, but we were from different worlds. In hers, everything lined up neatly and precisely according to set, unalterable rules. I didn't really believe in rules, something that had made our brief partnership difficult.

Since Olivia wasn't going to help me, I needed to call in some backup. I took out my cell phone and thumbed through its address book.

Indianapolis has a couple million residents, including a number of forensic pathologists in private practice. Some were willing to help out the law-enforcement community when we needed outside testing of a piece of evidence. One of them, Dr Mack Monroe, happened to be the head of the pathology department at my wife's hospital. Hopefully he'd still be at work.

He answered on the third ring.

'Mack, this is Ash Rashid from IMPD. How are you?'

'Be better if you guys paid my last bill.'

I probably should have expected that from my department. We hired Mack a couple of months earlier when an inmate we convicted appealed his sentence and was granted a retrial due to alleged mistakes in IMPD's forensics lab. The inmate's family hired an outside consultant to tear the lab's procedures apart, but Mack rebutted everything and argued that the case was sound. The jury ruled in the state's favor, so the inmate was back in jail where he belonged.

'How much do we owe you?' I asked. 'I might be able to make some calls and get it pushed through.'

'Forty grand.'

I swore under my breath.

'You worked for five days.'

'Yeah, and in those five days, I gave you boys a notch in the 'W' column. Good verdicts don't come cheap. Now what do you want, Ash?'

I took a breath before speaking. Forty grand was a lot, even for five days of expert testimony. The fee made me suspect there was something else going on, but I didn't ask.

'I'm working a case. I need a substance tested for cocaine. I wondered if I could hire you for it.'

Mack actually chuckled. 'You guys have some nerve, you know that? I'm not working with the city again until I'm paid.'

'This isn't for IMPD,' I said. 'Consider it a private matter.'

Mack paused before speaking, and I heard him draw in a deep breath.

'I like you. We don't know each other very well, but I like you. And I say this as someone who likes you. Your wife's not doing blow. I would have heard about it. And besides, you can't afford me. Frankly, you probably can't even afford a consult, let alone lab work.'

'This isn't about Hannah. I've got a case with two dead kids, and my department is ignoring it. If we don't do something, we'll probably have more to follow. I just need a little help.'

Mack growled into the phone.

'Jeeeesussssss,' he said, drawing out the two syllables. I heard him breathe deeply for a moment as if he were thinking. 'I volunteer in a charity hospital for children. I can't afford to do outside work without pay. What can you give me? Can you at least fix some parking tickets?'

'Probably. Tell me the car and I'll make some calls.'

'My girlfriend's Mercedes. It's in my name. I'm sure you can look it up. Last I checked, she had two or three dozen.'

I rubbed my brow. 'I'll do what I can about the tickets.'

'Good. Come by the hospital tomorrow at ten. I get coffee then.'

'Fine. I'll meet you there.'

I hung up the phone and stuck it back in my pocket. The meeting was in fourteen hours.

Hopefully I'd still be alive.

Chapter 11

I helped Hannah with the dishes for about twenty minutes before hopping in my car. It was earlier than I intended to head out, but I needed a drink and couldn't get one at home. I stopped at a sports bar near Plainfield and had bourbon with a beer chaser. I felt like myself after that. The bar was relatively uncrowded, so I imagined The Abbey would be as well. Even still, if Azrael made a living selling coke to would-be vampires, he'd be there.

I finished my drinks and got back in my car at a quarter after nine. I drove through the now-familiar countryside. The parking lot outside The Abbey was about half full. I saw several parking spots near the entrance, but I backed into a spot facing the exit on the edge of the lot. I didn't anticipate problems, but shit happens and I wanted to be prepared if I had to leave in a hurry. I checked my firearm before stepping out of the car and onto the gravel lot.

The wind was strong enough that it whipped across the old church's steeple, creating a low moaning sound. It was kind of creepy, actually. I slammed my door shut and pulled my jacket tight around me so my firearm wouldn't be exposed. There were a few other people in the parking lot, and from what I could see, they were all wearing black clothes and various shades of dark makeup. A good number had facial piercings. I ignored them and walked toward the old church. Rope lights bathed the limestone steps in purple incandescence.

I stopped at the foot of the steps. There were three bouncers at the top. Two of them were big enough that they could have been NFL lineman, while the third was smaller and held a clipboard. He looked like a Slim to me. They were checking driver's licenses and patting everyone down before they let them inside. I took my badge from my belt and held it up. The crowd parted in front of me until I reached the top steps. The larger two bouncers folded their arms across their chests, probably trying to look intimidating, while the smaller guy said something into a two-way radio. All three glared at me.

'Is there a problem here, sir?' asked Slim.

'Not if you get out of my way,' I said, holding up my badge. 'There's somebody in there I need to see.'

Slim looked from the badge to me and back. 'This is legit?'

'Yep. You can call IMPD's dispatcher to confirm it if you want,' I said. 'They'll vouch for it.'

Slim paused for a second, but then he shook his head.

'That's not necessary,' he said. 'Is there a problem that we need to know about?'

'Shouldn't be. I've got to see somebody. I'll be in and out. Don't worry.'

Slim looked over his shoulder to the two larger men, silently sharing orders. They stepped aside, clearing a path to the front door.

'If there's an issue,' he said. 'I want to know about it.'

I clipped the badge back onto my belt.

'You'll be the first,' I said, already walking past him. The club's music was so loud that it rumbled my chest like a mild case of indigestion. I stepped into the front room. It was dark and crowded, and the overhead lights cast a red incandescence made hazy by smoke. Every table looked full, and nearly everyone wore black from head to toe. I didn't recognize anyone from my niece's high school. The club must have tightened security after my conversation with Mick a few days earlier.

I pushed through the crowd, the music growing louder as I passed the velvet drapes that separated the church's narthex from its sanctuary. It was a good use of the building, really. Club goers who wanted to dance could do that in the remnants of the sanctuary, while those wanting a more relaxed atmosphere had it in the old narthex. The main room smelled like beer, cigarettes, and more than a hint of body odor. I took a quick look around. Couples, threesomes, and more grinded against each other on the dance floor. It was actually tamer than I had anticipated. Despite what Mick had implied on my last visit, no one was obviously having sex with anyone else. Maybe that was a Friday-night-only occurrence, sort of like marriage.

Mick was behind the bar. I walked to an empty spot and leaned against the counter to watch him at work. He had a bottle of vodka in each hand and a tray full of small, plastic cups in front of him. He emptied both bottles into shot glasses. I coughed, and someone behind me took that as an invitation to press her hips against mine. Mick looked up and waved her off before I could tell her to leave me alone.

'Thanks,' I said.

'Don't mention it,' he said, not even breaking stride with his drinks. 'Nice jacket. Did you beat up a philosophy professor for it?'

'Something like that,' I said.

Mick put the empty bottles down and waved over a blond in a T-shirt so tight I could tell both of her nipples were pierced. I'm sure her father was very proud of her. She took the tray and disappeared into the crowd.

'Order something.'

I looked around the bar for a draft tower, but didn't find one.

'Shot of Jack and a beer chaser.'

He handed me a bottle of a cheap domestic beer before filling a plastic cup with a generous shot of Jack Daniels. I pounded the shot and followed it with a swig of the beer. The beer was cold enough that it set my teeth on edge. Mick turned his attention to a girl beside me. She ordered a bloody gin and tonic. From what I could see, it was like a regular gin and tonic with a dash of grenadine. Mick moved so quickly behind the bar filling drink orders that I couldn't get his attention until the blond waitress came back with a tray full of empty cups and a thick pile of one-dollar bills. She handed everything to Mick. He threw away the cups, put the bills in a cash box behind the bar, and started making a new tray of shots beside me while the waitress waited.

'I haven't found anything about your girl,' he said as he poured. 'I told you I'd give you a call if I did.'

'I'm not interested in that right now. I need to know something about Azrael. Does he have a tattoo on his neck?'

Mick looked as if he were going to say something, but a white towel hit him in the shoulder. We turned at the same time. His assistant had five people shouting drink orders at him from the other end of the bar. I took another pull on my beer and turned around as Mick went to work.

On my first glance, I thought the club's patrons had all looked alike, but that was wrong. There were at least three distinct groups. Nearly everyone was young, but some dressed in form-fitting leather or vinyl outfits, some dressed in comfortable street clothing, and others wore silky, almost old-fashioned garb. None of the groups intermingled. It was almost like a junior high dance with the boys on one side of the room and the girls on the other.

'It's a Maori tribal symbol,' said Mick behind me. 'He's here tonight in one of our VIP rooms. Feel free to go up if you want to see him.'

That confirmed my suspicion even if it didn't make sense. Azrael had threatened my daughter. I turned back toward the bar, and Mick handed me another generous shot. I tilted it towards him, showing my thanks, and drank it in two gulps. The liquor bit into my throat and esophagus pleasantly. I washed it down with a sip from my beer.

'I don't need to see him,' I said. 'But can you give him a message?'

'I've got a waitress who can.'

I took two twenties and my business card out of my wallet. Before handing them over, I wrote 'fuck you' on the back of the card with a pen from my pocket.

'Give Azrael the business card. Do you know what he drives?'

Mick looked at my card and raised his eyes. 'You've got a real gift with people, Detective.'

'He threatened my daughter. She's four. This is me being nice.'

Mick looked back up at me. 'He picked up a girl I know. Took her home in a gray BMW 5-series. I think he parks behind the building so nobody will scratch it accidentally.'

I nodded and finished the beer before shuffling back outside. The parking lot had more cars in it than on my way in, but the line to get inside was shorter. I followed the club's exterior wall to a small, unlit parking lot around back. There were roughly ten cars there, most of which were older and American. A nearby dumpster reeked like rotting citrus.

True to Mick's word, there was a gray BMW in the middle of the lot. Like me, Azrael had backed into his spot, although I doubted it was out of a desire to escape quickly. I walked around the vehicle until my back faced the woods. Even behind the building, the club's music was so loud I could make out the lyrics. Something about crimson regrets, tourniquets and salvation. The woods behind me were silent.

I wrote down Azrael's license plate number and then grabbed my firearm. For the second time that day, I smashed a car window. I wasn't sure if the first guy deserved it; Azrael definitely did. The drinks were setting in by the time I got back to my car, and I was buzzing pretty hard. I thought about calling a cab, but as far from Indy as I was, I'd be dead sober by the time it arrived. I'd probably also be out fifty bucks for cab fare. I was slightly impaired, but everyone drove impaired. On my morning commute, I routinely saw women putting on makeup or men shaving. I had even seen someone reading a newspaper, but that one might have been taking it too far. I was fine; no worse off than anyone on a cell phone.

I exited the parking lot and headed toward the inter-state, feeling pretty relaxed. I almost made it, too. About a mile from the on-ramp, a pair of blue and red lights flashed behind me. The remnants of my buzz disap-peared, and I pulled into the parking lot of a strip mall. Except for a greasy spoon diner, all of the nearby busi-nesses were closed for the night. The officer pulled up behind me. The markings on his cruiser pegged him as a county sheriff, which meant I doubted we knew too many people in common. I sat up straighter, hoping my face wasn't as flushed as it felt.

The officer turned off his lights but didn't get out for a few minutes. Presumably he was looking up my license plate to make sure my car wasn't stolen. It was standard procedure. I closed my eyes and waited for what seemed like an hour before he got out of his car. He was middle-aged and heavy. His khaki and brown uniform had a sergeant's chevrons on his arms. I opened my window.

'So,' he said, leaning against my car. 'What's IMPD doing out here?'

'Covering a case,' I said. 'I'm on my way home.'

'And how much have you had to drink tonight?'

I guess there wasn't much point in lying. He'd field test me no matter what I said.

'A few.'

'A few as in two or three . . .'

'I don't count, Sergeant.'

He looked over the empty parking lot.

'Can you give me your license?' he asked.

I handed it to him. He stayed in his car for a few minutes, and when he came back, he was holding a breathalyzer. I blew a .10; it was over the legal limit, but not by too much. About ten years earlier, I wouldn't have even been considered drunk. The sergeant took the breathalyzer and my keys back to his car, where he stayed for another ten minutes, presumably calling for backup to drive me to the drunk tank. I didn't look forward to the conversation I would have to have with Hannah the next day.

The sergeant came back to my car, my license and keys in hand. He stared at me for a moment, shaking his head.

'I called my brother-in-law in IMPD's robbery squad,' he said. 'He said you were a good detective. He also said your niece just died.'

I wondered where he was going with this. 'Yeah, a few days ago.'

The sergeant looked around for a moment before reaching into his pocket and pulling out a business card. He scribbled something on the back.

'This is my cell number,' he said. 'I lead an AA Group. We're all sworn officers, and we've all been in your shoes. If you ever want someone to talk to, give me a call.'

I took the card. 'Thank you.'

'This is your only freebie,' he said. 'You've seen the statistics, and you've probably been to as many accidents as I have. If I see you driving under the influence in my town again, I'll haul you to jail faster than you can blink. Since your record's clean, I'm not going to jam you up if you promise to stay at that Waffle House for about an hour and sober up before heading home.'

I promised I would, and he handed me my license before walking back to his car. I slumped into my seat as he drove off. AA was a good organization from what I had seen, but it was for guys with problems. I didn't have a problem; I had a hobby that happened to involve drinking.

I closed my eyes. I don't know how long I sat like that, but eventually I took out my cell and called

Hannah's cell phone. It was our routine. If I had to call late, I called her cell so I wouldn't wake Megan up by calling the land line. Hannah picked up before the first ring finished.

'Hey, honey, it's me,' I said.

'How are you?' she asked. 'I was worried. I didn't know how late you'd be.'

'I'm fine, and it may be a little while yet,' I said, glancing at the Waffle House. 'I've got a couple of things to do before I head home. Might be an hour or so.'

'That's okay,' she said. 'I tried to call you earlier, but it went straight to voicemail.'

I pulled my phone away from my ear to make sure the battery was still charged. It was fine.

'Must have been out of cell range.'

'Yeah,' said Hannah. 'Megan and I aren't home right now.'

'Are you okay?' I asked, sitting up quickly.

'We're fine,' said Hannah. I heard her start and stop speaking. It took her a moment to form words. 'I feel silly. We were by ourselves, and it was dark. I got a bad feeling like someone was watching us. I feel like a kid.'

'Where are you now?' I asked.

'With Yasmina and Jack,' she said. 'I didn't feel comfortable at home. Do you think that's childish?'

Yasmina was Hannah's sister; she and her husband

lived near our mosque on the east side of town. I ran my fingers through my hair.

'No, that's not childish,' I said. 'Do you want me to come by and pick you up?'

'It's awfully late,' she said. 'I think we'll stay the night here. I'll call you tomorrow.'

'Okay,' I said. We settled into an uneasy silence after that. 'Are you sure you're okay?'

'Yeah, just a little paranoid, I think,' she said. 'I'm going to head to bed. I'll talk to you tomorrow, okay?'

'That's fine,' I said. 'I love you.'

Hannah told me she loved me, too, before hanging up. I closed my eyes and took a couple of deep breaths. My stomach twisted. I should have gone home earlier, and I sure as hell shouldn't have had as much to drink as I had. I felt guilty, but there wasn't much use fretting over what I couldn't change. I glanced at my watch. It was after eleven, so there weren't many productive things I could do except sober up. Even still, there was one. I thumbed through the address book on my cell phone until I found IMPD's central dispatcher. The guy who answered sounded even more tired than me.

'What do you need?' he asked.

'This is Detective Sergeant Ashraf Rashid. I need a trace on an Indiana license plate.'

'What's your badge number?'

After reciting the number twice, I gave the dispatcher

Azrael's plate number and a description of the car. Keys clicked intermittently as the dispatcher typed.

'Your Beamer's registered to a Plainfield company called Sunshine Blood Products, Inc.'

I grabbed a pen from the inside pocket of my jacket and wrote the company's address on my notebook as he read it to me. I wanted an actual person's name, but a company name was almost as good. They had to pay taxes, so there'd be a paper trail. I could follow that to Azrael. I pocketed the address, thanked the dispatcher for his time, and hung up.

The case didn't make a lot of sense yet, but things were coming together. Hopefully my life wouldn't fall apart before that happened. I spent the next forty-five minutes drinking coffee and reading the newspaper in the Waffle House. It wasn't the best use of my time that I could think of, but it beat sitting in a Hendricks County drunk tank.

I woke up the next morning when my cell phone rang. The sun beat against my blinds and birds sang outside. I sat up and swallowed a few times, trying to get my bearings. I was in my bedroom, and my head felt as if a thousand tiny jackhammers were pounding away at the interior of my skull. Mornings suck. I swung my legs off the bed and yawned before snatching my cell phone from the end table. It was my wife.

'Hey,' I said, glancing at my alarm clock. It was a quarter to eight. 'How are you?'

'We're fine. I wanted to call and make sure you were okay.'

'Made it in late last night, but I'm fine.'

'I'm glad to hear it, dear,' she said. 'I wasn't going to call you this morning, but Megan insisted. She's been up for a while.'

'Is she okay?'

'Yasmina gave her coffee with cream and sugar this morning. She hasn't stopped running since. I think she wants to talk to you.'

Despite my headache, a smile formed on the corner of my lips unbidden.

'Put her on.'

Megan's voice was so shrill and so fast that I could hardly understand her.

'*Baba*, *Baba*, *Baba*,' she said. 'Aunt Yasmina and Uncle Jack took me to McDonalds for breakfast. They had an indoor playground, and they let me go down the slide.'

'Really?' I asked, shaking my head and blinking to clear my vision of fog. 'That's really exciting. What else did you do?'

I talked to Megan for another two or three minutes before she dropped the phone mid-sentence and squealed. It sounded as if she was having a good time if nothing else. Hannah grabbed the phone and told me she had seen a deer outside. It's hard to compete with furry woodland creatures for a toddler's attention.

'Have you considered putting her on a treadmill?' I asked.

'If Yasmina and Jack had one, she'd probably already be climbing all over it,' said Hannah. 'We're going to the zoo today. You want to come?'

I grunted.

'I'd like to, but I've got stuff to do. Maybe we can go this weekend.'

'Sure, that'd be fun,' she said. 'I need to grab Megan before she starts jumping off the furniture again, so I'll let you go.'

'Good luck.' I said.

'I'll need it.'

Hannah hung up after that, and I threw the cell phone on the bed and rubbed my eye sockets with the palms of my hands. I didn't drink a lot the night before, but my mouth felt as if I had stuffed myself full of cotton balls before going to bed. Maybe I was getting sick. I poured myself orange juice in the kitchen and put on a pot of coffee before going to the living room and having morning prayers. Before rolling up my prayer mat, I made a special prayer, asking God to watch over Hannah and Megan. Hopefully He was listening.

I grabbed a cup of coffee after prayers and went to my office. I had a meeting at ten with Mack Monroe, but I had time to kill before that. I didn't want to waste it, so I grabbed my notebook and flipped through it to the page I had written the night before. Azrael's BMW was registered to Sunshine Blood Products, Inc. I hadn't heard of the company, but that wasn't too surprising. Drug fronts typically maintain a low profile.

Since the company was incorporated, there had to be records somewhere. I opened a web browser on my computer and navigated to the Indiana Secretary of State's website. When I first became a detective, I would have had to put in a formal request with a clerk at the Secretary of State's office to retrieve those records. It'd take about a week, and there'd be a pretty good chance we wouldn't find anything. Technology has come a long way since then.

I ran a business entity search for Sunshine Blood Products and got a partial listing. The company's actual articles of incorporation weren't available online, but the site gave me a summary, including the name and home address of the company's initial CEO and registered agent, Karen Rea. I doubted Azrael and Karen were related, but at least I had a real name. Karen was probably a dupe, just some sucker Azrael and his buddies used to start a company. I wrote her information down anyway, thinking I might be able to use her.

After that, I massaged my sinuses, hoping to quiet my headache. IMPD is a pretty big organization, but sometimes it feels like a small town. Gossip travels fast and wide, so there was a fair chance that my drunk driving was a topic of conversation that morning. If it had made its way to Susan Mercer, there was a pretty good chance my vacation would be extended indefinitely.

I logged into my department's webmail server to check my email. Most of it was junk, but there was one letter from an email address I didn't recognize. The subject was *From a friend*. I almost deleted it because most emails with that sort of subject turned out to be advertisements for penis enlargement pills or investment schemes. At the same time, Olivia had anonymously sent me the results from Rachel's preliminary autopsy with the same note attached, so it could have been from her. I opened it and found a link to a blog called fangporium.com. I hadn't heard of the website before, but I didn't think it would hurt to check it out.

On first glance, the page looked like every other blog on the internet. As my eyes focused, I could see that it wasn't. Fangporium.com was the official website of the Indianapolis Sanguinarian Society and platform of Mistress Karen, the society's founder and self-professed vampire. Maybe Karen Rea wasn't a dupe after all.

Like most blogs, fangporium.com was set up as a series of articles with public comments beneath. The first article was titled, *Murder in our community*. I skimmed it, and although names weren't mentioned, it was clearly about Rachel and Robbie. Karen claimed their deaths were the first salvo in a war between vampires and slayers, religious fanatics bent on eradicating vampires everywhere. She designated her lieutenant, Azrael, to form a response to the threat. About fifty people had commented, including Azrael. He said he'd be proud to serve and even had a plan to eradicate the threat.

I printed the article and read through it twice to make sure I hadn't missed anything. The site had pages and pages of similar postings. They were mostly delusional garbage and melodrama, but they told me something important. Azrael was only a soldier taking orders. Karen was the shot caller, and if her posts were any indication, she was bat shit crazy. Combined with the seeming loyalty of her followers, that made her extremely dangerous.

That's all I need.

I looked at my computer's clock. I still had almost two hours before my meeting. My house felt empty without Hannah and Megan, and I didn't like that. I hopped in the shower, got dressed, and called my wife back. It wasn't as exciting as an afternoon at the zoo, but I met them at a park near my sister-in-law's house. I pushed Megan on a swing and sat with Hannah on some picnic tables. We didn't say anything important, but it was nice to be with them.

I left at twenty to ten for my meeting. That should have been ample time, but there was a fender bender about three blocks from the hospital, which meant I ended up being twenty minutes late. I grabbed the Styrofoam cube I had taken from Robbie's safe from my trunk and ran inside. The lobby was bright, airy, and vibrant enough that it looked more like the front atrium at a nice hotel than a children's hospital. There were flowers everywhere and play sets for kids waiting to see their doctors. I took a lap around the room, but I couldn't find Mack anywhere. As late as I was, that was expected.

I slipped through the crowds and walked to the information booth beside the front door. A woman about my age in a pair of hospital scrubs adorned with Sponge Bob Square Pants smiled at me when I arrived. Her straight black hair was pulled back in a ponytail, and she had a headset on for the phone system. She was pretty.

'Can I help you, sir?'

'I hope so. I'm supposed to meet Dr Monroe. Can you page him or call his lab for me?'

Her face flushed red for a moment. I didn't know if that was a good thing or not.

'Mack was here earlier,' she said. She breathed in through her teeth. 'Uhm, are you Ash Rashid?'

I nodded. She bit her lower lip. 'He left you a message and asked me to deliver it word for word, but I'm not comfortable saying it.'

180

I raised my eyebrows. 'Can you paraphrase?'

'I'll just give it to you,' she said, plucking a Post-it note from her desk. She held it to me, blushing. 'I think it'd be best if you read it. Silently.'

I took the note from her hand.

Ash,
Fix my goddamn parking tickets or go fuck yourself.
Mack Monroe.

I looked up. The receptionist blushed again and looked apologetic. If nothing else, I was reasonably sure the note was authentic. I crumbled it and put it in my pocket.

'I was supposed to meet him for coffee. Do you have an employee cafeteria or break room where I might be able to find him?'

'He was in the coffee shop earlier,' she said, standing up. She pointed across the atrium at what looked like a bar. 'It's right over there. I didn't see him leave.'

'Thanks.'

I passed about three dozen kids on my way to the hospital's combination deli and coffee shop. It had a brass espresso machine on the counter in front and an L-shaped wooden bar behind it. A line of physicians, nurses, and hospital patrons snaked all the way outside. I walked past them and into the dining room. It smelled like coffee and bleach. Mack had a corner table and most of the surrounding floorspace to himself. He was reading a newspaper and sipping a cup of coffee large enough that it could have been a soup bowl. I crossed the room and plopped down across from him on a solid oak chair.

'Did you get my message?' he asked, not bothering to put down his paper.

'I think so,' I said. 'The receptionist was a little embarrassed to say it aloud.'

'Really?' asked Mack, his voice suddenly high. He folded his paper and put it on the table in front of him. He looked as if he hadn't shaved in a week, and he wore a T-shirt sporting the logo for Viagra. If not for his lab coat with DR MONROE stitched on the breast, most of the visitors probably would have thought he was a janitor. 'I took her out a couple of years back. You get a couple of shots in her, and she's got a mouth like you wouldn't believe. Says the sort of things you usually only hear if you pay four bucks a minute to a phone sex operator.'

'She sounds like quite a girl,' I said. I glanced to my right. A young couple was hastily gathering the remains of their breakfast while simultaneously shooting Mack the dirtiest looks they could probably muster. For his part, Mack stared right back, shrugged, and mouthed 'What?'

182

I could see why he drank alone. I cleared my throat, getting his attention. 'Are you ready to look into my problem?'

'Depends if you looked into *my* problem,' said Mack.

'I haven't yet, but I will as soon as I can. You've got my word.'

Mack leaned back and laced his fingers behind his head. 'I don't have a lot of free time, and you told me you'd meet me at ten. Now it's what, ten-thirty? I don't know if I can work with somebody who'd leave me hanging like that.'

'What else do you want, Mack?'

He winked at me and smiled. 'Do you know anybody in Goshen, Indiana? Elkhart County has a warrant out for Aleksandra's arrest, and I'd like that taken care of.'

Goshen was a small farming community in northern Indiana. It had a Mennonite college and a factory that made RVs, but not much else.

'She beat up some Amish people or something?' I asked.

'Close,' he said. 'She was buying Amish furniture for our place on Lake Michigan. Anyway, she was drunk, and some county sheriff took her in. When she didn't show up for her court date, the judge issued a warrant for her arrest.'

'Why didn't she show up for her court date?' I asked.

Mack wrinkled his forehead and looked at me as if I were an idiot.

'Goshen's three hours away. I can barely get her to sit still long enough to give me a lap dance, partner. You think she'd drive all the way up there for court?'

I closed my eyes and tried to think of any other forensic pathologists in the area who might help me out. Unfortunately, I came up blank.

'Okay,' I said, nodding and opening my eyes. 'I'll make some calls and see if I can get the arresting officer to drop the charges.'

'All right. That's what friends are for. Let's get out of here. These kids give me the creeps.'

I thought that was a joke, but it was hard to tell. Mack had an odd sense of humor. I think he liked kids. Or at least he liked fathering children. He had two of his own that he knew about.

We left the deli, and I followed him to a bank of staff-only elevators where he swiped his keycard while simultaneously informing a little boy standing beside us that if he ate his boogers, tomato plants would start growing in his stomach. The kid's finger immediately shot out of his nose and to his side. Thankfully the elevator arrived before Mack extolled more medical advice.

The pathology lab was in the basement, just one story beneath the lobby, but it was like another world.

The walls were cinder blocks painted white, and the overhead lights thrummed and cast an artificial, bluish-white hue. Goose bumps formed up and down my arms. Knowing Mack, I'm sure it was a state-of-the-art facility, but it didn't look very impressive. Unlike the forensics labs on TV, there were no flashing lights or attractive women with flowing hair. The most high-tech piece of equipment in the room was a microscope beside a computer in one corner. Mack moved a tray of specimen cups from the island in the center, clearing a workspace.

'Tell me again what you want me to test,' he said, washing his hands at a sink along the wall. I popped the top off the Styrofoam block I brought and laid it in the space he'd cleared.

'I picked these vials up at a crime scene. I want to find out if there's a high enough concentration of cocaine in them to kill somebody.'

He dried his hands on his lab coat and squinted at my vials and then to me and back again. He reached into his coat for a pair of glasses, put them on, and then pulled out a test tube from the styrofoam. I hadn't pulled the tubes out like that before, and nor had I handled the one Rachel drank from. The liquid inside was thinner than I had anticipated; light pierced it fairly easily, which meant it wasn't blood. I shifted as Mack furrowed his eyebrows at me.

'I need you to fill me in,' he said. 'Are you telling me these were actually packaged like this at a crime scene?'

'I pulled these tubes out of a safe. They were filled and sealed before anyone from IMPD touched them.'

Mack turned the vial over. The liquid cascaded down.

'Since I don't have a mass spectrometer, I can't tell you what's in here definitively. That said, we can at least run a Scott test to see if it has cocaine in it. That cool with you?'

I had no idea what a Scott test was, but I trusted Mack knew what he was doing.

'This going to cost me extra?' I asked. 'Maybe you've got a dead hooker in a trunk you need taken care of?'

'No, but I like the attitude,' he said, putting my tube back in the Styrofoam container. He walked to a gold supply cabinet along one wall, and I heard glass clink on glass as he moved things around. When he came back, he carried a tray holding two liquid-filled beakers, a couple of test tubes, and a number of eyedroppers. He had also put on some latex gloves.

'This is a simple test. We take a cobalt thiocyanate reagent, mix it with whatever's in your vial, and see what happens.'

I tried to look as if I knew what he was talking about. He popped the top of one of my vials. The smell was light at first, but it grew in strength. Wintergreen breath

186

mints. I shifted in my seat. Mack raised his eyebrow at me.

'You said somebody drank this?' he asked.

I nodded. He muttered something about 'fucking weirdos' before reaching for an eyedropper from his tray. He put a measured amount of my mystery substance in a clean test tube. He then laid the eyedropper to the side and used a clean one to put about twice as much of one of the liquids he brought over into the same tube. After that, he put a stopper on top and shook it up. A bright-blue mass formed at the bottom of the vial.

'Does that mean anything?' I asked.

'Just the first step of the process,' he said, reaching for a third eyedropper. He put a couple drops of another liquid into the test tube he was working with. The mass at the bottom turned pink. He looked at me over the top of his glasses as he shook the test tube. 'I hear Hannah's pregnant. It's your first, isn't it?'

'No, we have a little girl,' I said. I looked up. 'And Hannah's not pregnant.'

Mack stopped moving. I waited for him to say something, my stomach tightening slightly.

'Wow,' he said. 'This is awkward.'

My stomach felt like it had dropped about ten stories. Mack stayed silent as I thought. I love being a father; it's the most rewarding thing in my life. That didn't mean I was ready to have another kid, though. At least not right now. I closed my eyes.

'Sorry,' said Mack. 'I tested her blood a week ago. I thought she would have told you.'

I swallowed and tried to force the thought out of my head.

'That's okay,' I said. 'Can we focus on this?'

'Sure,' he said, taking the test tube he had been working with to a supply closet in the corner. I'm not sure what he did, but I heard glass bottles clink together. After that, he turned on some sort of tool that sounded like a dentist's drill.

'I wouldn't worry too much if I were you,' he said, shouting to be heard over the machine. 'I bet you're a good father. You're calm.'

'Thank you,' I said, shifting uncomfortably.

'Any time,' he said. He flipped off whatever machine he had been using and carried the tube back to our center island. The liquid inside had separated into two parts. It was clear on top, but the mass on the bottom had returned to a bright blue.

'It's a boy,' he said. He pointed to the tube when I didn't laugh. 'Because it's blue . . .' He paused and smiled slightly. 'I guess that's still a little early, huh?'

I glared at him, and Mack straightened up. He put the test tube in a wire holder and pulled off his latex gloves.

'Coke won't stay suspended like this in many solutions,' he said. 'My guess is that you have five vials of *agua rica.*'

I was a philosophy major in college, and as part of my major, I was required to take four semesters of a foreign language. I took Spanish. I rarely used it, but I still remembered a few vocabulary words.

'Rich water?' I asked.

'Yeah. That's what the farmers call it. It's one of the steps in the extraction of cocaine from coca leaves. You want the crash course?'

'Sure.'

He walked back to his supply cabinet.

'Coke's actually a pretty easy drug to extract,' he said, looking over his shoulder. 'Farmers will harvest about a ton of leaves from a coca plant and douse them in a bathtub or other pit with carbonate salt and water. After that, they'll toss in a solvent like gasoline or kerosene and stir that around for a while.'

Mack was quiet for another minute or so as he got things from his closet. When he turned around, he carried a metal tray laden with a squeeze bottle, a couple tablespoons of a purple powder, and a stack of beakers. He put the tray beside the test tubes he had been working with earlier.

'When the cocaine is extracted, the farmer will siphon off the solvent and filter it to remove any leaves or dirt.

189

Then he'll add diluted sulfuric acid to that mix. The acid converts the cocaine into cocaine sulfate. Once that's done, the farmer will siphon off the solvent again to reuse it. The leftover diluted sulfuric acid solution with the cocaine in it is called *agua rica*. That's what you've got here, I think.'

Mack picked up one of the vials I had brought and dumped its contents into an empty beaker on his tray. I furrowed my eyebrow and leaned against the counter.

'Why do you know this much about cocaine?'

'I used to volunteer for Doctors without Borders. Long story short, I went to South America a few years back with some nurse I wanted to bang. I fixed up a bunch of kids and nailed her when I could. On our last day, a patient's father asked if we wanted to see something the tourists don't usually see. I figured he was going to take us to some Mayan ruins, but he took us to his coca farm. There was a lab nearby, so we saw the whole operation from cultivation to the production of cocaine base.'

'You're quite the humanitarian,' I said, scratching my head. 'Why does it smell like breath mints?'

He shrugged. 'Someone probably cut it with winter-green oil to cover up the smell. I do that with acetone, too. Otherwise, it smells like a nail salon in here.'

I leaned back in my stool and tried to piece together everything Mack was telling me.

'So I brought you liquid cocaine?'

'I wish,' he said, chuckling as he pulled his ingredients tray closer to him. 'And on a side note, *agua rica* doesn't usually look like this. Most of the time, it's yellowish brown. Someone dyed this lot. It usually looks like beer or even blood plasma.'

I nodded, taking it in.

'How do you go from this stuff to what's on the street, then?'

'You oxidize it with potassium permanganate,' he said. He put a pinch of the purple powder he had brought into a beaker containing clear liquid. He then dumped the whole thing into the *agua rica* solution. A brownish black clump formed at the bottom of the beaker, leaving a clear liquid on top. 'Once you do that, you filter the liquid and discard the crap left over.'

He put a piece of cheesecloth on top of a third beaker and poured the clear solution over it. The black clump stayed on the cloth while the liquid fell to the bottom. He took off the cloth and threw it, along with the black clump, in the trash.

'What do you think we get if we add a base to this?' he asked.

I raised my eyebrows. 'Gummi bears?'

Mack grabbed a plastic squirt bottle labeled AMMONIA. He squirted a steady stream into the beaker. It was like a drug dealer's version of a snow globe. White particulate formed and fell to the bottom.

'That fluffy stuff at the bottom is about ninety-five-percent pure coke. A lot of people smoke that and get high, actually. If we were at a production lab, that fluffy stuff would be dried and then sent to another lab for further processing. It'd be mixed with ether and acetone. When that's done, it'd be packaged and sent to the streets for sale.'

'How much cocaine do you think is in these vials?'

Mack held up a vial and swirled it. 'Maybe five grams each. I can dispose of them if you want. I'm going to a party this weekend.'

I raised my eyebrows. 'My boss tends to get upset when I supply cocaine for parties. Just one of her quirks.'

He shrugged. 'Worth a shot.'

I ignored him and leaned forward, resting my elbows on the table. If Mack's figures were right, Robbie had been sitting on a fair amount of blow. It was no wonder Rachel had overdosed after ingesting part of a vial. I doubted she and Robbie would have done that if they had known what was inside.

'Do you think a dealer would have these?' I asked.

Mack shook his head.

'I'm not an expert, but I doubt it. I've never seen *agua rica* in the states before, and I've seen a lot of drugs in my time. These came from a lab. Even if your victim dealt kilos at a time, he wouldn't have these.'

I nodded slowly, trying and failing to fit the

information into my puzzle. I was about to thank Mack for his time when my phone rang. I motioned to Mack that I'd be a minute before glancing at the caller ID. It was my wife.

'Hannah, what's going on?'

'You need to come home.'

'Are you okay?' I asked.

'No. There's a detective with a search warrant on our porch.'

Chapter 12

I thanked Mack for his time and promised to make it up to him before jogging to the parking garage. My mind was running in about nine directions at ninety miles an hour each. I couldn't think properly. I took a breath, forcing myself to focus on one thing at a time. There were detectives at the house, but at least Hannah and Megan were safe for the moment. I didn't know what was going on, but at least I didn't have to worry about that. I was considerably less confident about my case.

I got in my car. Within five minutes, I was on I-465, a fifty-three-mile loop of asphalt ringing the city. The monotony of expressway driving gave me a moment to order my thoughts. I had known Azrael was pushing drugs, but evidently it was more than that. He and Karen were tapped into a lab somewhere. That took the case to a different level, but it still didn't tell me why Rachel and Robbie were killed. They were kids; even if they were involved with drugs, they wouldn't know enough to bring down the whole enterprise. All I knew for sure was that they had gotten into something over their heads and died for it. That was starting to frustrate me.

I pulled off the interstate and turned onto my street about fifteen minutes later. There were three marked patrol vehicles on my front lawn and an unmarked Crown Vic taking up most of the driveway. Hannah sat on the front steps while a uniformed officer stood watch. Since my driveway was taken, I parked in front of Mrs Phelps' house and jogged towards my front door. Hannah saw me, but she didn't move. Her shoulders were pulled back, and her posture was uncomfortably straight. She was in handcuffs.

Shit.

I ran onto the lawn. The uniformed officer put his hand up as if he were directing traffic, stopping me. He was older than I was, maybe fifty, and his skin was pitted and gray. He looked like a smoker who should have quit years earlier. At his age, he must have pissed somebody important off to still be on patrol.

'This is none of your concern,' he said. 'Move along.'

'Like hell it isn't,' I said. 'That's my pregnant wife, you moron.'

He took a step back and kept one hand up in the

stop motion while the other went to the butt of his gun. I put my hands up, palms towards him, to show that I wasn't going for a weapon, and took a step toward the sidewalk.

'We have a search warrant,' he said. 'She was interfering with that search. She didn't tell us she was pregnant.'

'That's because it's none of your business,' said Hannah, her voice gruff. 'You shouldn't even be here.'

'We have a search warrant, lady,' said the officer. 'We have every right to be here.'

'I'd like to see that search warrant,' I said. 'Get these handcuffs off my wife and get your CO out here right now.'

He glared at me as if I had affronted him terribly.

'You don't give me orders, son,' he said. 'Now back off, or I'm going to put you in cuffs like your wife.'

I'd like to see you try.

'I'm going to show you something. I'm not reaching for a weapon.'

The guy nodded, but he didn't remove his hand from his gun. I reached to my belt and unhooked my badge. The patrol officer took a step forward to get a better look. He took his hand off the butt of his gun and shifted on his feet uncomfortably.

'You're a detective?'

'Detective Sergeant,' I said. 'Now I'd suggest you get

the handcuffs off my wife before I file an excessive force grievance against you for handcuffing a pregnant woman.'

The guy didn't even hesitate. His shoulders sagged.

'I'll be right back.'

When he was gone, I helped Hannah stand up. She was sweating, and her face was red. Police-issue handcuffs use a standard key because it keeps things simple when transferring prisoners, and thankfully, I still had mine. I fished my key chain out of my pocket and unlocked Hannah's cuffs. She leaned against me, so I pulled her into an embrace and kissed her forehead.

'How long have you known I was pregnant?'

'About twenty minutes,' I said, pressing my face against her hair. It smelled like lilacs. 'Are you okay?'

I felt her nod against me.

'Mrs Phelps called my cell when she saw them kick down the door. That officer put me in cuffs as soon as I got here.'

'Did you say anything to him?'

She shook her head no. 'He locked me up as soon as I got here. I was just going to ask if I could watch.'

I ground my teeth.

'I'll take care of it from here,' I said. 'If you want, you can sit in my car. Hopefully it won't be too long.'

She hugged me again once I handed her my keys. I pointed my car out, and she walked up the street towards it while I put the deputy's cuffs on the porch. Lieutenant

Bowers came out a few minutes later. He wore a navy blue T-shirt with the word POLICE written across the chest. Like the last time I saw him, it looked as if he hadn't shaved in a few days. The bags underneath his eyes were gone, though; instead, there was almost a twinkle. The corners of his lips were upturned.

'Glad you finally made it. Thought I wasn't going to see you this morning.'

I crossed my arms. 'What are you doing in my house?'

'We're searching it. Being a detective, I thought you would have figured that out.'

'I understand that. What are you searching for?'

Bowers tilted his head to the side, the smug smile widening.

'This and that. And by the way, where'd you park? I want to search your car personally.'

I tilted my head to the side, considering how I wanted to respond. They could search my house all they wanted, but they'd never find anything. My car was another matter. It still had the vials of *agua rica* in it.

'You'll have to show me the warrant for that.'

'Gladly,' said Bowers, reaching to his back pocket. He held out a light-blue document and handed it to me.

Two things jumped out at me. They were searching for the missing vial from my niece's case, the one that supposedly disappeared from the crime lab. The vial was small, so it could have been hidden just about anywhere, which meant they could tear our house apart looking for it. On the other hand, the scope was narrow. The search authorized the police to search my house and *curtilage*, the standard terms our department used on search warrant affidavits.

'You know what the word "curtilage" means?' I asked.

Bowers stared at me blankly. 'Fuck you.'

'Didn't think so,' I said. 'Curtilage is a legal term. When a warrant says you're allowed to search someone's house and curtilage, it means you're allowed to search the home and surrounding grounds and buildings. My car is parked on the street in front of the neighbor's house. I would have parked in my driveway, and you would have been able to search it, but some dipshit in an unmarked Crown Victoria took most of it up. As a detective, I thought you would have planned for that sort of thing.'

The smile disappeared from Bowers' face.

'We'll talk later,' he said before turning around and walking through my front door.

I waited on the front porch for another twenty minutes for them to finish their search. They left in a big group: Bowers, Doran and Smith – the two detectives I had found staking out my house a day earlier – and three uniformed officers. None carried anything out. Hannah must have been watching because she joined me on the porch a moment later. Bowers smirked at us.

'Guess you guys were clean after all. Sorry about the mess. We had to be certain you weren't hiding anything.'

I ground my teeth, but didn't say anything. Hannah threaded a hand through the crook of my elbow.

'Can we go inside now, Officer?' she asked.

He nodded. 'Yeah. Have fun.'

She tugged on my arm, pulling me toward the house before I could say anything further. Hannah and I stepped through our front door a moment later.

I had executed a lot of search warrants when I was a detective and always made a point of reminding everyone in my search team that our suspect was innocent until proven otherwise. We treated his or her possessions with as much respect and care as possible. That's not a Constitutional requirement, just common courtesy. Most detectives have similar policies. Bowers was evidently not like most detectives, though, because our house was trashed.

We checked out the living room first. Our coffee table was overturned, the foam from our couch cushions had been removed and it looked like someone had run beside our bookshelves with his arm stretched out so he could knock everything off. The damage was cosmetic, though. Everything could be repaired.

I squeezed Hannah's arm and stepped down the hall to our bedroom. Every dresser drawer had been pulled out and overturned, and it looked like the contents had been sifted through. My wife's undergarments had been given special attention; they were strewn all over the floor. Our bathroom and closet had similar treatments. There were tubes of toothpaste on the ground in the bathroom, and our clothes had been thrown on the ground in our closet. It looked like an angry toddler had gone on a rampage.

The kitchen was the same way. I tried to be careful, but I stepped on a wooden spoon, a wedding gift from one of Hannah's aunts, cracking it. It was just stuff, and it could all be repaired and put back, but I felt violated. Worse, I couldn't have stopped them if I tried. They would have slapped cuffs on me and thrown me in jail. I clenched my jaw so tight I thought I was going to crack my teeth.

We walked into Megan's room last. It was the smallest bedroom in the house and had just enough room for a twin bed, a dresser, and rocking chair. There were clothes on the floor, and the rocking chair was overturned. The room could be cleaned, though, and the clothes could be put back. Those didn't bother me very much. I walked to the bed. There was a stuffed lion on it named Tom. I have no idea why the lion was named Tom, but it was Megan's favorite toy. My mom had given it to her.

Bowers' men had cut it open along its back and pulled out the stuffing as if they were searching for something inside. It was a kid's toy, and we could probably buy one just like it for a couple of bucks, but Megan loved it. And a stranger had come into my house and ruined it. I kissed Hannah's forehead and whispered that I'd be right back. I didn't bother looking at what I stepped on as I jogged through my house.

There was something in me that I hadn't felt before. I didn't get mad, not exactly. It was more like I relaxed the constraints that held my anger at bay. It was visceral, black and bubbling under the surface. I had been bottling it up since Rachel died and probably before that. Bowers and his men were still beside his car in the driveway, which meant they were probably signing the warrant so they could return it to the judge's clerk that afternoon.

I slipped through the crowd and grabbed Bowers' shoulder, spinning him around.

'You went too far, Lieutenant. If you want to come after me, do it. Don't you dare try to hurt my family again.'

The officers around me formed into a semicircle of blue with Bowers at the center. He smiled, but his eyes were as black as any I had ever seen.

'Are you threatening me, Rashid?'

I shot my eyes to the officers around me to see if any had gone for their weapons. They hadn't.

'No, I'm not threatening you. I'm giving you some advice. Stop paying so much attention to my family and start paying attention to your own. I hear your wife gets lonely when you work such long hours.'

That might have been uncalled for, but I didn't care about civility. Bowers stepped forward and grabbed my shirt. The officers around us shifted on their feet uneasily, and I noticed more than a few hands stray towards their weapons.

'What does that mean, Rashid?'

'Ask around. I'm sure any number of guys in your station will tell you exactly what it means. Probably in graphic detail.'

Bowers lunged at me as if to ram his shoulder into my midriff, but I stepped to my left and jammed my right knee into his side. I heard him grunt, but I didn't have more than a moment to enjoy the situation before I felt arms pulling me back and to the ground.

I hit the pavement hard. The jolt traveled through my body and into my spine. A sudden weight on my back pressed me forward, and my face was on the concrete before I could even gasp from pain. I twisted and tried to ball up, an instinctual move to protect my internal organs, but someone was pulling each arm flat to the side. I squirmed and thrashed, trying to get up anyway, but someone put his knee in my upper back and ripped my hands behind me. Steel cuffs bit into my wrists after that.

I tried to shout for Hannah to call a lawyer, but

someone put his knee on the back of my neck, pressing my face against the ground so I couldn't speak.

'You're under arrest for assaulting an officer. If you don't shut up, we will shut you up. Do you understand?'

I guess Bowers counted those as my Miranda rights because two of the uniformed officers threw me in the back of a squad car after that. One of the officers even made a point of putting the windows up. My entire body hurt, and I tasted something coppery and metallic. I was dizzy, but that could have been the heat. With the windows up and the sun blazing, the black vinyl seats were so hot they almost burned the exposed portions of my body. The back seat smelled almost vinegary from its previous occupant's body odor, but that was better than vomit.

As I waited, the heat scorched the hard edge of my anger away, and my rationality returned. Assaulting an officer was a felony, but Bowers wouldn't charge me with that. Not if he wanted the charges to stick. I partially instigated the attack, but he made the first move. I saw it, my wife saw it, and I'm sure some of my neighbors saw it. The officers on the scene would close ranks around their Lieutenant and say whatever they could to make it look as if he had acted in good faith, but it'd get ugly.

Hannah stood in the doorway. Her shoulders rose and

fell quickly, and her eyes smoldered; I was glad they weren't directed at me.

I don't know who made the call, but the patrol vehicle's back door opened about twenty minutes later, and Jack Whittler stuck his head in. 'You really pissed in somebody's sandbox here, Detective,' he said, sitting on the seat beside me. 'This car stinks. Hold on a second.'

He stepped out before I could respond. A moment later, one of the uniformed officers, a young blond guy this time, opened the door nearest to me and pulled me out.

'You're not going to do anything stupid if he takes off those cuffs, are you?' asked Whittler.

I said I wouldn't, and the officer unlocked me. I rubbed my wrists where the cuffs had been, hoping to regain circulation. Whittler put his hand between my shoulder blades and led me to a black Mercedes with dark tinted windows parked on the street. We sat in the back with the air conditioner blaring. The seats were supple black leather, and there were dark burl wood accents on the doors and vents. Under normal circumstances, I probably would have questioned how a public servant could afford the car; given what I was in there for, I thought it might have been inappropriate.

Whittler didn't say anything at first. He stared at me as if waiting.

'Did you nail this Lieutenant's wife?' he finally asked.

'I'm about the only one who didn't, from what I heard.'

'Did he nail yours?'

I shook my head no.

'Then help me understand what's going on. Because I stepped into a cluster fuck that I do not appreciate.'

I filled Whittler in on the details of my previous encounter with Bowers and with the surveillance detail he had put on me the night before. Whittler folded his hands in front of him and stared at them for a moment when I finished.

'The search didn't turn anything up, so you're fine there. Problem is you got into a goddamn fistfight on your front lawn. You know how that would look if that got out? A decorated lieutenant and one of my lead investigators? Jesus. I heard you were smart.'

The hidden undercurrent was 'do you know how that would hurt my chances in an election?' Whittler exhaled deeply and wiped sweat off his forehead before speaking again.

'I want you out of my office. Email a letter of resignation to my secretary. Say it's for personal reasons or that you got a better job offer from another department. I don't care. If you do that and keep quiet, I won't press charges.'

I figured that was coming. Unfortunately, it meant

the next stop on my rollercoaster career was probably a mall security office.

'Can I ask you something first?' I asked.

'What?'

'Did you see the affidavit Lieutenant Bowers used to secure the search warrant?'

'Of course I saw it,' said Jack, staring out his window. 'That's part of the reason you're not under arrest. The warrant was issued by Judge Thurman. I could shit on a piece of paper, and he'd sign a search warrant for the White House.'

'What was Bowers' probable cause to search my house?'

Jack ran his hand across his mouth before answering.

'Said he had a confidential informant who swore you had a test tube full of something called *agua rica*. He said you hid it in a stuffed lion in one of the bedrooms. Whole thing was bullshit, and you took the bait. If you had sucked it up . . .'

He kept ranting, but I tuned him out. Mike Bowers shouldn't have known about the *agua rica*, and nor should he have known about my daughter's stuffed animal collection. Whoever was tipping him off had been in my house. I spoke up when he finished speaking.

'Thank you. I'll get on that email.'

The Mercedes pulled away as soon as I shut the door. Bowers and the other officers followed shortly after. I met Hannah on the front porch and slumped beside her on the steps.

'I think you should go back to your sister's house.'

She looked over her shoulder at our hallway. 'We need to clean up first,' she said. 'Megan will be fine with Jack and Yasmina for a little while.'

'I'm not worried about her right now. You know those people who sent Megan flowers? They've been in our house.'

Chapter 13

Hannah stayed long enough to fill a duffel bag with clothes before driving back to her sister's house. I hated watching her go, even if it was for the best. She wanted me to go with her, but it was too late for that. Azrael and Karen Rea had already killed Robbie Cutting and Rachel. Unless I missed my mark, their organization had probably also taken out Rollo and James Russo. I doubted they'd hesitate to take me out, too. If I quit, Hannah, Megan, and I were dead.

I started to walk back inside but stopped in the front entryway. The frame around my front door was cracked, leaving a gap between the door and sill big enough that every bug in the state could crawl into my living room. I didn't have time to reframe it before dark, so I grabbed a sheet of uncut plywood from my garage and nailed it against what was left of the door frame. It wouldn't stop anybody from getting into my house if they were really determined, but at least it'd keep the squirrels from getting into my living room.

That done, I went through my kitchen door and grabbed a soda from the fridge. I rolled it against my forehead. It was fair to say that Azrael had gotten my message the night before and sent one right back to me. He might have been ready and looking for a fight, but I wasn't. I needed a new tactic. I gulped the soda and threw it in the trash before heading to my cruiser.

I turned on my car but left it in park as I flipped through my notebook. If the incorporation papers for Sunshine Blood Products were accurate, I had Karen Rea's home address. She and Azrael seemed to know a lot about me; it was time I learned something about them. According to my notes, Karen lived in Fischers, a wealthy suburb northeast of the city. I entered her address into my cruiser's GPS. It said the drive would take me twenty-five minutes, which would put me there at roughly two-thirty. I had plenty of time before most people came home from work.

I put my car in gear and headed out. Karen's neighborhood was typical of her area. The houses were roughly three-to-four thousand square feet, and all had yards large enough to field a baseball game. Very little was ostentatious or showy; it was a neighborhood where the upper class congregated to raise children outside the corrupting elements of the city. Unfortunately, a wrought-iron fence surrounded the complex and a guardhouse stood in front of the only entrance. That complicated things.

I pulled up to the guardhouse and opened my window. A young guy stepped out. He looked like he was in his early thirties. He was wearing a gray uniform that was a few sizes too small on a thick neck. As far as I could tell, he was unarmed, but he had a radio on his belt. He leaned over, and I caught sight of his name tag. John A.

'Can I help you, sir?' he asked.

I shifted on my hip to grab my badge. John put his right foot back and brought his hand to his belt as if reaching for a weapon. His movements were smooth, practiced, and deliberate. They taught cadets to do that at the Police Academy to protect their firearm.

'Take it easy,' I said. 'I'm getting my ID.'

John nodded but kept his right hip back. I held my badge out for him. His breathing became more relaxed after that. He leaned against my car.

'What can I help you with, Detective?'

'I'm here to see one of your residents. Karen Rea. She lives on Oakwood.'

'Is Dr Rea expecting you?'

Doctor?

'I hope not. And I'd like it to stay that way.'

John shook his head.

'Unless you have a warrant, I can't let you in without Dr Rea's permission,' he said. 'That's company policy.'

'I appreciate your policy, but I've got to get back there. Dr Rea has been ducking our subpoena for a week. If she knows I'm coming, she'll be gone before I get there. I'm making a delivery; I'll be in and out in ten minutes.'

'What's she being subpoenaed for?'

'You know I can't tell you that. It's important that I get this to her. I'm just doing my job.'

John's scowl didn't leave his face, but he held his right hand up, fingers spread apart.

'Five minutes as a favor to IMPD. I'll call Dr Rea in five minutes, so you'd better get over there before I do. Oakwood is the third cul-de-sac on the right.'

Five minutes was tight, but it was doable. I thanked him and put the car into gear. True to John's directions, Karen Rea's street was the third on the right. Like every other house in the neighborhood, her driveway was uneven cobblestone set in concrete, and her lawn was trim and green, a surprising luxury in the middle of a heat wave.

I climbed out of my car and onto an empty street. Karen had a single-story home with a two-car garage and a covered front porch. I walked up the driveway to her front door. White lace curtains blocked most of my view inside when I looked through the windows. I

212

couldn't see any furniture. I knocked hard to see if anyone was home. Nothing stirred. I looked through the windows again and then took a step back to look at the black house numbers tacked to the brick beside the front door. I was at the right place.

Maybe she's moving.

I looked up and down the street again but saw no one. I figured I still had some time, so I jogged to the backyard. Karen's lot was large enough that anyone looking through the windows of neighboring houses would need binoculars to make out my face. I figured I was safe as far as witnesses went. There were planters along the fence line, but the bushes looked like twigs and weeds sprouted everywhere. The lawn crunched like dead wood, and its green shade ended abruptly as I stepped behind the house. I bent down and squeezed some of the green grass between my fingers, but the tint came off like print on a newspaper. Paint.

I hate the suburbs.

I skipped a search of the yard and went directly to Karen's concrete patio. A pair of French doors led into a living room. I looked through the window. As expected, I couldn't see a stick of furniture. I was beginning to think the house was a dead drop. Our narcotics squad used them to communicate with confidential informants and officers under deep cover in the field. We'd rent an apartment, mail something to it, and our undercover officer could pick it up without having to meet us. It was a nice system.

As helpful as they were for us, though, they were even more helpful for organized criminals. A drug wholesaler could rent a house or apartment, stash his drugs inside, and be halfway across town by the time his dealers came and retrieved them. It wasn't uncommon to pop street dealers who hadn't even seen the guy they bought their stashes from.

I looked at my watch. Four minutes left. I took a deep breath and pressed down on the curved metal handle of one of the French doors while simultaneously throwing my hip into the frame. The tumblers inside the lock slipped, and the door popped open.

Cool air blasted towards me as I stepped in. Karen's living room was open to the kitchen. It had vaulted ceilings, dark hardwood floors, and enough windows overlooking the backyard that the homeowner wouldn't have to turn on lights during the day. I took a few steps around, my footsteps echoing as I did.

The builder hadn't skimped when he built the house. The molding around the windows and door frames was thick mahogany, and there were speakers mounted in the ceiling for a home theater. The kitchen was just as nice. The cabinets looked like mahogany too, and the countertops were two inch thick gray granite flecked with silver. It looked like a model home. The hardwood floor was clear of scuff marks, the stainless-steel refrigerator lacked magnets or pictures, and the stove top was pristine. The only things out of place were a black rice cooker beside the fridge and a teakettle on the stove.

Every dead drop I had ever seen was a shithole. With no one staying there, no one cared how the place looked. In fact, it was better if the place was messier. It's easier to hide things in a cluttered space than in a clean one. Karen's house felt wrong.

I opened the fridge. It had a pitcher of water, a bottle of soy sauce, and a green jar with Asian writing on it. Probably wasabi. I let the fridge door swing shut and opened a few of the surrounding cabinets. I found Tupperware in one and a few plates and glasses in another, but that was it.

I left the kitchen and followed a T-shaped hallway beside the living room. The left branch led to the garage and laundry room, but I didn't find anything exciting in either except for provocative black lingerie in the laundry room. The other end of the hallway held bedrooms, each of which had an attached bathroom. The first two bedrooms were empty, while the third, presumably the master, had a small bed, bookshelf, and computer desk alongside an en-suite bathroom. At least it was something.

I jogged to the bathroom. It had a jacuzzi tub and separate glass enclosed shower opposite the door. There was a double vanity sink to my left, while the toilet had its own separate room, allowing multiple people to use the bathroom at once. I opened drawers on the vanity and found Tylenol, heartburn medication, and generic Xanax prescribed for Karen Rea. I knew a couple of guys I could sell the Xanax to, but I left it in the drawer. I might have broken into the house, but I was still an investigator. One or two felonies a day was enough for me.

I went to the bedroom next. The room was big enough that it could have comfortably fit every piece of furniture I owned. I checked out Karen's desk first. It was laminated particle board, the sort of furniture sold in flat packs at discount stores and assembled with an Allen wrench. I pulled out the desk chair and shuffled to the waist high bookshelf nearby. The top shelf had a Latin–English dictionary, a copy of *Dracula*, and a few history books on Eastern Europe. They were probably source materials for her postings on fangporium.com. The other two shelves had thick green binders. I pulled one out and opened it to an academic journal from the Australian Society of Microbiologists. I slid it back onto the shelf and pulled out another at random. It had a similar academic journal, this time on virology.

I shelved the binder and clucked my tongue. So Karen Rea was a microbiologist. That was odd; I didn't find too many drug dealers with advanced degrees.

Since I didn't have much time, I ignored the computer and took a look at the desk. I picked up a coffee cup that sat beside the computer monitor and took a whiff. Green tea. I put it down and examined the only other thing on the desk. It was a picture frame. I picked it up to get a better look at it. The photo was faded and yellowing on the edges, but it had a young Asian family on it. The adults couldn't have been more than twenty-five. The only man in the picture wore a white shirt and thick, black glasses, while the woman had an infant on her hip. It was a personal memento, the last sort of thing I'd expect to find at a dead drop. Something was wrong about that place.

As I reached to put the frame down, time seemed to slow. I noticed a barrel-shaped, HD web camera with built-in microphone attached to the table. The green recording light was on.

Shit.

I vaulted forward, shaking the desk so violently I nearly knocked the monitor off its pedestal. I blocked the camera's lens with my palm. It must have been motion-activated. As I did that, the phone started ringing in the kitchen, signaling that my five minutes in the house were up. I looked around quickly, following the camera's cord into the computer. Chances were good that the video was being streamed somewhere over the internet, but I didn't have time to find out.

I scooted back from the desk and grabbed the mug of tea. In the off chance the video was stored locally, I tilted the computer forward, exposing the connection posts and air vents in back. I poured the tea inside. It sizzled as it hit the hot components, creating a cloud of plastic-smelling steam. The computer's fans ceased operating, but the hard drive still whirred, indicating the computer was still working. Hopefully it'd short out and overheat.

I jogged out of the house and pulled the French doors shut behind me. The yard was as bereft of life as it had been when I entered, so there shouldn't have been any witnesses to see me break in. I straightened my jacket and rolled my shoulders. I might not have found anything that would get Karen arrested, but at least I had learned something new. She was a microbiologist. I didn't know what to make of it, but it was interesting.

I walked around the building. My cruiser was on the street as I had left it, but there was a white pickup truck with a star painted on the door behind it. John, the gatehouse guard, was leaning against my car and staring at me with his arms across his chest. I nodded a greeting but didn't otherwise acknowledge him.

'Delivering your subpoena to Dr Rea's backyard?'

I stopped in the middle of the street. 'She didn't answer the front door.'

John raised his eyebrows. 'You were back there an awful long time, Detective.'

I looked up and down the street before putting my hands on my hips, flaring out my jacket and exposing my firearm.

'Yeah, I was. Is there something you want to say, John? Speak up, but be careful. I'd hate for you to say something you couldn't take back.'

I didn't know what that meant, but it sounded ominous in my head. John stared at me for a moment as if considering what he should do. Eventually, his posture softened and his shoulders relaxed.

'I'm sorry Dr Rea wasn't available,' he said, walking back towards his pickup. He opened his door and paused. 'If you'd like, I can have her call your office when she gets home.'

'There's no need,' I said, walking the rest of the way to my car. 'I left her my card.'

I got into my car and drove off. A lot of cops and ex-cops are genuine hard cases, so intimidating a guy who had been doing his job wouldn't have bothered them. I felt a little guilty about it, but I didn't have time to be self-indulgent. After my incident with the computer, Karen would know I wasn't just after Azrael. I hadn't dealt with her directly, so I wasn't sure how she'd react. I had to assume there'd be a reprisal and escalation, though, which meant my house probably wouldn't be safe much longer. At least my family was out of the way; that was something.

It was so hot outside that the air my cruiser blew at my face was lukewarm at best. Assuming I still had a job, I'd have to take the car to IMPD's vehicle services division and get the air conditioner looked at. I wiped sweat off my brow to keep it from falling into my eyes. I drove for a mile or two until I came across a strip mall. I parked in the lot under a ginkgo tree.

It was a little before three in the afternoon, which hopefully meant Mack would be near his phone. I thumbed through my cell phone's recent calls until I found his lab number and dialed.

No one picked up, so I left a quick message asking him to give me a call. After that, I let myself sink into my cruiser's well-worn seat, considering my options. First things first, I needed to get some clothes at my house while I still could. While I was at it, I also needed to warn Hannah not to come home any time soon.

I was about to put my car in gear and leave when Mack called back.

'You screening your calls or something?' I asked.

'Yeah. Aleksandra's pissed at me, so she keeps calling to bitch me out. I put her on an allowance 'cause she blew through three grand last month on shoes and hats. Let me ask you, how many pairs of shoes does Hannah have?'

I thought back to the pile on our closet floor and shrugged.

'Maybe ten or twelve.'

'Fucking-A. Ten pairs. Aleksandra bought more than that last month. You're a lucky guy.'

'Uh, thanks, Mack. I was calling to see if I could pick your brain for a moment.'

'Yeah, I've got a moment. Shoot.'

'I've been following up on some stuff we talked about this morning, and I came across some new information. What role would a microbiologist play in a cocaine lab?'

Mack was silent for a moment. I heard what sounded like a low growl in the back of his throat.

'I wouldn't think any. Coke extraction isn't microbiology, and the people who do it just have to follow directions. They don't need to know why anything works. Why do you ask?'

'One of my suspects had microbiology journals in her house. I thought it might mean something.'

'Tell you what. Your question was easy, so I'll hook you up. If your suspect is a microbiologist, I bet I can pull her CV off one of the hospital's databases. We recently hired an intern with a PhD in micro. She's hot; if you want, I can introduce you.'

'I don't need the introduction, but thank you,' I said, turning my car off so I wouldn't waste gas. 'My suspect is Karen Rea. That's Rea spelled R-E-A.'

I heard Mack typing a moment later.

'You got anything?' I asked.

'Yeah. Lots of stuff. Hold on, partner. Let me look at this.'

I heard more of Mack's throaty growl. Evidently he did it when he was thinking.

'You really think this lady's a drug dealer?' he asked a moment later.

'She's connected, but I don't know how yet.'

'Academic job market must suck pretty hard. She has a PhD in molecular genetics from Harvard with a postdoc fellowship at Stanford. If her CV is accurate, she taught at MIT for five years after Stanford. I don't have a calculator on me, but it looks as if she racked up about ten mill in research grants at MIT. It's too bad she's got kids. Otherwise she sounds like someone I'd like to meet.'

'I really doubt my suspect has kids,' I said, watching as shoppers went to cars around me. 'That might not be the right Karen Rea.'

Mack grunted again.

'It's the only Karen Rea in the database. And I'm only assuming she has kids. Her résumé makes it look like she took off in the middle of a pretty big research project a little while back. Usually only see that when a woman gets pregnant.'

I ran my tongue across my teeth and tried to remember

if anything at the house indicated she had kids even tangentially. The only thing I could think of was the picture on her desk, but it was at least twenty-five years old. If she had kids, surely there'd be something else.

'Does it say why she left?'

I heard Mack hum for a second.

'No, but she was gone for five years, and whatever she did, she fucked up. Went from Tenured Research Professor at MIT to Lecturer at Podunk University after her break. Her post-break teaching career didn't last long, either. About a year. After that, she disappeared.'

I nodded, processing the news. Mack might have been right. You don't go from academic all-star to no-name lecturer to drug-dealing vampire without a body or two buried in the backyard.

'Can you send me what you have on her?'

'Yeah. I can email it to you.'

'I appreciate it.'

I gave Mack my email address and hung up. I tapped my phone against the palm of my hand.

Who are you, Dr Rea?

Chapter 14

My front door was still nailed shut when I got home, which meant I wouldn't be sharing the house with the local wildlife or neighborhood kids. That was nice. It was mid-afternoon, so I figured I was safe for a while. Karen and Azrael wouldn't try anything during the day. There were too many potential witnesses, and it would be too easy to see them coming. I unlocked the side door to my kitchen and stepped into a mess that even my rumbling, empty stomach couldn't ignore. I grabbed fistfuls of silverware and utensils from the floor and dumped them into the dishwasher. The place looked a little more serviceable after that. At least I wouldn't have to worry about stabbing myself with a fork when I walked across the room.

Since I hadn't eaten lunch, I made myself a turkey sandwich and finished off a carton of potato salad in our fridge before going to my office. My computer was still running, so it only took me a few minutes to check my email and print off the document Mack had sent me. Karen Rea's curriculum vitae was more impressive than it had sounded on the phone. While Mack had mentioned her research grants, he hadn't mentioned her publications or professional presentations. That list went on for two pages.

I scanned it as I ate my sandwich. I may not have understood the first thing about Karen's research, but I did notice a pattern. She had co-written three articles with someone named Dr Doug Wexler. He had supervised her during a postdoctoral fellowship at Stanford. More telling than that, two of those articles were written before her break from academia while the third was written afterwards. The two of them might have kept in touch, which hopefully meant that he'd know where she had been. That could be helpful.

I wolfed down the remains of my sandwich, wiped my hands on my pants, and googled Doug Wexler. The first page that popped up was a faculty listing at Stanford University. Wexler's CV wasn't as long as Karen's, but like her, he had a PhD in genetics and several dozen publications. I read until I found his office phone number. I doubted he'd be in, but it was worth a shot.

I called the number on my cell and waited through two rings for someone to answer.

'Microbiology, how may I help you?'

Must have been his secretary.

'Yeah, hello. My name is Mike Bowers, and I'm calling from West Labs in Indianapolis, Indiana. I was wondering if I could talk to Dr Wexler about a former colleague, Dr Karen Rea.'

'Oh, Karen. We haven't heard from her in a while. How is she?'

I leaned forward. 'I presume she's doing well. She applied for a job in my department and used Dr Wexler as a reference. Did you know her?'

I opened a word processor on my computer.

'Not well, but she was a very nice woman. Always had a smile and always had nice things to say to people. Dr Wexler doesn't usually take calls, but I think he'll want to speak to you. I'll patch you through to his lab.'

I was listening to elevator music before I could respond, which gave me a moment to make a few notes. If the secretary was any indication, Karen was well liked by her coworkers. I doubted that'd be the case if they knew she cavorted as a vampire on the weekend. I waited about five minutes for the elevator music to end.

'Hi, this is Doug Wexler. Susan tells me you're calling about Karen. What can I do for you?'

'Good to meet you, Dr Wexler. As you were probably told, my name is Mike Bowers, and I'm calling on behalf of West Labs. We're considering Dr Rea for employment, and she listed you as a reference. I'm calling you to see if the nice things she wrote about herself are actually true.'

Dr Wexler chuckled. Hopefully that meant his guard was down.

'She's one of the most competent scientists I know, so I'm sure all the wonderful things you've heard are correct. You said you were calling from West Labs. I don't think I'm familiar.'

'We're an up-and-coming biotech firm in Plainfield, Indiana,' I said, thinking quickly. 'We're still small, but you never know what'll happen tomorrow.'

'Isn't that the truth?' said Wexler. 'Start-ups are exciting, and I'm glad to hear you're considering Karen. Been too long since I've read a Rea paper. What sort of biotech are you in?'

I coughed, thinking quickly.

'Our biggest contract is with the Department of Homeland Security, so I can't talk about our exact work.'

Dr Wexler paused. I was about to hang up and call it a dead end when he spoke again.

'And you're able to hire Karen?'

I raised my eyebrows. 'Is there any reason that we shouldn't?'

'Not at all, but Karen's work history is unusual. I presumed it would preclude her from attaining the requisite security clearance.'

'I'm not a security officer, so I can't comment on that.

I do have some general questions about her that you might be able to help me with. My notes tell me you supervised her postdoc fellowship at Stanford. Did you ever have issues or problems with her?'

I asked the question not because I was particularly interested, but because I thought it was the sort of question a prospective employer would ask. Dr Wexler told me that Karen was punctual, polite, and professional; she got along well with faculty and staff and her lectures were well attended by graduate students and faculty across multiple disciplines. I didn't think much of it, but I got the sense that Karen and Wexler's relationship extended well beyond the classroom. He said she had a beautiful mind and a gift for analytical thinking. I didn't ask if he found any other parts of her attractive, but I was tempted. Our conversation finally went back to her work history a few minutes later.

'You mentioned that Dr Rea has an unusual work history,' I said. 'I wondered if you could elaborate on what you meant.'

'Yes, of course,' he said. 'I was referring to her time with the South African Medical Services. I seriously hope you don't judge Karen by the research they conducted. You have to understand; she went as a scientist. She was given the opportunity to conduct pure research, unconstrained by political or commercial considerations. It was irresistible to someone with her acumen and curiosity. I don't know that she ever forgave herself for what she did.'

'What'd she do?'

Wexler paused for a moment and cleared his throat. 'Forgive me; I assumed you knew. I'd rather not discuss details.'

'Did Karen ask you not to speak about it, or . . .'

I let my voice trail off. Neither of us spoke for a moment. I could hear his breath on the line, so I knew he was still there. After a moment, I heard typing.

'Where did you say you worked? I just looked up West Labs and can't find anything. I don't appreciate—'

I hung up the phone before he could finish, my mind already forming new questions. A South African job that led to academic disfavor, associations with drug dealers, an empty house, and, judging by her lack of personal possessions, an even emptier life. I leaned back in my chair, processing the information. I may not have known where Karen's organization stored their drugs, but I was starting to get a better picture of her. I didn't like what I saw.

I flipped through my notebook until I found the address for Sunshine Blood Products. The company was a node in my investigation, a place where suspects and leads converged. It was also one of the few angles I had left to explore; if Karen had drugs somewhere, they were probably there. I packed a couple of days' worth of clothes into a suitcase and hopped into my car.

I put the address into my cruiser's GPS and drove for about forty minutes until I hit the Hadley Business Park, an industrial warehouse complex about ten miles outside of Plainfield. It had corrugated steel warehouses lined up like soldiers going to war with thin strips of dead, yellowing grass between. Despite the name, the only park-like amenity was a fountain off the main gate. At least I presumed it was a fountain; the reservoir surrounding it had dried up, and evidently the management decided it wasn't worth refilling. It smelled like rotting vegetable matter.

I drove past seven rows of warehouses until I found Sunshine's building. It was number thirteen, which I thought was fitting. I'm not a great judge of distances, but the building looked like it was about a hundred feet on a side. It had no windows, and the only entrance was an industrial-looking, glass-and-steel front door with red fabric awning over top. It wasn't inviting, but I doubt that was what Karen and Azrael were going for when they signed the lease.

I parked in front of the building. The only other car in the parking lot was a battered Honda Accord that made my cruiser look luxurious. Unless Azrael drove a Beamer by night and a junker by day, there must have been additional parking somewhere else. The wind tugged on my door as soon as I stepped out. Without trees or a break of some sort, the long rows of buildings funneled the air through the complex like a giant wind tunnel. My guess was that the designers had stolen the layout from Purdue University, my alma mater. It was the only place on Earth I knew of that the wind was in your face no matter where you turned.

I turned around, looking for vantage points and exits. I saw a soybean field to the west and warehouses to the north, south, and east. The highway to Plainfield was about a quarter of a mile to the west, but there was no easy access. The only way in and out of the complex was through the front gate. That'd be a bottleneck if I needed to get out quickly, but if I were fast, it shouldn't be a problem.

I thought I could do it. The complex was isolated enough that there shouldn't be too many people driving by in the middle of the night. More important than that, we were outside IMPD's jurisdiction. The nearest cops would be from the Hendricks County Sheriff's department. If they came from Plainfield, it'd take them at least ten minutes to get there.

I waited beside my car for about fifteen more minutes, but no employees or rent-a-cops drove past, and no one emerged from any of the nearby buildings for a smoke break. If the complex was that dead in the middle of the afternoon, it'd be even more dead that night.

I drove to a motel by the interstate in Plainfield. It was cheap, but the room was clean. It had a bed, a bathroom, and a TV. As soon as I got in, I sat on the bed and called my wife's cell phone using the room telephone. She didn't answer, so I left a message warning her that the house wasn't safe. I didn't think she planned to go back any time soon, but it felt important to tell her anyway. After that, I hung up the phone and put my keys and sidearm on an end table beside the bed. My muscles felt heavy and weak, and a dull weariness that went beyond exhaustion pervaded my body. I washed my face in the bathroom and had afternoon prayers before crashing onto the bed.

Chapter 15

I don't know how long I was out, but my eyes fluttered open to the sound of uncoordinated footsteps pounding down the hallway outside my room. For a moment, I thought it was Megan. Whenever she ran, it sounded as if she were half-falling and half-sprinting. I'm sure there was a medical reason to explain why kids ran like that, but I still thought it was cute. I scratched my head and sat up. No one had broken in while I was asleep. It's the small things in life that make it worthwhile.

I shook my head to clear any leftover sleep from my system and walked to the window. It was right before dusk, and there were two kids, both barely past the toddler stage, splashing around in the shallow end of the motel's pool. Their mother looked on from a white plastic chair. I was glad to see them; as long as they were outside, I doubted anyone would try to break down my door.

I ran my palm across my face. I hadn't shaved in a couple of days, so I was starting to feel like the Wolfman. I doubted Karen and her vampire buddies would care, but I preferred to avoid scaring small children with my appearance. I grabbed my toiletries from the bag I had packed earlier and went to the sink, stopping on the way to turn on the television for background noise. When I heard the anchor announce the lead story, I dropped my razor and sat on the bed.

The reporter stood in a parking lot in front of a familiar mottled brown cube. The building had narrow, rectangular windows and a banner hanging above the front door welcoming new students and parents to school. The camera panned past the front entrance to a mostly empty parking lot with basketball hoops and a softball field in the distance.

The last time I had been in that parking lot, Olivia and I had met Principal Eikmeier before interviewing some of Rachel's friends. He wasn't there any more. Instead, there were uniformed police officers erecting a perimeter beside the tennis courts. The camera panned back to the entrance and zoomed in on an attractive female reporter named Kristen Tanaka. She was well known in the area for her ability to scoop other stations on law enforcement matters; what wasn't quite as well known outside law enforcement was that she would sleep with anything that moved if it gave her a story.

'The scene here is still chaotic, and details are sketchy at this point. What we know is that two bodies, possibly students, were found near the tennis courts by a member of the school's custodial staff. So far, the police haven't officially released further information, but a source close to the investigation told me the bodies appear to have been burned repeatedly with a small round object. We're still waiting for word on what could have caused those.'

I tuned Kristen out as she continued speaking. Multiple round burns. Some boy in blue was going to get lucky for that tidbit.

I leaned back on the bed and allowed my mind to wander. Multiple burns indicated intentionality, maybe even torture. It takes a special kind of person to do that to a kid. I took a couple of deep breaths. Coincidences happen, but no one was thick enough to think four dead kids from one school was a coincidence. Something was happening, and the game was changing. Robbie Cutting had been murdered, but his death was quick, neat, and private. Someone took his time with these kids and then dumped them in a public spot. They were a message, but probably not from Karen and probably not to me. So far, her messages had been subtle and targeted. This was neither. We had new players.

As soon as the newscast went to commercial, I went back to the sink and finished shaving. New players or not, Sunshine Blood Products was getting a visitor that night, and I needed to be ready. My muscles felt tight, and my brain was firing on cylinders I didn't even remember I had. It was nervous energy. I used to get it before serving felony arrest warrants. It felt good to be that energized again. I had dusk prayers beside my bed, but it was difficult to pay attention. Hopefully God would cut me some slack.

Since I hadn't eaten much that day, I stopped by a Quiznos within walking distance of my motel and grabbed a sandwich. No one followed me, which was good. With luck, my visit to Sunshine would still be a surprise. After dinner, I watched a couple of local newscasts in my room, hoping to hear some new tidbit about the bodies at Rachel and Robbie's former school. Unfortunately, the reporters seemed to be as clueless as I was. Olivia might have heard something, but I doubted she'd be in the sharing mood.

I forced myself to forget about the bodies and focus on my task that evening. Even if there was an alarm, I figured I had at least ten minutes inside Sunshine before anyone could show up. That was plenty of time to find something worthwhile. Ideally, I'd find a document titled *Secret Plans to Take Over the World*, but I wasn't counting on it. There'd be something, though. I was confident of that.

I paced the short length of my room. My gun felt heavy in its shoulder holster. Part of me wanted to leave it behind. Breaking and entering was a felony, but it was a relatively minor felony. If the police caught me, I could plead to a lesser charge and get probation. It was a different crime entirely if I carried a deadly weapon while committing a burglary, though. I'd go to prison if I were caught. On the other hand, if Sunshine had a guard, chances were that he wouldn't be happy to see me. I needed a firearm in case I ran into somebody hostile inside.

After a while, I got so tired of thinking about my plan that I flipped on the TV, hoping for a late-breaking news story about the kids at the school. I went through the channels twice but couldn't find anything but sitcoms and crappy reality shows. I glanced at my watch. It was a few minutes after eight, and the sun was finally setting. I had another hour or so for darkness to settle on the area.

I decided that I couldn't force myself to wait around any more, so I changed into a black, long-sleeved shirt and dark jeans before heading to my car. Before leaving, I rooted through my evidence collection kit to make sure I had latex gloves. I had an unopened box of thirty-six. They were cheap and thin, but I didn't plan to use them for surgery. They'd work.

It wasn't quite full dark when I left the streetlights and strip malls of Plainfield behind me. The wind carried thick clouds that covered the moon and stars, leaving me in a world without shadow. My car rocked in the heavy gusts, making it difficult to drive. Half an hour after leaving my motel room, I was surrounded by dark fields, barns, and warehouses.

I pulled off the side of the road about a quarter of a mile from the business park. The soybeans danced around me in the wind. I shivered. Without streetlights, it was so dark that I couldn't see anything in three directions. I drummed my fingers on my steering wheel. Unlike the surrounding fields, the business park was lit as bright as day. Aside from the plants blowing in the breeze, nothing stirred.

In a perfect situation, I'd survey that building for a week. I'd develop dossiers of the employees, I'd track their average arrival and departure times, and I'd probably even make notes on who drove what vehicles. If the complex had a guard, I'd track him around the facility. I'd probably also make a schedule of when the State Police drove by. In short, I'd be well prepared. It's hard to catch a well-prepared criminal. Unfortunately, I didn't have time for any of that. This had to end before another kid died.

I watched for about twenty minutes more, but the complex was dead. I didn't see a single car come out or drive in. I reached into my glove box for the bottle of bourbon I had purchased a day earlier. I took off the cap and drank deeply. The liquid burned some of my nervous energy away and left me relaxed. It was going to be fine.

I drove the quarter mile to the main entrance but killed my headlights before going in. My knees felt stiff, and my chest felt tight. I could live with that, though. I parked in front of Sunshine's building and got out of my car. The breeze whistled through the complex, and cool air hit me in the face. I'd be in and out in ten minutes. That should be easy.

Sunshine's front door was glass in a steel frame. It looked flimsy, but from my years as a detective, I knew it probably wasn't. I saw a surveillance video a couple of years ago of a suspect throwing a brick against a similar door only to have it bounce back, hitting him in the head. The ricochet cut a gash in his forehead and damn near killed him. That's why I planned to use something a little less subtle than a brick.

I popped open my trunk and dug through my evidence collection kit until I found a Maglite flashlight. I put it in my pocket and reached back into the box for a twenty-four-ounce claw hammer. I hadn't ever used the hammer to collect evidence, but I kept it in there in case I needed to pry boards or something else up. If it didn't break the glass, I didn't know what would.

While I was in the trunk, I also tore open my box of latex gloves and snapped one on each hand. I glanced at my watch. Ten minutes.

Now or never.

I jogged to the door and smashed my hammer against it. The sound was loud enough to hurt my ears, but the glass didn't break. I hit it again, causing cracks to form. Maybe I should have brought a sledgehammer. I broke through on the third strike, and after that it was pretty easy to clear a hole big enough for me to crawl through without cutting myself. I dropped the hammer beside the door and stepped in with my firearm in one hand and my flashlight in the other.

The lobby was long and dark enough that I couldn't see the other end. I flipped on my Maglite and adjusted the focus to cast a wide beam. There was a receptionist's desk in front of a hallway directly ahead of me and a seating area to my immediate right. I didn't think old news magazines or appointment books would help my case much, so I skipped both and jogged towards the hallway. It was T-shaped with branches heading deeper into the structure to my left, right, and straight ahead.

I jogged straight and tried the first door I came to. It opened into an employee's break room. Nothing helpful for me. I closed the door and went to the next. The building creaked as the wind raked against it. I shivered. The place was creepy and not simply because its owners thought they were vampires. There were dark corners and doors everywhere, and there could have been someone waiting behind any of them. I didn't like it.

I threw open the second door I came to and stepped through with my firearm in front of me like a shield. I caught the smell before I saw anything. Wintergreen. I was in the right spot, at least. My adrenaline level spiked each time the building shifted in the breeze. I cast my light around the room quickly. I could see folding tables along the far wall, but the room was otherwise empty.

I shined the light on my watch. Eight minutes left. I breathed deeply to calm myself before jogging back in the hallway. I went through a door immediately across from me, but like the room I had previously checked, it was empty. It smelled like a nail salon. Acetone. Mack had mentioned something about that in his cocaine lecture. I may not have found any drugs yet, but my circumstantial case against Sunshine was growing.

I jogged back down the main hallway and hung a left. I found another empty room. It also smelled like acetone. If Karen used this building solely to process coke, she had quite an operation. Mack processed five grams of cocaine on a desk; Karen had to have been moving kilos at a time to need a building like this. I may not have found out what she was doing, but there was more than enough evidence in the building to bust her for narcotics trafficking.

I had a few minutes left, so I checked out the last room in the building. According to the nameplate, it was the office of Dr Karen Rea, CEO. The door was locked, so I took a step back and kicked it below the doorknob. The impact rocked me back and vibrated my teeth, but the door didn't move. I kicked again, this time ready for the jolt. The frame held, but I heard the crack of splintering wood. I kicked it a third time, and the door burst open.

The room was simply furnished with a desk in the center of the floor and filing cabinets along the walls. My heart beat a little faster. I skipped to the filing cabinets and pulled open a drawer. Invoices, receipts, certificates of inspection from US customs. It looked like Karen was moving about two cargo containers of blood products from South America to her warehouse every week. If they were all *agua rica*, that was a shit ton of coke.

I closed the drawer and tried two others, finding similar information both times. Karen's company kept better records than most accounting firms. If we could prove those invoices were about drugs, we'd have enough to send her to prison for ten lifetimes. I didn't think that'd be a problem, either. A lot of dealers write in code; there have even been Law and Order episodes about it. Once we proved there were trace elements of cocaine all over the building, even the most obtuse judge would have to see the documents for what they were.

I stopped for a moment, thinking. The situation wasn't

ideal, but with as much material as I had, I could probably get Detective Lee from narcotics on board. We could claim one of his more reliable confidential informants gave us a tip about the building. That wouldn't cost us much more than a simple payoff. Once we had that, we could apply for a warrant. With that, Karen and Azrael would be done for. If we made a big enough bust, Lee might even get a promotion out of it.

I felt pretty good for the first time in a long while. Things were coming together as they were supposed to.

I didn't bother looking at the rest of the filing cabinets. Instead, I started pulling open drawers on Karen's desk. I didn't see anything interesting until I came to one on the bottom left. It wouldn't budge. I ran my flashlight over its face and found a keyhole beside the handle. A locked drawer in a locked office in a locked building. With any luck, she'd have a stash right there.

I jogged back through the lobby and grabbed the claw hammer I had brought with me. Despite Karen's security measures, the drawer didn't take long to pry open. The drawer held an inch-thick manila folder. I opened it, feeling my stomach twist. It was my police jacket, the one from Internal Affairs. It had my contact information, copies of complaints against me, even psychological evaluations from the station's psychiatrist. She claimed I had mild post-traumatic stress disorder after being shot, moderate depression, anger issues, and serious issues with authority. That report was probably why I was bounced from homicide. I hadn't even seen it.

I turned pages slowly as the implication sunk in. Karen had a cop on the payroll, and whoever he was, he wasn't a rank-and-file officer. She had someone with access to personnel files. That meant Captain or above, which meant I had stepped into something way over my pay grade.

That's when I heard it.

Crunching glass.

Sunshine had new visitors.

Chapter 16

According to my watch, I had been inside for twelve minutes. That was a pretty good response time if someone had called the police. Knowing what went on in the place, I doubted I was about to run into my colleagues, though. I extinguished my Maglite and grabbed my gun, sweat dripping down my neck and back.

Without a flashlight, the building's interior was almost too dark to navigate. I could see the edges of walls, but that was about it. I crept into the hallway, hoping my footsteps weren't really as loud as they seemed. None of the new arrivals said anything, but I heard their feet plod forward softer than they had before. A thin, opaque wall separated us. Six inches of insulation, drywall and building studs. It wasn't much protection.

My muscles felt tight, and I had to fight the urge to spring forward, gun blazing. I paused against the wall, my breath coming in tight bursts. As I did that, I heard a shrill buzz, and then the air conditioner kicked on, creating a slight breeze that carried a whiff of gasoline. The air conditioner masked my footsteps, so I crept across the hallway and peeked around the corner. There were two men in the lobby; I couldn't see one well, but the other carried a subcompact machine gun. I only caught a glimpse of it, but it looked like an MP5. Our SWAT guys carried them on missions. It was fast, accurate, and definitely not what I wanted to see at that moment.

I crept forward to see if I could get behind the receptionist's desk for better cover. As if sensing my presence, the guy with the machine gun looked over. Our eyes locked at the same time, but he was the first to act. Automatic gunfire ripped through the lobby. I dove and landed flat on my Maglite. Pain ripped across my ribcage, while bullets pierced the drywall around me like paper. They thwacked into the receptionist's desk, causing shards of particle board to smack into my face. I stopped thinking. The world only had three things at that moment. Me and the two shooters.

The shooters yelled at each other, but it wasn't English. I army-crawled back to Karen's office for cover and squeezed three shots into the lobby. Glass broke and a bullet ricocheted against something metal. I knew I wasn't going to hit anything, but I needed room to breathe. If they thought I was unarmed, they'd storm the corner, and there was no way I could win a toe-to-toe fight against two guys with automatics.

One of the shooters returned fire in controlled, three-shot bursts. The bullets smashed through the drywall inches above my head, causing my eyes to sting with sweat and dust. The gasoline smell I caught earlier became stronger, almost overpoweringly so. I realized something, then. They didn't need to shoot me; they needed to keep me contained long enough to light the place up.

It was too dark to see clearly, but I could see shapes with my peripheral vision. I cast my eyes about the hallway, hoping I'd missed a window or emergency door earlier. I didn't have that kind of luck, though. My body tingled, signaling that it was ready to move at a moment's notice. I ducked my head around the corner to note the relative positions of the men.

My flashlight had served me well for a few years, but I'd rather lose it than my life. I crouched and threw it into the lobby. The heavy Maglite clanged against the far wall. The guy with the MP5 turned and fired at the noise. I fired five shots at his muzzle flare. In a movie, his finger would get stuck on the trigger, and he'd fall back, firing at random. Reality isn't like that. He thudded against the ground. I stepped around the corner, my weapon in front of me, searching for the second guy.

For a moment, the world moved impossibly fast. The air was thick with the smell of gasoline. I saw a blur as the second shooter ran towards the exit. Before reaching it, he stopped, flicked open a Zippo lighter, and threw it at the seating area on the far side of the room.

The gas smell disappeared, and the air was ripped out of my lungs as a fireball engulfed the sofa, love seat, and carpet near the door. The top layer of my skin felt as if I were under a broiler. I didn't have enough oxygen to breathe anymore. I had to move.

As I crossed the room, I spotted the guy I shot sprawled out in front of the receptionist's desk. His lips moved, but no sound came out. Attempted murderer or not, I couldn't let him burn to death. That wasn't right. I bent at my knees and hoisted him on my shoulder. He was heavy, but I was running on adrenaline. My ribs throbbed dully where I'd landed on the flashlight. I coughed, nearly choking on black smoke.

I sprinted across the lobby, my lungs and throat burning. The room hadn't seemed that long earlier, but two hundred pounds of dead weight and a fire can change perceptions. By the time I reached the door, the second gunman was peeling out in a Ford Mustang. The drywall and other building materials around me were catching fire, and black smoke billowed out around me. I stepped outside and sucked air. My legs shook, but before they gave out, I dumped my new friend on the hood of my car. The son of a bitch was probably going to leave a dent. At least it'd blend in with the others. He moaned, but said nothing coherent.

I slipped my gun into my holster and coughed so hard I nearly vomited as my lungs tried to expel whatever black matter had entered them. I breathed deeply, trying to catch my breath, and leaned on the hood. Pain coursed through my body every time I exhaled. It felt as if I had just run a marathon. As I stood panting, a rapid series of bangs erupted from inside the building. I jumped. Pain blasted through my side once again. The gunman's hands were empty. He must have left his weapon inside, and unless I missed my mark, the rounds he hadn't fired had cooked off. Thankfully nothing flew out at us.

We stayed for a few minutes like that. The heat was powerful enough that I could have roasted marshmallows from thirty feet away. Flame licked the aluminum siding around Sunshine's front door. The roof would catch soon, and once that happened, the fire would be noticeable for miles around. Unless I got out of there quickly, I was going to have company.

I dragged the semi-conscious guy from my hood and pulled him onto my back seat. He gasped, and I got my first good look at him. He was probably thirty and had sunken cheeks and a star tattooed on his neck. I had shot him in the arm and shoulder, so his wounds weren't immediately life threatening. If he got help, his biggest fear was an infection. And me, of course. I slapped him around until his eyes focused on me.

'You got someone you can call?'

He nodded, so I threw him my cell phone and climbed into the driver's seat. I didn't know much about my passenger, but I doubted he was on Karen Rea's payroll. Drug dealers don't often burn down their own facilities. More likely, he worked for a competitor. I tilted my rear-view mirror so I could see him. His chest bobbed up and down, so I knew he was alive even if he didn't otherwise move.

I exited the complex and floored the accelerator. The road was so dark that I couldn't see more than ten feet to my left and right, making me feel as if I were in a tunnel. Despite the fact that I was driving away from it, the orange glow in my rear-view mirror grew brighter and larger. My engine throbbed its way to ninety where I held it steady. The news about the fire hit my police radio when I was three or four miles out. Several units from the State Police radioed that they were en route a moment later. No one mentioned gunfire or fleeing suspects, so I was probably safe for the moment.

The first police cruiser blasted past with its lights blazing and siren wailing about five minutes later. A pair of fire trucks shot past not long afterward, rocking my cruiser in their slipstream. No ambulance followed, but that was just as well. If someone had been stuck in

Sunshine, he would have long since been burned to a cinder.

I slowed down as houses replaced the soybean fields. As I got closer to town, the yards shrank, and the houses bunched together to form small neighborhoods. By the time I reached a sign announcing that I was in Plainfield proper, the street had widened from two lanes to four and sodium lamps illuminated the blacktop. Car dealerships, shopping centers, and restaurants eventually choked off whatever greenery there might have once been, leaving me surrounded by concrete as far as I could see.

My phone beeped as my passenger finally dialed. He whispered, but when he finished he barked the name of a bar I didn't recognize before passing out. I twisted around and grabbed my phone from his curled fingers. With one hand on the wheel and one eye on the road, I searched through my phone's memory for the last number. I redialed and started talking as soon as someone picked up on the other end.

'Who the fuck is this?' I asked.

'Who is this?'

The speaker's voice was slow, and his accent was Slavic. I'd heard that voice on wiretaps a few times before. Generally speaking, Indianapolis didn't have major crime syndicates like Chicago or New York. Our criminals were mostly disorganized, loosely affiliated gangs. Still, there were rumors of organized figures muscling their way in.

Most of those rumors turned out to be false or highly exaggerated, but one rumor refused to disappear. Konstantin Bukoholov. By all appearances, he was a wealthy, respectable businessman with interests in bars and clubs across town. If the rumors were true, though, the illicit portion of his business empire stretched from prostitution to murder for hire. He was a regular hero for our downtrodden criminal class and a favorite role model for many lawyers across town.

'I'm the guy with your buddy on my back seat. The one he tried to shoot.'

Bukoholov was silent for a moment. Plainfield's main strip was dead at that time of night, but its stoplights were still as bright and as numerous as ever. I pulled to a stop as one turned red.

'What do you want?'

I breathed through my nose deeply and ground my teeth again. My dentist would probably never forgive me for that.

'Your address.'

Bukoholov never confirmed his identity, but he gave me the address of a bar in a part of the city I rarely ventured into. Fifty years ago, it would have been a thriving industrial center. Now it was a dump. Most of its buildings were old warehouses with broken windows and boarded-up doors.

As soon as I got off the interstate, I locked my doors and turned on my high beams so I could see the area better. I spotted two homeless men, one apparently sleeping, while the other received the attention of one of the area's many prostitutes. At least he wasn't spending his money on liquor.

I glanced in my rear-view mirror at the guy on my back seat. He skin was ashen, and his breathing was shallow. He hadn't died yet, which was helpful. I thought about dumping him on a corner and calling his boss but decided better of it. The people in that neighborhood could probably strip a corpse faster than they could strip a car. The guy'd be dead of exposure before his boss could even get to him.

I pulled up to the address my caller had given me and parked alongside the building. The curb was painted yellow, but I figured parking tickets were the least of my worries if a cop happened to come by. I undid my seat belt. The guy behind me moaned, so I looked in the mirror at him. His eyes fluttered.

'Don't go anywhere,' I said, opening my door. He moaned again, but I ignored him and stepped out of my car. The street smelled like sulfur and exhaust. I locked my car before slamming the door shut and stepping onto the sidewalk. Bukoholov had directed me to a bar called the Lucky Bastard Saloon. I hadn't heard of it before, which meant IMPD probably wasn't keeping it under regular surveillance. Knowing what I did about its proprietor, though, I doubted IMPD was the only law enforcement agency interested in his activities.

I kept my head down and stepped toward the bar. The front door had a metal frame with glass panels painted black. I noticed a bullet hole in the bottom with broken glass shards radiating away from it in a sunburst pattern. I pulled the door open and held it to air the place out. The smell of liquor, sweat, and cigarettes wafted outside.

The main room was about half-full. There were maybe ten tables, a handful of booths along the walls, and a long wooden bar directly in front of the door. There were no glittering bottles of expensive liquor or flatscreen televisions. The Lucky Bastard wasn't the sort of place its patrons went for a drink after work. It was the sort of bar you visited to get drunk, a state that most of its patrons were well on their way toward. I walked toward the bar. Most of the men I passed had more tattoos than clean skin, and all had rough, calloused hands. They were the men who made our city hum along, and their glares told me I wasn't welcome.

I ground my teeth and ignored them, walking towards the bar. The bartender's shoulders were broad enough that he probably had to turn sideways to make it through the average doorway, and he had faded black tattoos on both of his wrists. One was an elaborate star; the other looked like a knife tearing the flesh. If I had seen them on an American, I would have thought they were prison tattoos. Something told me this guy wasn't domestic, though. He leered at me. His top front teeth were chipped, and his nose had clearly been broken and never fixed.

'This is a private club. You're not welcome here.'

The guy's accent was as thick as Bukoholov's, but his voice was high, almost nasally. I fanned my jacket, exposing my sidearm; the bartender didn't raise an eyebrow.

'Give me a shot and tell your boss that his guest is here.'

The bartender leaned back on his heels and stared at me for a moment. Eventually, he nodded grudgingly and reached beneath the bar. When he stood upright again, he held an empty shot glass and a half-empty bottle of Russian vodka. He put them both on the bar top.

'Wait here.'

He walked to a small, dark hallway behind the bar. I poured a generous shot and choked it down. It was like chugging gasoline. I could feel it burn its way past my throat, down my esophagus, and into my stomach. It was terrible liquor, but at least it took the edge off things. I poured myself another and breathed in deeply. Rather than pound this one, I sipped it and turned around.

About twenty pair of hungry, greedy eyes were on me. I shifted on my feet and pulled my jacket back to expose my sidearm.

'You guys want something?' I asked, raising my eyebrows and leaning my elbows against the bar behind me. A few glares lingered, but most men looked away. I cast my gaze to those still remaining. After a moment, even they turned their attention back to their drinks. The bar's customers may not have liked me, but they knew I was there by Bukoholov's leave.

I scanned the room from left to right. None of the men paid me much attention, so I turned back around and was about to drink the rest of my second shot when the bartender emerged from the nook behind the bar. An older man stood behind him. He wore a black Oxford shirt and black pants. His shoulders were as thin as a coathanger, and the skin on his neck was loose and wrinkled. His eyes were gray and devoid of life.

'Mr Bukoholov,' I said, nodding. The older man inclined his head toward me slightly.

'I am,' he said. He placed his palms against the wooden bar and leaned forward. He made no move to shake my hand. I pulled out a barstool and sat down as the bartender went from table to table behind me, clearing the place out. The patrons went willingly. They knew their place on the pecking order. Bukoholov spoke again when we were alone. 'I appreciate your bringing my nephew here. We operate a facility nearby. We will take him there. After that, we need to talk.'

I pushed my stool back from the bar and stood up.

'I don't think so. I'm here to deliver. What you do now isn't my concern.'

Bukoholov's eyes darted over my shoulder, and I immediately felt a weight shove me forward into the bar. I should have been paying better attention to my surroundings.

'I'm asking you nicely,' he said. 'Please do as I request.'

'And if I refuse?' I asked.

'I'll insist.'

Chapter 17

We left the bar through the front door, and I immediately went to my car while Bukoholov and the Incredible Hulk got their vehicle from around back. My charge was still alive and conscious on my back seat. He even seemed glad to see me when I opened the door. It's nice to feel wanted. Bukoholov pulled up beside me a few minutes later in a lime-green Toyota Prius. I guess a black Lincoln Towncar was too cliché for him. The Hulk was in the driver's seat with Bukoholov in the back. Bukoholov didn't look at me, but the Hulk rolled his window down and stuck a meaty forearm out, motioning me to follow.

I followed the Prius for a few blocks. The neighborhood surrounding the Lucky Bastard was gentrifying, so the longer we drove, the less graffiti I saw. Eventually the abandoned, dilapidated warehouses were replaced by limestone and brick commercial buildings interspersed with old Victorian houses. We parked near the loading dock of a multistory office building, which, according to signs, had been converted to a veterinary hospital. I hoped Bukoholov had an actual doctor rather than some large-animal vet.

The garage door in back of the building rolled up almost immediately. From what I could see, the interior looked bright and clean. Three men wearing scrubs pushed a gurney large enough to hold a horse towards my car. No one said a word to me. They simply grabbed my passenger and left; Bukoholov evidently had pretty good health insurance. With my passenger gone, I checked out the rear seat. There were two bright red stains on the vinyl. A little bleach could take care of both without issue.

I gripped the steering wheel and leaned back with my eyes closed, taking stock of my evening. I think it was fair to say that I had just experienced one of the worst nights of my life. Not only had I committed a major felony by breaking into Sunshine with a loaded weapon, I shot the nephew of a very powerful gangster and then watched evidence that could have saved my ass burn. Some mornings I really ought to stay in bed.

A hard rap on my window broke me from my thoughts. The Hulk was standing outside and motioning for me to get out. I considered flooring it but ultimately decided against it. If Konstantin Bukoholov wanted to speak to me, he'd speak to me whether I was in the parking lot of a large-animal clinic, at home, or at work. I figured I might as well save everyone some trouble and see what he wanted.

I got out of my car, but before I could take more than a step toward Bukoholov's Toyota, the Hulk grabbed me by the shirt and threw me against my vehicle.

'Turn around.'

'Easy,' I said, turning around and putting my palms flat against my car's roof. The Hulk's hands were on my shoulders a moment after that. He disarmed me and took my keys and wallet. I shifted as his hands made a return trip up one leg. 'Watch your hands.'

'Shut up,' he said. Once he took his hands off me, I turned around. He stood about a foot away, glaring at me.

'Are you done?' I asked.

'For now.'

I straightened my jacket and pants. It was nice to have the weight of my weapon off my chest, but I would have gladly traded that minor inconvenience for a bit of protection. Not that a gun would have helped me much, though. The Hulk must have been pushing three hundred pounds. Even if I could get a couple of shots into him, he'd probably keep coming. And then even if I did manage to take him down, we were on Bukoholov's turf. I'd run out of bullets well before he ran out of lackeys.

I walked toward Bukoholov's Prius. The aging gangster rolled the rear passenger window down when I approached.

'We need to talk. Get in.'

'No. I did you a favor, but now I'm going home.'

Bukoholov's already cold eyes narrowed.

'You shot my nephew. Get in the car before my brother-in-law kills you.'

I glanced to my right. The Hulk was staring at me. His face was red, and a vein throbbed across his forehead. Shooting his kid would explain the hostility. Rather than wait around for the big man to get angrier, I climbed into the Prius and sat beside Bukoholov. The car still had the fresh-from-the-factory smell of plastic and adhesives, but I thought I caught a slight whiff of marijuana, too. I would have leaned over to check the ashtray in the front console, but Bukoholov and I were packed tight enough that I would have bumped into him if I had. The Hulk climbed into the driver's seat and tilted his seat back far enough that he might as well have been sitting on my lap.

We left the parking lot without saying a word. Since I didn't know that part of town well, I memorized streets as we passed. It wasn't a particularly helpful activity, but it beat the alternative of doing nothing. The buildings became taller and more upscale the longer we drove. For whatever reason, the Hulk seemed attracted to Monument

Circle. That was okay by me. I knew that area. Cops patrolled it heavily.

'Where are we going, Mr Bukoholov?' I asked.

'Around. You never know who's watching.'

Paranoia was probably a helpful character trait for someone in his line of work.

'If we're here for a tour of the city, I'd just as soon get out now.'

Bukoholov shrugged. 'You can get out anytime you want. You're not my prisoner.'

'Then pull over anywhere.'

'I said you're free to leave anytime you want. I didn't say we'd slow down.'

I heard the Hulk snicker. If I had the room, I would have kicked the back of his seat. As tight as the car was, though, I could barely move.

'What do you want from me?' I asked.

Bukoholov shrugged again. He seemed to be fond of doing that. 'I'm curious what a detective was doing breaking into that building.'

'I'm on the job. As soon as my colleagues hear what you've done, you're going to have so many cops crawling up your ass that a visit to work will be like a visit to the proctologist's office.'

'That's a truly disgusting reference, but I'll take my chances,' he said. 'Even if you are a detective, we both know this is off the clock.'

'You're not going to get away with kidnapping me.'

I grimaced as soon as I said it because it sounded like something Daphne would have said on *Scooby Doo*. Bukoholov chuckled again and patted my knee like my grandfather would have done.

'You might be surprised.'

I shifted in my seat and swallowed.

'What do you want from me?' I asked for the second time that night.

'I want to talk. Share information. You and I both know what goes on in that warehouse. We might be able to help each other.'

If Bukoholov knew what went on at Sunshine, he knew more than I did. I wasn't going to say that, though.

'Fine. Karen Rea killed my niece and her boyfriend. She also killed a friend of mine. That's why I was there.'

Bukoholov squinted at me. 'So you're taking care of your family. I like that. We can work together.'

Before I could ask what that meant, Bukoholov shouted something to the Hulk in Russian, and we made a U-turn so sharp that two of the Prius's tires might have actually come off the road.

'I need you to see something so we can understand each other,' he said.

'Whatever.'

We drove for another fifteen minutes and ended up outside a nightclub occupying an old Masonic temple downtown. The exterior was gray limestone and had columns out front, making it look like an old courthouse. A line stretched halfway around the block, which, in my experience, meant there was more than likely a cop somewhere within shouting distance. I had the option to run, but at the same time, I wasn't exactly replete with allies at the moment. If Bukoholov wanted to help, I wasn't in a position to turn him down.

I crossed in front of the car and met Bukoholov on the sidewalk. The Hulk drove off. The frail Russian held his hand in front of him and gestured for me to precede him inside.

'After you, my friend.'

I didn't know we were on friendly terms, but I stepped forward anyway. Bukoholov apparently knew the bouncer because he let us inside without even having money exchange hands. That got us some angry stares from people in line. They were easy to ignore, though.

The club's interior was big enough that there were activities for just about everybody. There was a burnished concrete bar along one wall with video games and electronic dartboards beside it. I couldn't see it, but I figured there was a pool table amid the people there, too. If patrons were more interested in dancing, there was a raised platform in the middle of the room and cages suspended a few feet above the ground. The music was so loud I couldn't even understand Bukoholov when he leaned into me and yelled almost directly in my ear. He put his hand on my upper back and guided me past the bar to a hallway in back.

At first, I thought he was leading me to the bathroom, which would have been strange, but we pushed past them and turned a corner. It was so dark that I could barely see the guy standing in front of me or the door he was standing in front of. The walls muffled the music enough that we could speak. The bouncer took a drag on his cigarette, momentarily illuminating the space immediately around him in a dull amber light.

'The restrooms are back that way,' he said, gesturing to the hallway behind us with the glowing tip of his cigarette. 'Nothing but offices back here.'

'I realize that,' said Bukoholov. 'Open the door.'

'Oh, sorry, Mr Bukoholov,' the bouncer said, knocking on the door behind him. A peephole slid back like at a 30s-era speakeasy, and the bouncer had a quick conversation with someone on the other side. The door opened a minute later, and Bukoholov and I were waved in. The back room looked like a men's lounge at a long-forgotten resort. There were high-backed leather chairs against the wall and cigar smoke in the air. My skin prickled as goose bumps formed up and down my arms. Six men huddled around a card table in the middle of the floor. Surprisingly, I recognized one. Jack Whittler.

Bukoholov stepped in and greeted the men at the

table before waving me over and introducing me as a friend of his. Whittler never took his eyes off me, and I only took my eyes off him to greet the other players. Alongside Jack, the highest-ranking law enforcement official in the county, I met two reps from the Indiana House of Representatives, a circuit court judge, the deputy mayor, and the CEO of a regional bank head-quartered in the city. I was totally out of my league.

Thankfully Bukoholov didn't linger around the table, and we stepped into his actual office a few minutes later. Unlike the card room, the office was pedestrian. Bukoholov had an antique-looking desk in the middle of the room as well as a couple of chairs and a small couch. There were no windows and little ornamentation. It was absolutely silent.

'How much do you know about cocaine, Mr Rashid?' asked Bukoholov, taking a seat behind his desk. I took that as my cue to sit down.

'Never tried it.'

'You should. It might loosen you up,' he said, leaning over and reaching into one of his desk drawers. He pulled out two sandwich bags and dropped them on the green felt blotter that covered his desk. Both bags held white powder, but one sparkled like snow while the other had dull yellow tones in it.

'This is mine,' he said, holding up the bag with the yellowing powder in it. He then picked up the bag with the sparkling white powder. 'This is Miss Rea's. My stuff is good. It's seventy-percent pure, and it has no harmful additives. Ms Rea's stuff is too good. It's ninety-five, ninety-seven percent pure. Customers take their usual amount and overdose. There's no room to screw up.'

That told me something new about Bukoholov. I hadn't heard he dealt with drugs. Murder and prostitution, but never drugs.

'Why does this concern me?' I asked, folding my arms across my chest.

'Because it concerns me. That bitch is destroying a market that took me fifteen years to develop. And I'm not the only one she's hurting. Chicago, St. Louis, Cincinnati, Louisville. It's the same thing everywhere. I know my competitors. We talk and set prices together. It keeps us all safe. This crazy bitch doesn't talk to anyone. She moves in with her cheap shit, and prices go through the floor. We're losing money and market share.'

Bukoholov leaned forward and picked up one of the bags. He held it to the light before throwing it down.

'And her goddamn dealers are children,' he said. 'It's disgusting. We caught one a few weeks ago. She was fifteen. She called me a slayer, whatever that means. Karen Rea has no principles. You don't work with kids. It's wrong.'

You might sell them coke, though.

I kept the thought to myself. If Bukoholov was telling me the truth, it told me something else important.

'Did you see the news tonight?' I asked.

Bukoholov sighed and made the sign of the cross over his chest.

'If you're referring to the two kids at the high school, I heard,' he said. 'Some of my competitors lack the moral constraints that I possess. They believe they can put Miss Rea out of business by destroying her network. I'm not willing to do that, which is why I need your help. You'll stop her for me.'

'I'm not a killer, and your men destroyed every piece of evidence I had against her when they lit that warehouse up.'

Bukoholov smiled. Rather than setting me at ease, it chilled me. He reached back into his desk and pulled out an IV bag full of a brownish-yellow liquid.

'Do you know what this is?' he asked.

Show and tell?

I shook my head no.

'It's blood plasma,' he said. 'My nephew followed one of Miss Rea's employees to work one day, and he gave us a cooler full of these.'

Bukoholov handed the bag to me; the liquor was thicker than I expected. I raised my eyebrows and looked up. 'So Sunshine is a legitimate business?'

'Yes and no. This man told us they brought in a lot

of plasma and blood from poor people in South America. They brought in more than that, though. Have you ever heard of *agua rica*?'

'It's a diluted sulfuric acid solution containing cocaine sulfate. It's a step in the production of cocaine base.'

Thank you, Mack.

Bukoholov looked at me and smiled knowingly. I handed him the bag.

'That's how they're bringing their stuff through customs. It looks like plasma, they refrigerate it like plasma, they even mix it with a legitimate shipment. They process it at that warehouse. We took care of that. Your job is to take care of the rest. If you do that, you'll have your revenge, and I'll have my business. We both win.'

'I'm not after revenge.'

Bukoholov's eyes were cold. 'Bullshit. You call it justice, but we all know what it is. She hurt you, so you want to hurt her. It's revenge. The sooner you realize that, the sooner you'll understand the world you live in.'

I nodded as if I agreed. People in law school made the same argument for the death penalty. They called it the retributive theory of justice, which is a pretentious way of saying eye for an eye. The old adage is that it makes the world blind. In reality, it makes the world bitter and empty.

'If I do this, if I stop her, I don't want to hear from you again.'

Bukoholov stood up. He was smaller than I was, but he seemed to tower over me.

'I appreciate your intestinal fortitude, but you shot my nephew. You live by my leave. Collect your possessions from Nicolai outside and tell the bartender to call you a cab.'

I didn't think staying and arguing the point was a good idea, so I stood and took a final look around the room before departing. Bukoholov slipped the bags of cocaine back in his desk, seemingly oblivious of the county prosecutor twenty feet away.

I felt dirty, scared, and more than a little conflicted. Like it or not, I was going to do as he asked. It may not have been my intention, but I was going to help a drug dealer solidify his position in my city. While Bukoholov's competitors went after each other directly, he'd sit on the sidelines until it was over. After I took out Sunshine and the people who ran it, he'd pick off any weakened competitors still surviving. It was a plan straight out of *The Art of War*.

I didn't stay long in the back room, but I noticed Jack Whittler and one of the Indiana House representatives were gone. They probably had late-night trysts with prostitutes. The Hulk must have come by because the bouncer guarding the back door had my gun, ID, and wallet. I put everything back in its proper spot and hailed a cab in front of the club. I gave him the address of the animal hospital at which I had parked. Memorizing the street names turned out to be the only good thing I had done that day.

Chapter 18

When I got back to my motel, I fell onto the bed and was out before I even thought about taking off my clothes. Not that the bed was that comfortable. I probably could have fallen asleep on a concrete slab. I woke up at about noon when a clap of thunder slammed through the building, shaking the furniture and causing me to jump. When I regained my senses, I closed my eyes again and breathed deeply. It sounded like the first good thunderstorm the city had seen in the past few weeks. Most people in town were probably pleased for some relief from our month-long drought, but I would have gladly traded the rainfall for another hour of sleep. I tried closing my eyes and drifting away again, but a second rumble reverberated through the room as soon as my eyes were shut. Apparently God wanted me up.

I swore under my breath and swung my legs off the bed. My head throbbed, and I winced as pain lanced down my spine. I ran a hand along my side. My ribs felt tender from landing on the flashlight the night before, but nothing felt broken. I'd live for a while longer. I stumbled to the sink and made a cup of complimentary black coffee in the room's single-serving pot. I doubted it would live up to my wife's black-as-pitch coffee, but hopefully it'd wake me up.

While the coffee brewed, I cleaned myself up and had morning prayer. I felt a little calmer after that. Once my prayers were done, I got off my knees and sat on my bed. Aside from summer work when I was in college, I had never been anything but a cop. I went to the police academy when I was twenty-two and never looked back. My investigation into Robbie and Rachel was my first foray outside the public sector. Already, I had burned a building to the ground, shot a guy, become indebted to a drug-dealing Russian gangster, and uncovered a major drug-trafficking ring with ties to a vampire cult. No one could say I didn't get shit done, at least.

I turned the television to a noon broadcast of the news on one of the local stations. While the reporters talked about the mayor's latest proposal to fuck up my morning commute by 'fixing' some downtown roads, I got my coffee. It was thin but nearly boiling, so I was reasonably sure I wouldn't get a horrid disease by drinking it. That was all I could hope for from a motel coffee maker.

About ten minutes into the newscast, the reporter finally stopped talking politics and mentioned the fire at the Hadley Business Park. The actual story had scant details, but the accompanying video told me everything I needed to know. Sunshine's warehouse was gone. The reporter said the business park had improperly laid water mains, so firefighters had to truck in water instead of using the on-premise hydrants. No one mentioned shell casings or gunfire, but that'd come eventually when the arson investigators sifted through the ashes. With luck, though, I still had a few days.

I was about to turn off the TV when the studio anchor came back and updated us on that morning's breaking story. The Chief of Police had released the names of the bodies dumped near Rachel and Robbie's school the day before. Alicia Weinstein and her boyfriend Mark Patterson. The Chief confirmed that both had been burned repeatedly. No matter what those two were into, neither deserved to be tortured to death. Maybe helping Bukoholov eliminate his competitors wasn't such an ignominious activity after all.

I turned the TV off and paced my small room. Olivia wasn't going to like it, but she needed to hear what I had found out at Sunshine. She put her life in her colleagues' hands every time she went to work. If one of those colleagues was willing to sell my information to drug dealers, they'd probably do the same to her without hesitation. My hope was that she'd actually let me finish speaking before sending a patrol car to arrest me.

I sipped my coffee and thumbed Olivia's desk number into my cell phone. She answered on the second ring.

'Olivia, this is Ash. We need to talk.'

'I'm sure we do, but not right now.'

'I only need a minute. You need to hear this. Somebody in your department—'

'Stop,' she said, interrupting me. 'This is not the right time. If you want to talk about work, meet me at The Park in half an hour.'

'You're serious? The Park?'

'Of course I'm serious,' said Olivia. 'I love The Park. If you have something to say to me, meet me there.'

'Can you make it an hour?'

Olivia agreed and hung up immediately after our conversation. I ran my tongue along the front of my teeth. Indianapolis has a lot of parks, but only one has significance for Olivia and me. Our park was a patch of grass and dirt on the city's near-North side. We caught a homicide there a few years back that bothered us both. The victims were four teenage boys. Each of them had been castrated and shot multiple times. None of them had ID, and none were ever reported missing. We buried them as John Does. As far as I knew, their case was still open.

Olivia wouldn't have suggested meeting me in The Park unless she had a damn good reason. I took a deep pull on my coffee and mulled the situation over. I was already hip-deep in a pile of rancorous shit, and for some reason, my old partner had asked me to step into the sewer.

I took a shower and brushed my teeth before heading out, sure that Olivia would appreciate both. Even though I hadn't been to The Park in a few years, it wasn't hard to find. I drove to the worst neighborhood in town and followed the sirens. After about twenty minutes of driving, I noticed signs outside the bars requesting patrons leave their gang colors outside. That's when I knew I was getting close. A couple of minutes after that, I hung a left at Three Little Pigs Ammo and Supply and saw Olivia's car parked about half a block up.

I parked behind her and stepped out. The neighborhood stunk like sewage, probably because there was an open manhole on the sidewalk not ten feet from my car. In most parts of town, that would indicate someone was working underground. Near The Park, though, that meant someone had probably stolen the manhole cover and sold it for scrap. It was downright entrepreneurial.

I looked around quickly as soon as I got out of my car. The police department didn't go into that area very often, and when they did, they went in force. The hackles on the back of my neck stood up. The saddest part of that neighborhood was that most of its denizens were good people. They had jobs, they went to school, they raised their kids as well as they could. They happened to be poor and live in a neighborhood infested by drugs and gangs. It was unfortunate, but there wasn't much anyone could do about it.

As I stepped forward, I saw movement in my peripheral vision and shot my hand to the firearm inside my jacket. A heavyset white guy stepped out from behind a bush and onto the sidewalk, pulling his pants up. He saw my weapon and froze, his hands in the air. A woman followed. Her fishnets were torn, her hair was in disarray, and her gaze was glassy and absent.

'Get scarce,' I said, inclining my head towards the street. The guy scampered away, but the prostitute he was with didn't move. She looked high, so I doubted she comprehended English at that moment. There was little I could do for her, so I ignored her and walked towards some picnic tables beside a rusted swing set a dozen yards away. It was eerie being in that place again. After my last visit, I didn't think it could get much worse, but evidently, I had been wrong. The hookers didn't usually show up until dinnertime.

Olivia was sitting at one of the tables. She wore an orange sleeveless shirt and dark jeans. Her purse was slung around one shoulder and was open. Even if I hadn't known her, I would have known she was a cop. Her head never stopped moving as she observed her surroundings, and nor did her hand stray too far from her purse, where I presumed she kept her service weapon. I called her name so I wouldn't startle her and walked over.

'You've got a tap on your cell phone,' she said, sniffing. 'And by the way, you smell like burned plastic.'

I looked down at my jacket. It was the same one I had worn the night before to Sunshine.

'It's a long story. I'll tell you it some other time. The cell tap. Is it Bowers?'

Olivia nodded.

'What's he looking for?'

'I haven't got a clue,' she said, shaking her head. 'He's covering the body dump at the High School, so he's got every politician in the state pressuring him to find a suspect. My guess is you were convenient.'

'It's nice to feel loved,' I said, straightening. 'I'll worry about that when I can. In the meantime, somebody in your department crossed. I thought you ought to know.'

Olivia's back straightened, and I heard her inhale deeply. 'What do you mean?'

'I found my police jacket in a warehouse near Plainfield. It had psych evaluations from the station's shrink, copies of formal complaints lodged against me, even a picture of the two of us on a stakeout. It was my complete file.'

She stared at me for a moment as if she were thinking. Eventually, she nodded slowly. Her gaze looked far away. 'Do you have it with you?'

'No. It's gone. Burned last night.'

She sighed.

'Without the physical file, there's not much we can do. I can go to records and see who's been looking you up, but chances are they didn't use official channels. If you had the actual file, we could at least dust it for prints.'

'I know there's not much we can do. I just thought you should know,' I said, standing up. I looked around to see if there was anyone watching us. 'Watch your back.'

Olivia put her hand on my arm. 'Don't go public with this yet,' she said. 'If you do, it'll be like sticking your dick in a hornet's nest. This is bigger than the two of us, so I'll find something. If you have to contact me again, buy a disposable cell phone from Wal-Mart. And where are you staying now? I know you're not at your house.'

'A cheap motel in Plainfield.'

She nodded.

'Did you pay with a credit card?'

'Cash.'

'Is the room in your name?'

'Yeah – the clerk needed a copy of my driver's license, so I didn't have a choice.'

'Okay. You should still be fine,' she said. 'Even if the place is in your name, it will be hard to trace you there, so stay. Is your family with you?'

'They're at my sister-in-law's house.'

Olivia paused and closed her eyes.

'They ought to be fine there,' she said. 'If you're right, we can't trust anyone on this. Keep me in the loop, and I'll do what I can for you on my end.'

'I'll do that.'

'This is too important to play cowboy on,' she said. 'If you screw this up, someone will get hurt. Are you with me?'

'Yes.'

'Good,' she said, standing up. 'And get a disposable phone.'

Olivia took one final look around the area and trotted back to her car. It was one of the quickest meetings I had ever had with her, but I felt good, almost energized. For the first time in a long time, I felt as if I had an ally I could trust again.

Chapter 19

Despite Olivia's assurances to the contrary, I figured I had a fifty-fifty shot of surviving my ordeal even with her help. I figured that I might as well forget about my cholesterol and live it up while I still could. Rather than drive back to my motel, I stopped by a greasy spoon my wife would never let me go to and gorged on fried eggs, hash browns and more turkey bacon than the average man eats in a year. After breakfast, I decided to take a chance and run to my house. I hadn't packed many clothes when I left, and after the fire at Sunshine, I was running low on those that didn't reek of burning building supplies. Plus, it'd be nice to make sure the neighborhood kids hadn't bashed down the front door.

To be safe, I drove up and down the side streets around my house for about twenty minutes, looking for surveillance teams. I didn't find anything out of the ordinary, though.

I parked in the driveway. The rain earlier that day had slackened off, and the late-summer heat was taking its place, making it feel as if I were in the Amazon. I walked around the house, looking for broken windows or damage, but it was as I had left it. With a boarded front door and lack of lights, it looked abandoned, a state that wasn't too far from the truth with my wife and daughter gone.

I went inside, grabbed a soda from the fridge, and headed to the bedroom. The place was still a mess, but it'd have to wait. I grabbed a duffel bag from the closet and stuffed it with shirts and pants. Once that was full, I hung my plastic-smelling jacket on a bedpost and grabbed an old brown one from my closet. I had lost weight since the last time I wore my brown jacket, so its arms and shoulders were a little roomier than I remembered. It still fit, but barely.

I took my duffel bag to my office and leaned against the door frame. If I were going to get Mike Bowers off my back, I needed to give him someone else to look at. It was daytime, so I doubted Karen and Azrael would come after me yet. I still had time. I sat at my desk chair and flipped through some of the notes and papers I had printed off recently. I stopped on Karen Rea's CV. Her former colleague Dr Wexler told me she had spent time with the South African Medical Services and felt guilty for whatever she had done. More than that, whatever she did sent her career down the toilet. It wasn't much, but it was a start.

I turned on my computer and spun around in my chair to think while it loaded. College professors are relatively tolerant of colleagues with eccentric views. The only professor I could think of who was universally panned by his colleagues was a California law professor who argued that torture was legally justified. I doubted Karen tortured anyone, but it got me thinking.

As soon as my computer finished loading, I googled *South African Medical Services, biological weapons.* That netted me a hundred thousand results, most of which discussed what would happen if South Africa were attacked. I modified the search and added the dates of Karen's trip. The number of results plummeted, and most had a common theme, something called Project Coast. I clicked a link to a scholarly article from the Brookings Institute and read the abstract.

'You evil bitch.'

From what I read, Project Coast wouldn't land Karen in jail, but it wouldn't earn her too many friends, either. The project was long-since closed, but in the eighties and early nineties, it had been apartheid South Africa's response to a growing Soviet presence in Africa. The country's leaders recognized they couldn't compete with the Soviet Union's nuclear technology or its conventional weapons, so they created a clandestine chemical and biological weapons program for self-defense. According to the article, they had stashes of Ebola, Rift Valley, and Marburg viruses. If the descriptions I saw were correct, they made the bubonic plague sound like fun.

The project was focused on more than the Soviet Union, though. It also had a domestic component. The article was sketchy on details, but it described a project to develop a virus that would selectively infect and sterilize the country's native African population in order to ensure future white supremacy. It was ugly, and I would have dismissed it as a racist fantasy except that the article referenced a memo initialed by the lead scientist, K.R. I stopped reading for a moment, considering. That would explain why Karen Rea wasn't teaching undergraduates anymore.

I leaned back from the desk. Maybe I was being paranoid, but I flipped through my paperwork until I came across a page I had printed a few days earlier. Karen claimed that Robbie and Rachel had been murdered by slayers, and Azrael had claimed he had a plan to strike back. When I first read it, I thought the article was weird but not terribly threatening. Now I wasn't so sure. I leaned back from my computer. I needed to find out what she was actually capable of. Luckily, I knew someone who might be able to help me. Before I did that, though, I needed to take care of something for him.

I called up my email program, and, as per Jack Whittler's request, I sent a generic letter of resignation citing personal issues to his secretary. I also added two small postscripts.

PS. Dr Mack Monroe kindly requests the office pay his most recent consulting fee. In addition, he requests that any and all outstanding parking tickets given to the Mercedes registered in his name be voided.

PPS. I enjoyed seeing you at the poker game.

Jack was facing an uphill election for a second term as Prosecutor in a few months, including a challenger in the November primary. Allegations that he was involved with one of the area's biggest criminals would sink his campaign faster than if a photographer snapped a picture of him snorting cocaine off a dead hooker. If Whittler cared about his political future, Mack's bill would be paid and his girlfriend's car would be ticket-free in no time. Hopefully that'd be enough.

I called Mack's cell phone, but it immediately went to voicemail. I told him that his parking tickets would be taken care of soon and asked him to call me back as soon as he could.

While I waited for my callback, I took my gun to the workbench in the garage. The Prosecutor's Office convicted a lot of murderers because they were too cheap to get rid of their guns after shooting someone, making ballistics matches easy. I suppose I couldn't blame them on some level. A reliable firearm was pricey. My Glock ran more than five hundred bucks; I wouldn't want to part with it, either. Unlike most of the people we caught, though, I knew how a modern forensics lab worked, and even though I wasn't a gunsmith, I knew how to replace my weapon's barrel and firing pin. I could at least make a match difficult in case the arson squad found my shell casings at Sunshine.

After twenty minutes in the garage, I tossed the old firing pin and barrel from my Glock into a trash bag and threw it onto the back seat of my cruiser for disposal later. As I did that, I thought I heard a car down the street, but it never crossed in front of my house. Must have gone to a neighbor's place. Mack called as I opened my kitchen door. Olivia had warned me that Bowers had my cell phone tapped, but I didn't care. I trusted Mack, but I didn't plan to tell him anything incriminating.

I answered before it went to voicemail.

'Just got off the phone with parking enforcement,' he said. 'Aleksandra's SL is clean. I didn't think you'd pull through until now. I appreciate it.'

I pulled a chair from under the breakfast table and sat down.

'I have the feeling you'll be getting a check from the Prosecutor's Office soon, too.'

'Fucking A, Rashid. I ought to do more favors for you.'

'Glad to hear that because I've got something to ask

you. Last time I talked to you, you said you had hired someone with a PhD in microbiology. You think I can talk to her?'

'I'll introduce you to whoever you want. Just hold on a sec.'

Mack didn't put me on hold; instead, it sounded as if he just carried the phone with him to his newest hire's lab. It only took him about five minutes to get there, but in that time, I heard him ask one woman if she wore space pants for her out-of-this-world ass, and I heard another woman squeal as he presumably squeezed some part of her anatomy. I made a long-term mental note to never allow Megan around Mack when she came of age. Eventually, I heard the phone clatter as he put it down.

'Ash, you're on speaker phone. Dr Michelle Weiss is here, so go ahead and talk.'

I hadn't intended to be on speaker, but I guessed it didn't matter much.

'Hi, Dr Weiss. My name is Ash Rashid, and I'm a detective with IMPD. I was hoping I could ask you a few questions.'

She hesitated at first, and I thought I heard her exhale deeply before speaking.

'I'm sorry, but I refuse to talk to this man,' she said, presumably to Mack. 'And I'm disgusted that you're talking to him.'

I coughed. 'I think I missed something.'

'Wow, this is awkward,' said Mack, chuckling. 'I thought you were going to stiff me a couple of days back, so I told people you pick up girls at the local high school. It's silly, but I was pissed. I take it all back now.'

'That's swell of you, Mack,' I said.

Dr Weiss cleared her throat.

'Sorry about what I said,' she said. 'Since you're not a child molester, I'd be happy to answer your questions.'

'Thank you,' I said, flipping my notebook to a blank page and shaking my head. I took a breath. 'My questions will sound a little strange, but they've come up in a recent investigation. Let me ask you right away. Are you familiar with something called Project Coast?'

'Not off the top of my head,' said Dr Weiss, her voice distinctively less sharp than it had been earlier. 'You know anything about it, Dr Monroe?'

I heard Mack grunt. I interpreted it as a thoughtful no.

'How about a biological weapon that targets specific racial groups?' I asked.

'Genetically sensitive therapies are a hot field right now, but I've never heard of a racially sensitive weapon.'

I made a note of it.

'Is it possible to develop one?'

'Maybe, but I doubt it,' she said. 'This is outside my

area of expertise, but race is more of a social convention than genetic category. What we refer to as race is, in reality, a loose conglomeration of genes and geography. And frankly, human beings are so interbred I imagine it'd be virtually impossible to target one race rather than another.'

I leaned back in my chair and scratched my chin.

'What would happen if someone developed a weapon they thought was targeted but wasn't?'

'It could fizzle, or it could infect everyone on the planet. There are too many variables to say.'

'If you wanted to build one, what do you think it would take?'

Dr Weiss was silent for a moment, and I leaned back in my chair, waiting for her to respond.

'You thinking about a new hobby?' asked Mack.

'Not exactly. I need to know if it's possible.'

'Maybe for a big corporation,' said Michelle. 'You'd need at least a level-three biocontainment facility, commercial-grade peptide synthesizers, and licenses from the government. And even if you had those, there are only a few dozen people in the world with the knowledge to even begin.'

I didn't say anything, but my suspect had not only the knowledge, but experience. Worse, she genuinely seemed to believe she and her misfit friends were persecuted by a religious order hell-bent on eradicating them.

If she and Azrael thought they could eradicate that group by targeting their genetic makeup, I had little reason to doubt they would. A biotechnology company which invested heavily in blood products was pretty good cover, too.

'Assuming you could get the proper licenses, how much money would it take to set up a lab like that?'

'Twenty or thirty million dollars, maybe. I really don't know,' said Dr Weiss. 'But even if you had money, you'd need specimen viruses to work with. You can't get those at any cost.'

Dr Weiss would probably be surprised at what money could buy. I pushed back from my table and looked up at the ceiling, struggling to put what I had heard into my growing puzzle. Indianapolis wasn't a huge city, but it had a couple of million residents. I didn't know how much the local cocaine market was worth, but I had to assume even a small piece of it was enough. If Karen was funneling everything she had into her lab, it would also explain why her house was empty. I ran a hand across my face and considered whether my speculation was worth calling Olivia about when something hard and heavy pounded on my front door. My muscles tensed.

'You okay there, buddy?' asked Mack. 'Sounded like you dropped a television.'

There was another crash and the now familiar sound

of wood splintering. My heart thumped and my chair fell over as I vaulted up.

'Someone's breaking into my house,' I shouted, ripping my weapon from its holster. 'Call the police for me now.'

Without waiting for Mack to reply, I dropped my phone and ran into the hallway. The wood bracing on my front door buckled, and after that, everything moved so fast that I didn't have time to think. Men swarmed into my front hallway. The first two carried some sort of black battering ram, while those behind them carried the same sort of automatic weapons I had seen the night before at Sunshine. I never got a shot off; hell, I never even raised my weapon. Before I could react to my new guests, something sharp and hot tore through my shirt and into my chest. After that, every muscle in my body exploded at once and I felt more pain than I had experienced in years.

Chapter 20

They shot me with a taser, which has an upside and a downside. On the one hand, getting shot with one indicates that your shooter doesn't want you dead. That's always nice. On the other hand, though, having every muscle in your body fire at full strength for thirty seconds is about as pleasant as spending a night in a Mexican prison.

When I came back to my senses, there were four men staring down at me. Unless roving bands of vampire assassins started wearing Kevlar vests and carrying automatic weapons, they were members of my department's Special Weapons and Tactics team. We used them when serving high-risk, felony warrants on drug dealers and other violent offenders.

'Normally you guys knock first,' I said, trying to sit up.

'Stay down.'

I got a boot to my chest by a young guy I didn't

recognize. Thankfully, he declined to taser me again. I slid my hands up to my head. Someone must have taken my gun from me because I didn't know where it was.

'Take it easy. I'm on your side. I'm a detective.'

At least I used to be a detective. I didn't think that moment was the correct one to tell the world about my abrupt career change.

'Stay down, Ash. We're checking the house.'

I recognized the voice this time. Under normal circumstances the speaker was a plainclothes detective in our gang intel unit named Jim Price. He was a good man, and he knew the local gang scene better than anyone else on the street. The Prosecutor's Office convicted at least four gang bangers in the past few months because of his tips. He leaned over me. There was sweat on his forehead and nose.

'Trust me on this,' he said. 'Do what I say, and I'll make sure you make it through safe.'

I nodded before laying my head back down on the ground. Price and his men went from room to room, presumably checking the closets and anywhere else large enough for someone to hide. After a few minutes, one of the SWAT guys rolled me onto my stomach and secured my hands behind me with a zip tie. They let me sit up after that and lean against the wall. Detective Price slid beside me a moment later and pulled a pack of cigarettes from his utility belt. I thought about telling him my wife and I had a nonsmoking house, but I didn't see the harm at the moment. It's not as if we had working doors to hold the smoke in. He lit up, took a puff, and offered it to me. I declined.

'Glad you finally made it by the house,' I said. 'I would have had you earlier, but school and the job keep me pretty busy. You should have brought your wife. We could smoke a chicken or something out back.'

Price laughed softly and stared at the cigarette dangling from his fingertips. He didn't look at me. I paused for a moment, processing.

'How bad is it out there?' I asked.

'Bad.'

'Media?'

He took a drag on his cigarette.

'That Asian chick from Channel Seven,' he said. 'She got here before we did.'

'I don't suppose you'll let me slip out the back and pretend you didn't see me.'

Price chuckled and shook his head. 'When I give the all-clear, Bowers and his boys are going to come in and arrest you. I thought I'd give you a minute to breathe.'

'I appreciate that.'

'Don't mention it. Ever. And a bit of advice. You've still got people in the department you can trust, but not many. Watch what you say around Bowers. Rumor is we're not playing on the same team.'

I was glad to hear I wasn't the only person with that thought. Price took a final puff of his cigarette before leaning forward and standing up.

'Remember what I said. Watch your back.'

As soon as Price left, I pushed myself back against the wall and twisted my hands, trying to loosen the zip ties securing my wrists. The sharp plastic bit into my skin as it stretched. It was going to leave a mark, but with the ties loosened, I could move a bit. I rolled my shoulders, while Price went to my living room and radioed an all-clear to the officers outside.

Mike Bowers was the first man through the remnants of my front door. The last time I had seen him, he had been practically giddy. He had aged since then. His face was pale, he needed to shave, and, judging by the rumpled state of his suit coat, he could have used a fresh change of clothes. He leaned over me, and I caught a whiff of citrus-scented aftershave. He probably threw it on in lieu of a shower; it wasn't a very good substitute.

He gestured for me to stand up.

'This is a prime opportunity to kick me while I'm down,' I said. 'Might as well get your licks in while you can.'

'Get up, Rashid. I haven't got all day.'

I floundered around for a moment, but made little actual movement to stand until a pair of uniformed deputies slipped their arms through the crooks of my elbows and pulled. Bowers sighed.

'You have a back door to this place?'

I raised my eyebrows.

'You don't want to pose for the cameras?'

'No, I don't want to pose for the goddamn cameras.'

I took a deep breath and leaned my head back as if I were thinking deeply.

'Then no. We don't have a back door.'

Bowers muttered something inaudible before walking down the hall toward the kitchen, presumably to see if I had lied to him. Hannah and I did, in fact, have both a back door and side door, but my house was small enough that even if Bowers led me out one of them, we'd just end up in front of the media anyway. He must have realized that there was no point in trying to escape that because he grabbed me by the elbow as soon as he came back from the kitchen and led me down the hallway. The plywood erected to cover my front door was broken in two, but there was little additional damage to the frame. At least I had that going for me. I squinted as I stepped onto the porch. It was overcast outside, but it was still hot and muggy. There were two news vans parked in front of the house. This was going to be a hard one to explain to Hannah.

Bowers led me straight to his unmarked police cruiser without a word. Most cops in his situation would have wanted to savor the limelight as long as they possibly could, but Bowers had spent a significant portion of his career undercover and probably didn't want his face broadcast on statewide television. As someone whose family has been the target of criminals, I could respect that. I made little move to call additional attention to us and climbed into the back of his cruiser.

'You're not going to let me put my seatbelt on?' I asked once Bowers sat in the seat in front of me. 'That's a nonmoving violation. Somebody could give you a ticket, not to mention the safety issues.'

'Pray we don't get into an accident.'

I leaned back into the seat and tried to get comfortable, a difficult task with my hands secured behind my back. Unlike a patrolman's vehicle, Mike's cruiser didn't have a computer or mesh screen separating the front and rear passenger compartments. It was more like a taxi than anything else, and Bowers drove it as such. We ran two red lights and damn near hit a group of pedestrians before making it to the downtown police station.

He parked in a garage beneath the building, patted me down, took everything out of my pockets, and led me to an interrogation room. There was a polished metal table bolted to the floor in the middle of the room with a matching metal chair bolted in front of it. Unknown to most suspects, the legs of the chair had purposefully been cut short so that a suspect would have to look up to his interrogators, and the table was too far out of reach for the average person to lean against and become comfortable.

Bowers cut the zip ties from my wrists and gestured toward the center of the room.

'Have a seat. I'll be right back.'

I took a step in and leaned against the table, rubbing my wrists where the plastic had worn my skin raw. 'I think I'll stand, but thank you.'

Mike shook his head. 'Have it your way.'

He walked through the room's stainless-steel door and shut it behind him. I knew it wouldn't budge, so I didn't bother trying to open it.

Plain and simple, a good interrogation is about power. Mike was going to do everything he could to take me out of my comfort zone and make me feel powerless. More than likely, he was going to crank the air conditioner as low as it would go and watch me squirm for a good half hour. After that, he'd come in and apologize for the delay and the temperature and offer me a cup of coffee to warm up with while he finished paperwork. It would seem like a nice offer except that I'd eventually have to use the bathroom, thereby giving him something else to hold over me. I pulled myself onto the table and laid back with my legs hanging over the edge.

The smartest thing a suspect can do in an interrogation room is to sit down, shut up, and ask for an attorney.

Since I didn't seem to have that option, I closed my eyes as if I were going to sleep.

Mike walked in about twenty minutes later with a cup of coffee in one hand and a manila folder in the other. He set the coffee cup on the table beside me. I sat up and yawned.

'Peace offering,' he said, motioning towards the cup with his chin. 'For earlier. I was doing my job.'

'You're going to pay to have my door reframed; I'm telling you now.'

'Don't worry about your door,' he said, starting to take a step backwards. 'Drink the coffee, and I'll get the forms for you to fill out for the city to reimburse you.'

'Cut the shit. If you leave, you won't be back for another half hour. No games. I want to get this over with. Tell me what you've got on me, and I'll tell you why it's bullshit.'

Bowers smiled. 'Cocky, aren't you?'

'Innocent.'

He leaned against the wall beside the door and crossed his arms.

'You know there's a camera recording this, so don't try anything,' he said, flicking his gaze to a corner of the room behind me. 'Tell me what you know about Caitlin Long.'

I climbed off the table.

'The redhead?'

'Yeah,' said Bowers. I shifted and shrugged.

'She was my niece's best friend. I might have met her when she was a kid, but I don't remember. She was supposed to give me a call, but she never did.'

Bowers unfolded his arms and tossed the manila folder on the table.

'That's the extent of your relationship? You never talked to her on the phone? You never met her after that?'

I shifted again uncomfortably and took a seat in the room's only chair. That was probably what Bowers wanted, but I didn't care.

'No. Why do you ask?'

Bowers took a step forward and leaned against the table. From my angle, I had to crane my neck to catch his gaze.

'Never flirted with her? Asked her on a date?'

I started to say no, but stopped myself quickly. Bowers wouldn't have asked the question unless he had heard something. My legal sense was screaming at me to shut up, but an even louder voice was telling me to explain myself. Bowers counted on that second voice; every detective does. I leaned forward and put my hands flat on the table.

'I wanted an *appointment* with her to talk about Rachel and Robbie. That was it. I never got in touch with her, though.'

Bowers nodded as if he understood. 'Do you try to set up a lot of appointments with young girls?'

My stomach fluttered, but I forced myself to chuckle and lean back in my chair.

'If you broke down my door for this, I think I'll be walking out of here pretty soon. This is fucking ridiculous.'

'Is it?' asked Bowers, sliding the manila folder he had tossed on the table toward me. 'Check it out and then tell me how ridiculous it is.'

A pit grew in the bottom of my stomach. Folders weren't good. I hesitated and looked at Bowers for some sort of tell, but he didn't blink. I swallowed, opened the folder, and almost immediately felt my stomach clench. I've seen a lot of crime scene photos, but you never get used to seeing dead young people. It was an outdoor shot with pine needles and thick tree roots on the ground. Caitlin Long's lips were blue, and her red hair was splayed out around her head. There was an ugly ligature mark on her neck.

'She put up a good fight,' he said. 'She had bruises on her palms and skin under her fingernails. I noticed you were limping, Rashid. Can you explain that?'

'I jumped over my fence and twisted my ankle a few days ago. Where were these taken?' I asked, leafing through the photos. The second photo was a wider angle shot. The girl was wrapped in what looked like a bed sheet or maybe a large roll of fabric. I looked up.

301

'Eagle Creek Park,' he said. 'Where were you last night at around nine?'

I ignored the question and continued flipping through the contents of the folder. There were multiple pictures of objects found around the body, including a wrapper from a condom.

'Was she assaulted?' I asked.

'She's fucking dead. What do you think?'

'Sexually?'

'That is yet to be determined, but judging by the fact that she was nude and wrapped in a sheet, I'm guessing yes. So let me ask again. Where were you last night and what was your relationship with Ms Long?'

My stomach lurched. I had a pretty solid alibi, but I doubted telling Mike that I was in a gunfight with a Russian gangster would improve my situation greatly.

'We had no relationship. And I don't remember where I was at nine last night. I was drinking.'

Mike reached across the table for the folder. 'Was anyone with you?' he asked, flipping through its contents.

'Not that I remember.'

'Must have been quite a night,' he said, pulling a sheet of paper from the back of the folder and sliding it towards me. 'This is a dump of Ms Long's last hundred calls. She called your house five times yesterday afternoon. Maybe you were too drunk to remember.'

Fuck.

I leaned forward and looked at the paper Bowers had pushed towards me. He was telling the truth. Someone had even conveniently highlighted the calls. Four were less than ten seconds, but one lasted a minute and a half. Since I hadn't spent much time at home for a while, I hadn't checked the answering machine in the past day or two.

'I gave my business card to my sister so she could give it to Caitlin. That's how she had my number.'

'So you talked to her?'

I shook my head.

'She must have left a message.'

'So why'd you give her your home phone number? Why not your office phone?'

'I gave her my business card. It has my home number on it for emergencies.'

Bowers nodded, but paused before speaking. He leaned forward.

'Did you give her the card before or after your wife left you?'

I closed the folder so I wouldn't have to see the body anymore.

'Hannah didn't leave me. She took Megan to her sister's house for a few days. They're visiting, like a vacation.'

'Vacation,' said Bowers, smiling. 'That's what my wife said, too. She left you, but let's focus on what's important. You're dealing coke with your partner, Detective Rhodes. You gave some to your niece, and she gave it to her boyfriend. She OD'd on your product. Shit happens, right? Robbie is upset and offs himself. Your wife finds out and leaves you. Meanwhile, Caitlin's not too pleased with you after your shit killed her best friend, so she threatens to out you. You get drunk and decide to shut her up, so you took her to Eagle Creek Park last night, assaulted her, and strangled her. That sound about right?'

I didn't say anything for a moment as the story sunk in.

'That sounds insane.'

'Really? Rachel Haddad, dead. Robert Cutting, dead. Alicia Weinstein, tortured and dead. Mark Patterson, Alicia's boyfriend, tortured and dead. Caitlin Long, raped and dead. James Russo, dead. Rolando Diaz, dead. You sense the pattern here? They meet with you, and then they die.'

I swallowed and looked up.

'I want to talk to my lawyer.'

Chapter 21

Bowers stood up, grabbed the folder full of pictures, and left as soon as I said it. My heart was pounding so hard I could hear the blood rush in my ears. I leaned forward and rested my face in my hands.

Shit.

If I had been in Bowers' position, I'd probably be doing the same thing he was. I wouldn't have arrested a suspect so early without substantial physical evidence, but that might not have been his choice. With so many dead young people, the entire judicial system would have been pushing for an early, quick resolution.

I closed my eyes. Caitlin's death didn't fit into my puzzle. She went to a different school, hung out with a different crowd. She was a bystander as far as I knew, and her death didn't help anyone. On the other hand, it sure did hurt me. I wanted to vomit.

'Detective Rashid,' said a deep, booming voice.

I looked up and noticed the figure in the doorway. He was black and tall with graying hair and deep brown eyes. Danial Reddington. He was the Chief of Detectives, one of the most powerful men in the police force. 'You're free to go at this time. Make sure you're available for the next couple of days because we'll probably want to talk to you again. There's a car waiting for you out front. The driver already has your possessions.'

I stayed in the chair for a moment. Something wasn't right. They shouldn't have released me like that, and they sure as hell shouldn't have handed my belongings over to whoever was picking me up. Someone was pulling strings and throwing an awful lot of weight around, which gave me the feeling that I was about to incur a debt I couldn't afford to pay. I wished I had a choice in the matter.

I nodded to Reddington and stood up. He escorted me out of the station without saying a word. It was awkward. The interrogation rooms were deep inside the station. I knew half the people who worked in that building, some of them very well. Most pretended they hadn't seen me, which I was grateful for.

There was indeed a car waiting for me outside. It was a big gray Mercedes. Konstantin Bukoholov's number two, the Hulk, leaned against it, smoking a cigarette. He lifted his chin at me as soon as Reddington and I stepped through the glass front doors.

'You're out of here, Detective,' said Reddington. 'Our office will be in touch.'

'Thank you,' I said. Reddington didn't wait around to see me off or even respond to my thanks. He disappeared into the station. That was probably a smart move on his behalf; it wouldn't have been very political for him to be seen escorting a suspected murderer to a suspected crime boss. I took a step forward, but stopped before I got within an arm's length of the Hulk. He nodded at me, threw his cigarette down, and ground it under his foot.

'Kostya's waiting for you. Get in, please.'

I hadn't anticipated a polite exchange, so it took me a moment to come up with an equally polite response.

'Is your son doing okay?' I asked.

'Get in the fucking car.'

That was more like it. I walked to the rear passenger door and climbed inside. When I saw it a few days earlier, I had thought Jack Whittler had a pretty nice Mercedes. Bukoholov's car was in a different class, though. There was enough leg room that my wife could have given birth in there, and there was a console between the two rear seats with a built-in cigar humidor and controls for the radio and air conditioner.

'Did you guys buy this from Saddam Hussein or something?' I asked, rolling the rear window down. The glass was at least half an inch thick. Armored. The Hulk ignored my question and walked around the car to the driver's seat. As soon as he climbed in, my window rolled up and would no longer respond when I hit the switch.

Asshole.

'Do you have the stuff the police took from me?'

The Hulk threw a manila envelope at me without looking over his shoulder. The envelope was light.

'They give you my firearm back?'

The Hulk grunted, which I assumed was a no. That was disappointing but not unexpected. I opened the envelope and dumped it on the seat beside me. I slipped on my watch and thumbed through my wallet to see if anything was missing.

'Did they give you the cash from my wallet?'

I saw the Hulk smile in the rear-view mirror, but he made no other indication that he had heard me. I swore under my breath. The ride was no more than five minutes. The Hulk pulled into an alley near the club Bukoholov had taken me to the night before. The buildings were black with grime and soot, and the road was pockmarked with potholes and broken concrete. There was garbage everywhere. We drove for about half a block before parking beside a nondescript black door.

'Kostya's waiting for you inside.'

I stepped into the alley, straightening my shirt. A sickly sweet smell wafted from a dumpster about ten yards to my left, and flies buzzed continually around it. I looked around for a moment, memorizing my surroundings in case I had to make a quick exit later. As I did that, the Hulk sped off, leaving me alone.

With my driver gone, there wasn't much left to do but see what Bukoholov wanted. I pounded on the door the Hulk had dropped me off at and waited for a moment. The guy who eventually opened it appeared to be in his mid-thirties and had a buzz cut as if he had recently gotten out of the army. He wore a pair of jeans, a black shirt, and a black pocketed apron across the lower half of his body.

'What do you want?' he asked.

'Bukoholov summoned me.'

'That's Mr Bukoholov,' he said, stepping back and ushering me inside with his arm. The club was a mess. There were plastic cups stacked on several tables and full black garbage sacks in the center of the dance floor. The air was stale and stuffy; evidently Bukoholov didn't like turning on the air conditioner without party goers.

'I assume you know where you're going?' asked the bartender. I said I did, and he grabbed a garbage sack and continued clearing tables and putting the room back in order. I took a breath and plunged into the back hallway. There was no bouncer this time, only a blank wall. I knocked, and the peephole slid back.

'Final-fucking-ly.'

The door slid back, revealing the speaker. He looked like a younger, better-dressed version of the bartender. He wore a black, silk shirt, and black dress pants. He waved me in.

'Uncle Kostya's waiting for you,' he said as I stepped inside. I took stock of the room before stepping in. The air was cold and smelled fresh. Evidently Bukoholov installed a different HVAC system for his personal abode than for the rest of his establishment. There was no card game this time; the kid and I were the only people in the place.

'He in his office?' I asked.

The bouncer nodded, so I walked to the room's only other door and knocked. Bukoholov shouted for me to come in. He sat at his desk with a ledger in front of him. He wore a pair of thin gold bifocals and a white Oxford shirt beneath a black silk vest. He looked more human than he had the night before, more like an elderly accountant than an aging crime boss. He looked up, his eyes featureless and cold.

'You were in the police station for more than two hours. What did you tell them?'

'Nothing concerning you.'

If it were possible, Bukoholov's eyes actually became even more chilly. His lips cracked into a thin smile, and he leaned forward. I involuntarily pushed myself away from the desk.

'That's not what I asked you. What did you tell the police?'

I didn't trust him, and my instincts screamed at me to shut up, but I told him everything that had transpired. From my early morning meeting with Olivia to my suspicions about Karen Rea's activities in South Africa to Caitlin Long's death and my arrest. Bukoholov sat back and took it in, asking questions at opportune moments so I could clarify points.

We were both silent for a moment once I finished. Eventually, Bukoholov searched through one of his desk drawers before straightening up and pressing a business card toward me.

'I keep a law firm on retainer. Call them when you are picked up next. Do not speak to anyone else.'

I glanced at the card before picking it up. Jonathan L. Meyers and Associates. If I were on my own, I'd have to mortgage my house to afford him. I hesitated. I needed a lawyer, but I wasn't sure if I wanted to let Bukoholov sink another hook into my skin. I looked at the card and then to Bukoholov.

'That's not a request, Mr Rashid.'

I picked up the card and swallowed. 'Thank you.'

'Of course. I take care of my associates. What's your plan now?'

I had hoped he wasn't going to ask that, because I honestly didn't know.

'The police confiscated my weapon,' I said, stalling. 'There's not much I can do without that.'

'Guns are easy. What are you going to do?'

'I can't let them kill another kid.'

'I'm not concerned with your goals,' Bukoholov said, his voice sharpening. 'I want to hear what you're going to do.'

I swallowed. 'I don't know yet.'

Bukoholov leaned back from his desk.

'I have a source in your department who tells me that, as of this afternoon, you will have two detectives watching you at all times. What would happen if you pulled a gun on me in front of these men?'

'After your partners shoot me?'

Bukoholov's lips drew back into a thin smile that wasn't entirely devoid of humor.

'Yes, after that.'

'The police would probably try to find out who you are and why I pulled a gun on you. They'd also probably be curious why you had so many armed men around you.'

The old man nodded.

'So that's what you have to do. Confront Miss Rea in public and let your old colleagues figure out why.'

Bukoholov's plan was certainly simple, and it did have the advantage of ample field testing. Big game hunters had been using it while on safari for as long as safaris have existed. Of course, it didn't always work out so well for the bait.

'I'd need a gun,' I said, stalling again.

'Agreed. On your way out, tell my nephew to give you the Sig. It's clean, and he has no need for it. Now that you have a plan, you can go. I've got work to do.'

That was it. I swallowed. I didn't know if I actually had a working plan or not, but it was obvious that staying in the office was out of the question. I stood up and walked to the door.

'Good luck, Mr Rashid,' said Bukoholov, putting his glasses on.

'Thank you.'

I left through the club's front door a few minutes later with a Sig Saur P226 tucked into a holster on my belt and two clips of forty-caliber Smith and Wesson ammunition in my pockets. I hadn't checked the gun beyond a cursory examination, but it looked like it was in working order. A lot of cops carried Sigs, so I knew they were reliable weapons. I also knew they usually had a serial number stamped on the gun's frame; mine didn't.

I took a cab back to my house. I had to pay by credit card because I didn't have any cash. My lawn was a mess. The SWAT team's van had parked on it, leaving a double row of muddy tire marks across the grass so deep that I'd have to reseed. A piece of two-by-four held a fresh sheet of plywood across my front door. I was grateful for that. The police were legally required to seal a residence after breaking its door down, but they didn't always do a very good job. It seemed someone still respected me enough to do it reasonably well.

Once the cabbie was gone, I slipped through my kitchen door. I didn't know how much I could trust the detectives who were supposedly watching me, but I was too tired to care. If they killed me in my sleep, at least I'd go quietly. I kicked off my shoes and went to bed.

Chapter 22

It was seven that evening when I woke up. The sky outside my bedroom window was streaked with oranges, reds, and purples as the sun set and twilight began its evening rounds. My stomach rumbled, reminding me that I hadn't eaten since my fried egg orgy that afternoon. I rolled out of bed and went to the bathroom to wash my face and hands. I had dusk prayers in the living room but stayed on my knees long after I had finished. My family was the most important thing in my life. I prayed that God would take care of them if I didn't make it.

After prayers, I stood and went to the kitchen. Hannah was the resident chef in the family, and with her absent, my dinner options were limited. I made two grilled cheese sandwiches and heated a can of cream of tomato soup. While my soup simmered, I grabbed the cordless phone from the office and dialed my wife's cell.

Our conversation was quick because she needed to

tuck Megan into bed, but it was a comforting reminder that I still had a few good things left in my life. I even got to talk to the kiddo. She had gone fishing with her Uncle Jack on the Geist reservoir and caught a catfish she claimed was big enough to swallow their boat. When Hannah got back on the phone, she called it a minnow. They were having fun, but they both wanted to come home soon. I told her that I was doing my best to make that happen; what I didn't tell her was that my best option to do so would probably land me in jail. Some things are best left unsaid. She promised to call back the next evening.

After my call, I poured my soup into a bowl and took it along with my sandwiches outside to eat. The area was surprisingly quiet for a Friday night. When the weather was nice, the kids next door used my front lawn as part of their soccer field, so I could usually hear them all the way in the back. They were good kids and didn't hurt anything, so Hannah and I didn't mind. I guess my recent arrest made their parents leery of letting them play around my house.

I ate dinner quickly and silently. As I saw it, I had two realistic options to get my family back. Show everything I had to Mike Bowers or shove a gun in Karen Rea's face. Neither were particularly good choices, although I was moderately less likely to get shot with Bowers than with Karen. The problem was that I doubted

Bowers would do anything. He'd filter whatever I told him through his own assumptions and throw me in jail while he sought more information. That would leave Karen on the street, doing whatever the hell she was doing. On the other hand, if I could provoke Karen, there was a pretty good chance we'd both be in jail while Bowers continued investigating. I wasn't a fan of jail, but if I had to go, I might as well take Karen and her lackeys off the street first.

I cleared my dishes from the table and walked back inside, trying to think things through. The plan Bukoholov gave me hinged on IMPD's unwitting cooperation. With Bowers' animosity toward me, I didn't feel as if I had much to worry about in that regard, but insurance is always helpful. I went to my office. I had dropped my cell phone earlier that afternoon when I was arrested, but it still had a charge. I dialed Olivia's home number.

'Ash.'

I could practically hear her grinding her teeth on the other end of the line.

'I'm taking care of Karen Rea tonight. I have the feeling that she's going to be at The Abbey. It's a bar in Plainfield. I'm going to swing by at about ten and end this before someone else gets hurt.'

Olivia was silent for a moment.

'What do you mean "end this"?'

'Use your imagination,' I said.

'Have you, uhm . . . do you . . .' began Olivia. I heard her sigh. 'We should talk about this in person. I'll meet you somewhere.'

'No. I appreciate the offer, but I'm done talking. I've got to end this now before someone else gets hurt.'

'Okaaaay,' said Olivia, drawing the syllable out, as if she were thinking. 'I'll meet you there. If I go with you, we can talk this through. Do it together.'

'No. The place is going to be crowded enough as it is. I wanted to call to let you know what was up in case something happens.'

'Think about this. It's not a good idea.'

'I have, and I haven't got a choice. Take care of yourself if anything happens to me. I'm probably going to stir up some trouble tonight.'

'I'd really prefer if you didn't.'

'I don't have an option. Take care, Olivia.'

I hung up before she could respond. If Bowers and his men truly had my phone tapped as Olivia had said earlier, they now knew where I was going to be and when I planned to leave. The only way to be more explicit would be to send them an email with directions in case they got lost. I grabbed the bottle of bourbon from my car and took it to my back porch to enjoy what I figured might be the last free night I'd have for quite a while.

*

Before I left, I wrote two letters, one to my wife and one to my daughter, and put them on the coffee table. I had never written letters like those before, but the words came easily enough. I told my wife that I loved her, and I told Megan that I was proud of her. Hopefully they'd never have to be read.

When that was completed, I hopped in my car and sped off. It was early, a few minutes after nine, but I was antsy. My street was dark and had relatively few cars, which made it easy to see if anyone was following me. I occasionally saw flashes of light in my rear-view mirror as headlights turned a corner, but no one was close. It wasn't until I turned out of my neighborhood that a late-model Pontiac caught my attention. It stayed a few cars back, but it slowed when I did and turned every time I did. My shoulders relaxed a bit, and my breath came a little easier. I may not have had much, but at least I had backup.

The drive to Plainfield was thirty-five minutes of monotony until I came to The Abbey. The place was busy as hell. There were cars circling its gravel lot looking for spots, while many in four-wheel-drive vehicles simply parked on the neighboring fields. I'm sure the farmers loved that. There were people everywhere, many of whom were drinking beside their cars before going in. I imagined the club's management would have put a stop to that if they had known about it, but the bouncers were so busy checking IDs and frisking party goers that I doubted they had even seen it.

I drove slowly, the gravel crunching under my car's tires until I came to the small employees' lot behind the building. Like the front, every parking spot was taken, but I didn't care. I parked behind Azrael's gray BMW, blocking him in. I looked around before turning off my car. I couldn't see the Pontiac, but hopefully it was still around.

My heart thudded against my breastbone, so I took a couple of deep breaths to get it under control. I'm not sure why, but reality took that moment to hit me. I was going to shove a gun in a cocaine dealer's face while surrounded by her supporters. When put in that light, it didn't seem that bright, even if it was the best plan I could come up with. I took more breaths, forcing my heart to resume its normal pace as I opened my door.

Slim was still in charge of the bouncers at the front door. I skipped the line and flashed my ID at him. He looked at me from my head to toe as if gauging my intentions before telling the other bouncers to let me through. Since I knew where I was going this time, I skipped the front room and went straight to the club's main room. There were a hell of a lot more people there than the last time, but none stood out on my quick scan of the room.

I forced my way through the crowd. The club goers

were drunker than they had been on my previous visit, and several ran into me along the way. Some offered slurred apologies while others ignored me. One girl in a lacy white bustier even licked her lips, exposing artificial fangs, and motioned me forward when I came near. Old guys were in, apparently. I put my hands up and smiled no thanks as I made my way towards the bar area. Mick tossed ice and bottles of beer into a cooler as I leaned against the counter. He didn't notice me.

'Hey.'

I shouted to be heard over the music until Mick looked up and tossed me a beer. I twisted off the cap and mouthed 'thank you' as he stood straight.

'You want to tell some of my other customers off?'

'Not tonight.'

The auxiliary bartender shouted something I couldn't understand, and Mick leaned under the bar and grabbed a pitcher of thick red syrup and a stack of clear plastic cups the size of shot glasses. He filled each cup halfway with the red syrup and slid them down towards his partner who finished the drink with vodka. A redheaded waitress grabbed a tray full of them and disappeared.

'What do you want?' he asked, taking a break and leaning against the bar once the drinks were dispensed. 'I've got shit to do.'

'Wrap it up because something's going down tonight. How many fire exits does this place have?'

Mick furrowed his brow and cocked his head at me. 'Enough. Why?'

'Because you need to make sure they're unlocked. Trust me.'

Mick stared at me, then pointed toward the exit.

'For your own good, get out before you do something stupid,' he said. 'These people you're messing with are seriously pissed off, and I'm getting there myself.'

I looked around the room. 'I'm not going anywhere. You've got plainclothes detectives in your parking lot and inside. My advice is to stay near an exit.'

'You're an asshole, you know that?'

'I'm sure you don't mean that,' I said, taking a step back from the bar and looking over my shoulder at the balcony overlooking the dance floor. I motioned towards it with my head. 'Those are your VIP rooms, right?'

I didn't think Mick was going to answer for a moment, but he eventually nodded.

'Remember what I said,' I said. 'For your own good, make sure every exit is open. Try to stay near one if you can.'

Mick muttered something else, but I couldn't hear him above the club's music. His tips would be down for the night, but long term he'd be better off if I took out the trash for him. I put my beer on the bar and slipped back through the crowd. I noticed at least one skirt hitched up higher than it ought to have been as a couple gyrated against each other on the dance floor. The two were so intent on groping each other that they barely noticed me as I passed.

The stairway to the VIP room was in the old narthex. The crowd was much more sedate there, and the music was softer. I looked around, hoping I could see a face familiar from my days with the department, but came up with nothing. They had to have been there, though. I did everything but specifically say I was going to kill Karen Rea on the phone; Bowers had to act on that. I reached behind me and felt the gun Bukoholov had given me to make sure it was still there. Locked and loaded. Now or never.

I stepped across the room toward a narrow winding staircase on the right side. There was a rope across the opening with a sign hanging from it that said the balcony was closed. I ignored it and started climbing steps. I felt the wood slip under my feet, but the music was so loud I couldn't hear it creak.

When I reached the top of the stairs, there was a tight turn before I entered the VIP room. I paused there for a moment and caught my breath before rounding the corner and getting my first peek of Karen's private world.

The balcony ran the entire length of the old sanctuary. At one time, it probably had seats for forty or fifty people. Now there were tables in the center and chaise lounges along the walls. Unlike the regular club goers, those in the VIP room had glass champagne flutes and actual glasses. One entire table was covered in bottles of vodka and other liquors. Several faces turned towards me as I walked up, including an Asian one with a Maori tribal symbol running from his cheek to neck. Azrael leaned over to talk to the woman he was standing beside.

She cocked her head at me and raised an eyebrow as Azrael whispered. Unless I missed my mark completely, I was looking at Karen Rea. She was Asian and wore a lacy black top, which she filled out very nicely. I could appreciate that even on a crazy person. I crossed the balcony towards an open spot overlooking the club's main room and waited for her to walk over. From my vantage, I could see the entire dance floor, so if Mike's men were watching, they'd see everything I did.

Karen smiled at me. Her lips were full, and her eyes had crows' feet at the corners. Judging by the dates on her CV, she was probably in her mid-forties, but she looked as good as any of the twenty-something girls on the floor. She stood so close to me that she could probably rest her head on my chest had she wanted to. She smelled like Dove soap.

'You broke into my house and now you're following me when I'm out with my friends. Better be careful, your pretty wife might get jealous.'

'You killed my niece. My marital welfare should be the least of your concerns, bitch.'

The smile dropped from her face, and she took a step back, every pair of eyes in the balcony on us.

'Sticks and stones, Detective Rashid. If that's all you have, please leave.'

I shot my eyes around the space. There were at least eight people on the balcony in addition to me, and so far, they were staying back. I needed a scene.

'I'm not making accusations. I'm stating facts,' I said, straining my voice to be heard over the music. I fixed my eyes on a college-aged kid with spiked pink hair. He wore a mesh shirt and was drinking what looked like champagne. 'What'd you tell your followers about Rachel Haddad?'

The blond kid's lips curled to reveal a pair of fake fangs, but he made no other move. At least I was getting a reaction.

'What I tell my friends is none of your concern.'

I looked over the crowd.

'How about Caitlin Long?' I asked, sweeping my gaze back to Karen. 'Did you tell your friends that you had a teenager raped and murdered?'

Azrael stepped toward me, but Karen put her hand across his chest.

'If you're trying to shock us, it won't work. I'd like you to leave, now.'

'Or how about Alicia Weinstein? She was tortured for being your friend,' I said, casting my eyes around the group. I rolled my fingers above my arm to illustrate the point. 'Cigarette burns all over her body. Even for a vampire that must have hurt like hell.'

Several of Karen's followers stood. I was getting somewhere.

'Leave or you're going over the balcony,' said Karen.

I hesitated for a moment. Being thrown off the balcony would get attention; it'd also get the jackasses who did it arrested immediately, which could be quite helpful. An attempted murder charge carried a lot of weight. I'd seen suspects flip on family members to avoid it. On the other hand, if I went over the edge, I'd probably break my legs, something I wanted to avoid if at all possible. I reached behind me and felt the gun Bukoholov had given me.

'I'm not done talking,' I said, taking a few steps back and pulling the weapon from its holster. Karen's chest rose slightly as she inhaled, but the surprise didn't reach her eyes. I glanced at the crowd below us. I was pretty hard to miss, so Mike's men would storm the place at any moment. All I had to do was hold on. 'Back up.'

'Oh, Detective,' said Karen, shaking her head and walking towards me. She stopped about a foot away from my outstretched arm, the soulless smile back on her lips. 'Was this your plan? Pull a gun out and see what happens?'

She stepped closer so that my gun's muzzle rested against her chest.

'I hate to tell you this, but nothing will happen,' she said, her voice nearly a whisper. 'My people won't act without my say, and your people aren't here.'

Sweat beaded on my forehead, and my legs felt heavy. I fought the urge to take a step back.

'Unless you want to find out if your breast implants are bulletproof, I'd back off.'

Karen didn't. Instead, she tilted her head to the side and her smile broadened. My hand was starting to feel heavy from the weight of my outstretched gun, and my wrist was starting to shake. Her gaze traveled from it to my face and back.

'I've read your file. You may be depressed, but your department psychiatrist says you have a deep sense of morality and personal responsibility. I'm as safe with you as a babe in its mother's arms.'

I swallowed and took a stutter step back to give myself some breathing room.

'You read a police psychiatrist's report about me,' I said, trying to make my voice as hard and loud as I could. 'I told her what she wanted to hear so I could get a job.'

Karen chuckled.

'Of course. You're a real badass. Put down the gun,

and I'll let you walk out of here. Spend the night with your wife and daughter. It will probably be your last chance for the next thirty to forty years.'

I stood up straighter. 'What are you talking about?'

She shrugged. 'You didn't see the news tonight, did you? Somebody found a pair of bodies executed near Military Park. They were members of a drug cartel from Mexico and were shot with a nine-millimeter Glock 17. Speaking of which, didn't the police confiscate that same weapon from you yesterday?'

'I should shoot you right here.'

'But you won't,' said Karen, taking another step forward. I matched her movement by taking a step back. 'For your own sake, put down the gun and forget we ever met.'

'No.'

Karen crossed her arms across her chest and raised her eyebrows.

'I tried to be reasonable. Remember that,' she said. She flicked her eyes above my shoulder. 'Stick him.'

Before I knew what was happening, I felt something pinch the skin on my neck, and almost immediately my vision blurred.

'You should have done as Mistress Karen asked.'

I spun around to face my attacker and found the muscles in my legs had become limp. I slipped and grabbed a table, knocking bottles and glasses to the ground and dropping my firearm in the process. I scrambled forward, cutting my hands and chest on glass. My body wasn't responding right. I tried to stand, but I was so dizzy, my legs fell from under me. I pulled myself to my feet on a nearby chair and leaned against it.

The guy who had stuck me leered. He looked like he was about twenty and wore a tight black shirt over an athletic build. He was big with black hair and sunken eyes. The collar of his shirt was popped up, making him look like a college-age version of Bela Lugosi playing Dracula. I tried kicking his knees, but it felt like I was in a swimming pool. My legs were slow, and he side-stepped me easily. I fell forward, landing on the arm of a chaise lounge.

'What did you do to me?' I asked, slapping my neck where I had felt the pinch. I felt a welt like I had been stung by a bee.

'I gave you something to make you cooperative.'

My chest felt heavy, and I could barely hold up my arms. I shook my head trying to clear it, but that didn't work. I had to get out of there. I launched myself forward, pushing past Dracula with my momentum and stumbling headlong into the wall beside the stairs. Rather than go down, I steadied myself by grabbing the handrail. Karen's men were on me before I could stand, so I flailed my arms until I caught something hard and metal on the wall. It was the fire alarm; I pulled it, causing floodlights to pop on and a piercing screech to replace the rhythmic pounding of the music. For a brief moment, it seemed like everyone in the club was silent, stunned.

Then they started screaming.

I lost my sense of time after that. Dracula threw me over his shoulder as easily as I would have done to my daughter, while the club's patrons downstairs collectively freaked out. From my limited vantage point, the dance floor below looked more like a slowly writhing mass than a group of people desperately trying to escape an enclosed area. Everyone ran in different directions, knocking each other to the ground. Mick jumped on top of the bar, shouting and waving a towel like a traffic guard, but I couldn't tell if he was helping or hindering. Hopefully he had at least taken my advance warning to heart and made sure the exits were open.

While the crowd panicked, Karen Rea directed her minions like a well-practiced soccer mom. Her crew lined up like a kindergarten class and filed out orderly and neatly. Dracula and I were the last to go. He hit my head on the winding staircase twice, and I'm pretty sure it was on purpose both times. I writhed against his arm and tried kneeing him in the face, causing him to slam my head against the wall hard enough to make my blurred vision turn black momentarily.

The first floor was chaotic. There were club goers everywhere. I tried shouting for help, but it came out garbled. My vision blurred with every step, and I felt what little strength I had fading. Some of the more sober party goers asked if I was okay, but Karen explained that I had passed out from smoke inhalation, and they were rushing me to the emergency room. I tried shouting for help again, but my mind couldn't form the words.

By the time we got outside, I was fading in and out of consciousness. I remember the limestone steps in front of the club, and I also remember being put down and Azrael kicking me in the ribs when he found I had parked behind his BMW. All I remember after that are bits and pieces. I remember an SUV with a black leather interior and a rough road. I kicked and screamed as well as I could until I felt a searing pain in my neck, like I had been stabbed with a red-hot needle. For a few minutes, colors danced in front of me, but then the world went black.

Chapter 23

My eyes fluttered open to what seemed like blinding light. I was in a hospital bed, and I wore a pair of generic blue pajamas that looked like something from a prison dispensary. I swallowed and sat up. My lips were dry and cracked, and my throat tickled like I was getting a cold. I rubbed sleep out of my eyes and looked around. There was a cardiac monitor beside the bed and an IV bag on a stand shooting clear liquid into my arm. The rest of the room was like a hotel. The carpet was short and gray and there was a beige recliner alongside the far wall beneath a flat-screen television. Sunlight pierced through a pair of red drapes covering the windows.

I ran my fingers through my hair and to my neck. A pair of quarter-sized bandages covered the welts where Karen's goons had shot me up. As far as I could tell, whatever they gave me hadn't done permanent damage. That was something.

I stretched, swung my legs off the side of the bed, and looked for a button to call a nurse. I didn't find one, so I did the next-best thing to get someone's attention and peeled the electrode connecting me to the cardiac monitor off my chest. It screeched and within thirty seconds a middle-aged nurse with brown hair bounded into the room, breathing heavily and uncoiling a stethoscope from around her neck. As soon as she saw me, she skidded to a stop so quickly I thought she had lost her balance.

'Where am I?'

'Why don't you sit back, Mr Rashid,' she said, walking over and hitting a switch on the cardiac monitor. Once the monitor stopped screaming, she tried to guide me back into the bed. Her hands were chilly, and she smelled like the sort of soap found in public restrooms. 'You've had a long night.'

'I've had a long week,' I said, refusing to budge. 'Where am I?'

The nurse took a step back, and I noticed the name tag on her chest. Mary Ann.

'You're in the Indiana University Hospital. You're safe. There are people who want to talk to you, but in the meantime, I want you to lay back.'

Neither Mary Ann nor I moved for a moment. She raised her eyebrows and smiled, giving me the same patient, commanding look my wife gave my daughter when Megan was being stubborn. I thought about ripping the IV out of my arm and walking out, but I didn't think I'd get very far, certainly not home. I didn't have a car nearby, and in my limited experience, cab drivers tend to stay away from men in pajamas, even if they are near a hospital. I ran my tongue across the front of my teeth and leaned back. Mary Ann smiled.

'Good. Now how are you feeling? Any dizziness or nausea?'

I shook my head. She put her hands on my forehead and held open my eyelid.

'I'm fine.'

'Good,' she said, leaning over. She extended her index finger about a foot away from my nose and slowly moved it to the left and right. 'Follow my finger with your eyes.'

Mary Ann gave me a quick examination, presumably checking for shock or indications of brain injury. Among other things, she asked me what year it was, what city I lived in, and who the President was. I must have received a fair bill of health because she called the hospital's information desk when she finished and said I was awake. Lieutenant Mike Bowers sauntered into my room about five minutes later followed by two guys in suits. Bowers looked more haggard than usual. He wore jeans and his Oxford shirt was wrinkled. There was at least two days of growth on his chin, and his eyes were red.

'Anybody tell you lately that you look terrible, Bowers?'

Bowers ignored me and collapsed into the chair near the television. He closed his eyes while the two men wearing suits stood at the foot of my bed.

'Glad to see you awake, Detective Rashid,' said the first of the two men with Bowers. He was in his mid-forties and was tall, black, and completely bald. His facial structure was almost serpentine; his eyes were far apart and dark, and his nose was hooked downward. He flashed a badge at me long enough for me to see that he was with the FBI. 'Special Agent Howard Tallie.'

Tallie gestured toward the guy beside him. The man was white and athletic-looking. He was probably in his late twenties or early thirties, which meant he was still green on the job. Judging by his buzz cut, I figured he was recruited out of the army. I knew the type; still young enough to be idealistic and naive enough to believe his work was meaningful. That could have been me not too long ago. I nodded a greeting at him.

'My partner is Agent Brian Osbourne,' said Tallie. He turned and gestured to Bowers, already nodding off in my chair. 'Lieutenant Bowers informs us that you two are already acquainted.'

'We go way back,' I said, propping myself up on my

pillows. I was dizzy for a moment, but it went away quickly. 'So are you guys here to tell me what's going on?'

Tallie and Osbourne looked at each other.

'We were hoping you'd tell us,' said Tallie.

'I woke up in a hospital ten minutes ago with track marks on my neck, and you're asking me what's going on?'

'That's exactly what we're asking you, Mr Rashid,' said Osbourne. There was a tinge of Southern to his voice.

I would have laughed, but they were serious.

'I went to a bar last night to meet somebody and got stabbed with a pair of needles big enough to vaccinate a fucking elephant. Whatever I was shot up with knocked me out. End of story. That's all I've got.'

'Probably Ketamine,' said Bowers. I didn't think he had even been awake. He yawned. 'We find it in clubs every now and then. Did you have weird dreams while you were out?'

'Yeah, sort of. I remember seeing lots of colors.'

I also tasted sounds, felt music, and danced with a panda, but I didn't think it was appropriate to bring those up. Bowers stood, but stayed near the chair.

'You were high, Ash.'

Tallie put his hand up and glanced over his shoulder, stopping Bowers from speaking again. The Lieutenant sat back down and shook his head.

336

'Who were you meeting in the bar?' asked Tallie, turning his attention back to me. The man really did look like a snake. I half-expected to see his tongue dart out when he wasn't speaking.

'I went to see a woman named Karen Rea. She killed my niece and probably a bunch of other kids, too.'

The FBI agents exchanged lingering glances but neither looked back at Bowers, who had gone back to sleep. Tallie took charge first.

'Let's back up,' he said. 'How do you know Konstantin Bukoholov?'

'I don't, really,' I said, shrugging. 'I met him a couple of times while investigating Karen.'

Tallie and Osbourne both took notepads out of their jackets and started jotting things down.

'And Karen is one of his employees?' asked Osbourne.

'More of a competitor. And shouldn't you be asking her these questions?'

Tallie wrote something on a notebook he took from his hip pocket.

'It's not the policy of the Federal Government to discuss ongoing investigations with outsiders,' he said without looking up. 'How did Bukoholov come up in your investigation?'

I paused before saying anything. I doubted the FBI were Bukoholov fans, but I didn't think telling them I had shot the guy's nephew would help me. I shrugged as if I didn't know, stalling. The two agents stared at me intently.

'I guess I met him in a bar.'

'The Lucky Bastard?' asked Tallie.

'That sounds right,' I said.

'How many meetings have you had with him?' asked Osbourne.

'Two.'

'The one at the Bastard and where else?' asked Osbourne again.

'Lieutenant Bowers arrested me yesterday, but he let me go pretty quick. Bukoholov's brother-in-law picked me up from the station and took me to see him at his club downtown.'

The FBI agents looked at each other and nodded, but said nothing.

'What are you guys looking for?' I asked after a moment of silence. 'If I know, it might help me give you the information you need.'

Tallie glanced at his partner before speaking. Osbourne shrugged.

'We're part of an anticorruption task force,' said Tallie. 'We have reason to believe there are compromised individuals in some local agencies. When you met Bukoholov, were there ever other representatives from the Prosecutor's Office present?'

I didn't say anything for a second as that sunk in.

'You're not here about drug trafficking?' I asked.

Osbourne shook his head. 'Narcotics are no longer an agency priority. If you'd like—'

'Tell me you at least have Karen Rea and her crew in custody,' I said, interrupting the FBI agent. He looked to Bowers, who shrugged.

'I'm sure we'll get another shot with her,' said Bowers. 'We caught three homicides last night, so we didn't have the manpower to bring her crew in safely. You're lucky you still had a detective watching you.'

'So what, you let everyone go?'

'We didn't let anybody go,' said Bowers, his neck red. 'As soon as Detective Doran flashed his cruiser's lights, the bitch dropped you and took off. Doran drove you to a hospital because he thought you had been poisoned. He might have saved your life.'

I paused a moment, thinking, and then panned my gaze to the two FBI agents.

'Bukoholov has a poker game downtown at a club called Mist,' I said. 'It's in the back room. Go on a Friday or Saturday night, and you'll probably find someone interesting.'

Tallie shifted on his feet and nodded.

'Anything else you can tell us?' he asked.

'Those homicides IMPD caught last night,' I said. 'Were two of them in Military Park?'

'Yeah,' said Bowers, crossing his arms. 'What do you know?'

I ran my tongue across my teeth before speaking.

'When you get ballistics, they'll match a Glock Seventeen registered to me.'

Even the FBI guys raised their eyebrows at that. Bowers walked to stand beside my bed.

'Are you confessing something?' Bowers asked.

I shook my head and coughed, clearing my throat. 'You confiscated the firearm when you arrested me yesterday.'

Tallie glared at Bowers. 'I thought you had your station under control,' he said.

'I thought I did,' said Bowers, his face blank. The room was silent for another second.

'Make sure Lieutenant Bowers has your current contact information,' said Tallie, tearing his glare from Bowers and directing it towards me. 'We'll talk again soon.'

The two FBI agents left, leaving me alone with Bowers. His skin sagged on his neck and jowls, and his hair was graying. He looked older than he had a week earlier, if that was possible. For a moment, I thought he was going to stare at me and then leave, but eventually, he opened his mouth.

'How you doing, Ash?'

'Peachy. I didn't know we were on a first name basis, Mike.'

'Yeah, of course,' he said, straightening up. He pulled my cell phone out of an interior pocket in his jacket and put it on the end table beside my bed. 'This beeped every five minutes last night, so I turned it off to save your battery. You should check your messages more often.'

I reached over and picked up the phone. For a moment, I thought I saw something in Bowers' face that resembled actual human emotion. It was almost a pained expression, but it was gone before I caught more than a glimmer.

'Thanks,' I said after a pause. 'You look like you could use some sleep.'

'No rest for the weary. See you later, Rashid.'

Bowers left after that, and I sank into my pillows. My plan had been an abysmal failure on nearly every level. I rubbed sleep out of my eyes and sighed. Karen won. That's what it came down to in the end. I gave the case my best shot and all I got out of it was a five-minute meeting with two FBI agents intent on arresting a politician. Hopefully somebody else would pick things up later, but I was done. I loved Rachel. She was a good girl, and she would have done good things with her life, but there wasn't anything else I could do for her. If God wanted justice for her, He was on His own. All I had left to do was put my life back together while I still had one.

I turned on my cell phone and glanced at the screen. As Bowers had said, somebody had left me a message. It was a text from a number I hadn't seen before. It was short, but it had a picture along with it. I stared at it for a while, my hands feeling numb. Eventually, I dropped the phone and closed my eyes.

Karen had Hannah and Megan.

Chapter 24

Call me. Tell no one. KR

The picture accompanying Karen's message was grainy, and the colors were off, but it clearly showed my daughter and wife. They were in a car with black leather seats. Megan slept in her car seat, while my wife sat beside her. Hannah's back was straight, and her eyes were dull. I thought the picture was fake until I saw my wife's hands. She held them at her waist, so the photographer probably hadn't even seen them. Her left hand was flat, while her right was balled into a fist on top with her thumb pointing up. It looked as if she were playing paper, rock, scissors with my daughter, but the message was clear. Before Megan could talk, we had taught her some basic signs so she could communicate. Hannah was giving one of the few I remembered.

Help me.

For a moment, I couldn't form a coherent thought,

343

and my stomach felt as if I had stepped off a cliff. I stayed like that for a few minutes, my hands shaking and my throat dry. Eventually I managed to collect myself enough to pound the return call button. Karen picked up on the third ring.

'Mr Rashid, I'm glad to hear from you so soon.'

I tried to speak, but my voice didn't work at first.

'What do you want?' I asked.

'This and that. Before I say anything else, though, I want to tell you one thing,' said Karen. 'Your daughter is adorable. She's been telling us stories since eight this morning when she got up. And you'd better watch out because I think she has a boyfriend at day care.'

Every muscle in my body felt rigid. I gripped the phone tight.

'If you hurt her, I will kill you and everyone you've ever cared about.'

Karen laughed.

'I'm sure you would, but it won't come to that. I need a favor from you. Do it and I'll let your family go. You'll live long and happy lives together. Refuse and I'll slit your daughter's throat and shoot your wife in the head. I'd rather avoid doing that, so please play along.'

I choked back a lump of anger that threatened to bubble to the surface. I bottled it in some recess of my soul for future use. My hands no longer trembled, but the muscles in my legs and back quivered. I ground my teeth and counted to five before I spoke.

'What do you want me to do?'

'I need you to deliver something to Hong Kong. It'll be a quick trip. Twenty hours there, twenty hours back. Walk around the airport, do some duty free shopping if you're interested, and come home. It'll be a long weekend, but that's it; I'll even buy the ticket. As soon as you land, your family goes free, and you'll never hear from me again.'

'If it were that easy, you'd do it yourself.'

Karen chuckled.

'So suspicious, Ash. I would do it myself, but the People's Republic of China labels my family undesirable, so neither I nor my nephew are allowed in. You, I'm sure, would have no problem.'

The door to my room was open, and I saw movement outside with my peripheral vision. An elderly man in a pair of pajamas much like mine pushed a walker down the carpeted hallway while a little girl about my daughter's age tottered behind with a juice box in hand. She smiled at me. I smiled back and lowered my voice.

'What would I be delivering?'

'Something so small and light you will hardly know you're carrying it.'

'Do you think you could be a little more specific?'

Karen practically purred. It was nice to know one of us was in a good mood.

'How do you feel right now, Ash?'

'Pissed off.'

I said it louder than I probably should have because one of the nurses popped her head in my room after that and pulled my door shut. At least she smiled as she did it.

'Physically, I mean. Are you achy? Does your throat hurt? Feeling sinus pressure? Anything like that?'

I wouldn't have indulged her, but as soon as Karen stopped speaking, the tickle in the back of my throat increased so rapidly that I had to cough.

'Something like that,' I said.

'You have a very special cold. I gave it to you last night,' said Karen. 'When combined with a very special vaccination, you'll develop a very special illness. It won't hurt you, but that's what you'll deliver.'

I balled my free hand into a fist.

'Is this something you developed while in South Africa?' I asked.

'You've done your homework,' she said. 'My work in South Africa made this possible, yes. If you're really interested, we can talk more in person tonight. I'm thinking eleven. I'll send you the location when we're set up.'

'I'm in the hospital. I don't know if they'll release me by then.'

'Oh, I'm sure you'll be there. If you need motivation,

pretend your daughter's life is on the line. I'll see you tonight, Mr Rashid.'

Karen clicked off after that, and I stayed still for the moment, feeling sick to my stomach. Outside of James Bond movies, criminals don't kidnap and hold people who can disrupt their plans, and, no matter what they say, they never let witnesses walk out. My family was dead unless I did something. My heart and shoulders felt heavy. The tension that had built up over the past week rose and gripped my lungs in a vise. I didn't have superpowers, I didn't know karate, I didn't even have a gun. My stomach clenched, and I almost vomited.

It took about ten minutes for the nausea to pass, and when it did, it left me feeling numb. No matter what I did, I needed to get out of the hospital, which meant I needed clothes. No one had checked on me since Bowers and the Feds left, so the hospital staff obviously wasn't too worried about my condition. I'd be fine discharging myself.

I rolled over and swung my legs off the bed. The IV in my right arm was secured with two rows of soft white tape. I unfurled both and grasped the clear plastic top of the IV and pulled parallel to my arm. It slid out easily, leaving a trickle of blood behind. No needle came with it, so I felt around my arm for anything hard but found nothing. Hopefully that was okay.

I laid the IV tube on my bed and stood. The blood

rushed from my upper body, blurring my vision and almost causing me to fall backwards. I blinked and shook my head, hoping to clear the fog. It took a few seconds for the world to come back to focus, but even then, I felt like I was a couple of shots in on a raucous Friday night. It was probably the residual effects of whatever Karen had drugged me with; that was going to take some getting used to.

I put my hand on the bed for balance and opened the drawer on the end table beside it. Medical supplies. Not what I was looking for, but helpful. I grabbed a square bandage, tore it open, and pressed it onto my arm. It'd tear off hair when I had to remove it, but it beat having an open wound.

After that, I searched a dresser beside the chair Bowers had sat in earlier. I found my jeans and a white T-shirt in the first drawer and my shoes, keys, and wallet in the bottom. I would have liked some underwear, but I could settle. I changed in the room's adjoining bathroom and put on my shoes without socks. No one would mistake me for a doctor or even a reasonably well-dressed handyman, but it'd do.

Five minutes after leaving my room, I walked out the hospital's front door as if I were a visitor; no one even looked at me more than once. The hospital and my law school were just a few blocks apart, so I knew the area fairly well. There were restaurants, bookstores, and other services geared towards students all around. I headed south towards the University's Campus Center, and for a moment, I got so dizzy that I had to stop and lean against a lamppost to catch my balance. Apparently I had been shot up with more drugs than I thought.

Eventually, I regained my equilibrium and continued walking, albeit at a slower pace. If I were going to survive the next twelve hours, I needed a few things, not the least of which was a firearm. I couldn't get that on campus, but at least I could get some money. I withdrew fifty bucks from one of the ATMs in the Campus Center and called a cab to pick me up. While I waited, I glanced at the receipt that came with my cash. Hannah and I had a little less than three grand in the bank, most of which was from her most recent paycheck. She wasn't going to like it, but I needed to use a good portion of that.

The cab pulled up about five minutes later. Rather than have him drive me home, I gave him directions to The Abbey so I could pick up my car. It was in the back lot where I had left it, but the front bumper was smashed and one of the headlights was broken. Evidently, Azrael hadn't wanted to call a tow truck, so he rammed his way out. That was just inconsiderate. Thankfully, it started fine.

I needed a gun without too many questions, and as a former homicide detective, I knew where I could get one. I drove home, but only stayed long enough to change into a clean pair of clothes before heading to a pawn shop about ten miles from my house.

Frank's Pawn and Gift shared a strip mall with an adult bookstore and theater on the city's near-North side. I suppose pawn and porn made good neighbors. Both attracted customers who didn't like questions or attention, and cleanliness wasn't high on either place's list of business needs.

I pulled into a parking lot laced with cracks, weeds, and broken bottles and parked as close to the exit as I could in case I had to run. A group of young guys in shirts with some fraternity's logo emerged from the bookstore. Two carried grocery-sized sacks of pornography while their friends laughed hysterically. I guess their weekend was planned.

Frank's Pawn and Gift smelled like stale cigarettes and gun oil. Ostensibly, it was a standard pawn shop, but in actuality, it was more like a gun shop specializing in pawned firearms. I skipped the aisles of cheap, Chinese-made handcuffs and throwing stars and walked to the back. There were probably two or three hundred rifles hanging from racks along the rear wall and a long counter in front prominently displaying ammunition and handguns.

A buzzer beeped when I got near the counter, and a fat guy with a graying goatee walked from behind a curtain amid the firearms. I hadn't met him in person before, but the description I had heard from one of my old confidential informants fit. I was being helped by Frank himself.

'What can I get for you?' he asked.

'You're Frank, aren't you?' I asked, putting out my hand. He shook it. 'Joey Walls tells me you've got a good selection.'

Frank smiled. Joey was a low-level pot dealer who worked one of the college campuses. He was more of a slacker than a hardened criminal, but he schmoozed better than any used car salesman I've ever seen. Because of that, he knew a lot of people and heard a lot of things, so we let him deal a little in exchange for information. I hadn't talked to him in a few years, so I hoped his name still had some street cred.

'Joey's a good boy. Heard he's in school now, studying business or something. You see him, tell him we could use someone like him around here.'

'I'll do that,' I said, leaning forward on the counter. 'I'm here because I need a handgun. Maybe a nine-millimeter semiautomatic.'

'We can do business,' said Frank, bending down and unlocking the display. He reached in and pulled out a rack holding four firearms. Three were too small and flashy for my needs, while the fourth was a large, steel monstrosity with a Slavic-sounding manufacturer printed on the barrel.

351

I raised my eyebrows. 'I'm looking for something for self-defense, not a rap video.'

Frank snickered. 'Most people don't know the difference. What do you have in mind?'

'Something concealable with stopping power.'

'I've got what you need.'

Frank bent down again and this time picked up a slim aluminum case about twelve inches on a side. The weapon it held was flat black and small. I picked it up. It was a little heavy for its size, but it felt nice. I looked at Frank for information.

'It's a forty-caliber Beretta 9000 with a ten-round magazine. If you want stopping power with a small footprint, that'll do you. New in box. Six hundred.'

That was more than I wanted to spend, but the weapon fit my hand well. It'd work.

'I'll take it. Give me fifty jacketed hollow-point rounds for this. And while I'm here, give me fifty rounds of thirty-eight caliber jacketed hollow points and a holster that will clip on my belt.'

'You want a shotgun while you're at it? Gave one to my mom for Christmas, and she says she sleeps a lot better at night. I'll make you a deal for the whole thing.'

I looked at the rack behind him, considering. A good shotgun has a lot of merits, but subtlety isn't one of them. If I went in with one of those, Hannah and Megan would be dead before I got a shot off. I shook my head no, so Frank began to search for my ammunition.

'I'm going to need to see three forms of ID for these,' he said, reaching into boxes beneath the counters. He found what he needed quickly and dropped two cases of Remington ammunition on the counter beside the aluminum case housing the Beretta. 'You can hunt for a holster that'll fit you on the shelves, and while you do that, I'll get the paperwork started.'

'I hoped we could do this one between the two of us. Joey told me you might be willing to help a guy out.'

Frank squinted at me and crossed his arms.

'We can do a private sale, but it's gonna cost you. You buy from my business, and you get the price on the tag. You buy from me personally, and then we've got to talk. Nine hundred for the Beretta and ammo, and I'll give you whatever holster you want.'

'Seven for everything.'

'This ain't a negotiation. You want this firearm, you'll pay my price. Nine hundred.'

I thought about taking out my badge and laying it on the counter, but decided against it. That'd hurt my old CI more than anything else. I took my credit card out of my wallet and paid the guy. I was out of the store in under an hour and back in my house twenty minutes after that. Karen hadn't called yet, which didn't surprise me. If she were smart, she wouldn't call until the last minute so I wouldn't have time to set up an ambush. I had an idea about getting around that, but I had more pressing things to do for the moment.

I microwaved three egg and cheese English muffins from a box in the back of our freezer. They were probably older than my daughter, but at least they kept my stomach from rumbling. When I finished those, I went to my car and grabbed Robbie's revolver from the evidence kit in my trunk. I held it straight in front of me and checked the alignment of the chamber and barrel. It was a good bit out of whack, but it was serviceable.

I took the gun to my workbench in the garage. When I worked a beat, my backup weapon was always a revolver. It could only hold six rounds, but it was as reliable as any firearm could be. I disassembled Robbie's firearm; thankfully, it came apart just like my old revolver. I spent the next twenty minutes cleaning its chamber and barrel of residual gunk before oiling the moving parts heavily and putting it back together straight and true. It wasn't the best weapon I had ever possessed, but the parts were free of rust, and it was in fair shape mechanically. It'd fire, I hoped.

I went back inside and strapped the revolver to my ankle and the Beretta to my waist. Physically, I was as ready to go as I'd ever be. Now I needed some intel.

Chapter 25

The roads in central Indiana take a beating every winter, so it's not uncommon to find potholes six inches deep and several feet across. Generally, the city does a good job of patching them up, but there are neighborhoods where even the toughest road crews won't venture. That was going to come in handy. After twenty-five minutes of driving, I pulled to the curb beside Three Little Pigs Ammo and Supply and reversed so my left rear wheel dipped into a pothole bigger than the inflatable kiddie pool I bought for my daughter a few months earlier. The rear of my car dipped about six inches, hopefully making it look like the tire was flat. With the front end smashed, it fit into the neighborhood well.

I got out of the car and leaned against it while I searched through my cell phone's memory for Olivia's number. She answered quickly, but I spoke before she could say anything.

'It's Ash. I need to see you. Can you meet me in The Park?'

'Uhm—'

'It's an emergency,' I said, interrupting. 'Please.'

She was silent for a moment.

'Okay. Give me forty-five minutes.'

'Thank you. I'll see you then.'

I hung up before she could respond. It was late afternoon, so the stores were still open, and I could hear conversations through windows and doors propped open by rocks and sticks. A group of little girls drew flowers on the sidewalk in front of a barbershop. I said their drawings were pretty as I walked by, so they smiled and waved.

The Park itself wasn't as busy as the surrounding neighborhood. Two kids played on a swing set, while four teenagers stood near the picnic tables in the center, passing something around. I didn't see any hookers, but I didn't look very hard, either. The teenagers scattered as soon as I came close, probably thinking I was a cop. One tossed a rainbow-colored glass pipe onto the ground while another threw a Ziploc bag into the bushes. Those kids could probably get another bong or crack pipe as easily as I could fill up my gas tank, but I picked up their pipe anyway and threw it into an open garbage can, breaking it against a bottle of Boones Farm strawberry wine. The bag was empty except for a few seeds.

Cheap marijuana; at least it wasn't heroin. I threw it in the same garbage can I had thrown the pipe and then sat on the picnic tables to wait.

Olivia had said forty-five minutes, but it only took her twenty. She drove by twice, presumably looking for a parking spot. I pulled my Beretta from its holster and held it behind me as she approached. She wore a pair of faded jeans and a navy blue top that was ruffled around the chest. I wasn't pleased with her at the moment, but there was no denying she looked good. She nodded at me when she got close enough. I couldn't see a weapon on her, so if she had one, it was in her purse.

'Hey, Ash. What's your emergency?'

I took my arm from behind my back and leaned forward with my firearm resting on my knees. Olivia's back went straight and she breathed in.

'We need to talk, Olivia.'

'Okay,' she said, putting her hands in front of her and shrugging her purse off her shoulder. 'Let me get something from my purse first.'

I shifted so the muzzle of my firearm pointed at her midsection. My thumb slipped from the grip to the barrel, disengaging the safety with an audible click.

'I'd drop that if I were you.'

Olivia stayed still and looked around, assessing the situation. Her posture was rigid.

'What do you want, Ash?'

'I want you to drop the purse.'

She looked around for a moment, but the teenagers and kids were gone. We were alone. She dropped her purse and tilted her head to the side.

'What now?' she asked.

'I want to talk about why you sold out my family and how you can help me get them back.'

Olivia's eyes never left mine.

'I don't know what you're talking about.'

'Really?' I asked, leaning back. I reached into my jacket's inside pocket with my free hand and pulled out my cell phone. I threw it at her. 'Check the last text message.'

'I don't know—'

'Do it.'

Olivia was quicker with the phone than I was. After about a minute, the color ran from her face, and her shoulders dropped. She looked up and swallowed.

'I'm sorry,' she said. 'I didn't know.'

'Bullshit. Maybe ten people know my cell number, and fewer than that knew where Hannah and Megan were. You're the only person on both lists.'

Olivia put her hands up in front of her and stepped towards me.

'Put the gun down,' she said. 'We'll talk about this and figure it out together.'

I pulled my Beretta's slide back, chambering a round. Olivia stopped moving.

'You're not going to shoot me with people watching.'

'You think witnesses matter in this neighborhood?'

Olivia took a step back. Her lower lip trembled.

'What do you want?' she asked.

'Where is my family being held?'

'I never would have said anything if I thought she was going to hurt your family,' said Olivia, shaking her head. Her face was white. 'She told me she was going to scare them to get you off the case. That's all.'

'Where are they?'

Olivia's chest rose and fell as she breathed deeply.

'Karen owns a refrigerated warehouse north of town. Your family's probably there.'

'How do I get there?'

The directions were complicated, so I had her repeat them twice so I could memorize them.

'How many men will she have with her?'

'She trusts three. If this is important to her, they'll be there. There are too many for you to take on your own. I'll go with you if you want.'

'I've had enough of your help on this case,' I said. 'What'd she put in me last night?'

'Ketamine and GHB. It's clean. They don't put anything extra in it. That's why it sells so well.'

'What else?' I asked.

'I don't know.'

I stared at her for a few moments, but Olivia didn't blink.

'If I see you at this warehouse, I'll shoot you on sight.'

Olivia knelt in front of me, almost pleading. 'I tried to keep you out of this. I really did. I even asked Karen not to kill you. That's why you're still alive. I'm sorry.'

The textured grip of my firearm bit into my hand as I squeezed.

'You came to Megan's birthday parties,' I said. 'We had you over for Thanksgiving. I hope whatever Karen paid you was worth it.'

'I'm sorry,' she said again. 'I didn't think it would come to this.'

'You have until ten tomorrow morning to turn yourself over to the police,' I said, holstering my firearm. I kept the safety disengaged in case I had to pull it quickly. 'If you don't, I'll give your name to Konstantin Bukoholov and tell him you know where Karen Rea keeps her main stash.'

'He'll kill me. You know that.'

'Eventually. He'll torture you to get the location first. And if my family is hurt tonight, start running. Consider this your head start.'

I stood and walked away. Olivia called after me and asked me to stay so we could talk things through, but I had already said everything I had to say.

When I got back to the car, I called IMPD's dispatcher. I didn't know Bowers well enough to have his personal cell phone number, so I had the dispatcher send him a message for me. I told him I had plugged one of the department's leaks and asked him to give me a call if he wanted to hear more. Evidently he did because he called me back right away. I repeated what Olivia had said, and we spent the next ten minutes working out a plan. I gave it fifty-fifty odds; Bowers thought that was generous.

He was probably right.

Chapter 26

My eyes popped open and I jumped as my cell phone rang. The world was dark and blurry. I blinked as the dream world faded and reality came into focus. I was in my living room, and it was dark except for my television. The evening news was on, so it was sometime after ten. I coughed to clear my throat and snatched the phone from the coffee table.

'I'm here,' I said, rubbing my face to get the blood flowing. The drugs must have been wearing off because I wasn't dizzy as I sat up.

'I thought you weren't going to pick up,' said Karen. 'That would have been disappointing.'

'I'm sure it would have been. Where's my family?'

Karen's directions were nearly identical to the ones Olivia had given me earlier. Her warehouse was about a forty-five-minute drive from my house, which meant Mike Bowers and his crew could probably make it from their station in thirty-five with their lights and sirens blaring. Ten minutes wasn't a big enough gap for them to get set up.

'I'll be there when I can.'

'You'll be there at eleven, which means you need to leave now.'

My heartbeat ticked up a few notches, so I coughed to keep my trepidation from showing in my voice.

'I'll be there when I'm able. It's late, and I'm hungry. I'm going to stop by a drive through to get something to eat, and I'll be over right after that.'

Karen chuckled, but her voice sounded harsh, almost strained.

'This isn't a social call. If you don't come by eleven, I'll kill your wife.'

My fingers trembled. I closed my eyes. The picture Karen had sent earlier popped into my imagination unbidden. Visceral, raw anger spread through me, crowding out everything else I felt. I spoke clearly and slowly, much as I would have done when talking to Megan after she misbehaved.

'You're going to do whatever you want no matter what I do. We both know that, so I'm going to get a hamburger while I can, and then I'll come see you. Okay?'

Karen didn't answer for a second, so all I could hear was her breath.

'You just killed your wife, Detective Rashid. Now

363

you're working on your daughter. I'd suggest you come on time.'

The line went dead after that. I stared at the phone, my stomach knotting and my breath coming in short gasps. Intellectually, I knew that the threat had been bluster and bravado to scare me into compliance. As long as Karen needed leverage over me, Hannah would be fine. At the same time, knowing that was true and believing it were two different things. I shivered. My mouth felt dry as I dialed Bowers' number. He answered with a grunt.

'It's a go,' I said, hoping my voice didn't crack. 'Same address. Eleven o'clock.'

'We'll be there. It's going to be fine, Rashid. We'll get them back.'

'I know.'

He hung up before I could wish him luck. I didn't like our plan, even if it was the best we had. My job was to go in and secure my family. Ten minutes after I went in, Mike and his crew would cut the building's power and subdue Karen's men in the dark. It sounded simple, but there was a lot that could go wrong. We didn't know the building's layout or even how many men would be inside, so we were going in blind; I guess that was better than not going in at all, though.

I grabbed a sports coat from my closet and headed to the car. My head hurt and my chest felt constricted, but

I couldn't let that bother me. I focused on the situation. In total, I had thirty-six rounds of ammunition on me. Thirty were for the Beretta in my belt holster, which Bowers and I figured Karen would confiscate. Our hope was that by giving her something to stare at, she'd miss the revolver strapped to my ankle. Six shots wouldn't amount to much, but it was better than nothing.

As I anticipated, it took me roughly forty-five minutes to drive to Karen's address. She seemed to have an affinity for warehouses in the middle of nowhere. Unlike the one Bukoholov's men had burned, though, this one was in a nice complex. The grass around it looked relatively green, and most of the surrounding buildings had signs, indicating they held legitimate businesses. Karen's warehouse had a solid block foundation with extruded, white metal siding above. There were windows evenly spaced around the exterior and a rock-lined drainage ditch in front. I could see a thicket of woods behind and to one side of the building.

I parked a block away and got out of my car. I couldn't see Bowers or his team, and for a moment, I was tempted to give him a call. I couldn't risk it, though, not with the possibility that someone was watching. I was going to have to trust him. The night air was crisp and clean, but it did little to still my nerves. My muscles felt tight, and I jumped every time a moth buzzed my head or something scurried across the ground. I reached behind me for my Beretta and squeezed the weapon's grip. I felt better with it there even if I were going to lose it.

I pulled a Swiss Army knife out of my pocket and, as per Mike Bowers' request, stabbed the rear tires of each car in the lot, including a gray BMW with a broken taillight and dented trunk. If my Cruiser had feelings, I'm sure it would have felt vindicated. Once the tires were flat, I straightened, adjusted my shirt, and glanced at my watch. It was five after eleven, right on time.

I collapsed the knife, stuck it in my pocket, and walked to the building's only door. No one came to greet me, so I took out my cell phone and dialed Karen's number.

'I'm here.'

I hung up before she could respond and sat on the folding chair propping open the door. I couldn't see far into the building. Just a long hallway that led left and right. I took a deep breath, calming my nerves. My family was in there somewhere.

I heard Karen's men before I saw them. At least one had keys or change in his pocket, and the other wheezed as he walked. I had seen them in the club the night before wearing all black, but this time they wore matching khaki pants, black polo shirts, and name tags. It looked as if they had come right after work. Tony and Byron. Tony had deep track marks on his neck as if he had been scratched by an animal, and Byron had a raspberry-shaped bruise on his cheek. Byron pulled a gun

366

from a hip holster, so I started to put my hands on top of my head.

'I think I saw photos of some work you boys did on a girl in Eagle Creek Park,' I said, standing. 'As a father, I hope to kill you both before the night's over. I thought I'd give you fair warning.'

The two of them snickered.

'Sometimes work has its rewards,' said Byron. He looked at his partner. 'Search him.'

Tony was as gentle as a rabid pit bull. He pounded my chest looking for weapons and then moved down my body until he found the Beretta strapped to my waist. I had considered strapping the revolver to my waist and hiding the Beretta on my ankle, but Karen's guards would have known something was off as soon as they found it. Very few officers in IMPD still carried revolvers, and most of those who did were near retirement age. I'd rather sacrifice the Beretta than lose them both. Tony pulled the firearm from my holster, showed it to his partner, and raised his eyebrows.

'You got anything else?' he asked. He flipped his hand around, grabbed the barrel of my gun, and used the grip to hit me in the crotch before I could move. A wrenching pain exploded across my abdomen. I couldn't breathe, and I doubled over without thinking. Tony laughed. 'Whatever you had, it's gone now.'

I tuned the two of them out. Since I was bent over,

my revolver was a few inches from my hands. I probably could have grabbed it before they even noticed. My fingers trembled, and I looked up. The jackasses were still laughing, so I put my hands on my knees, pretending to catch my breath. It would have been nice to take them out of the game before seeing Karen, but my job wasn't to play hero. They'd get theirs. The laughter died to periodic chuckles and then even that stopped.

'You ready, Cinderella?' asked Byron, gesturing for me to stand with the muzzle of his weapon. I shot my eyes from Byron to Tony. I didn't recognize the gun Byron carried except that it was a semiautomatic about the same size as my Glock 17. Guns that size usually held ten to fifteen rounds, so even if he were a bad shot, he'd have plenty of opportunities to put holes in me. I was less worried about Tony. He aimed my Beretta at my chest, but he had kept the safety on, so it wouldn't fire no matter how hard he pulled the trigger. It was hard to be intimidated by stupid henchmen.

I straightened and put my hands back on my head.

'I'd like to see Karen, now.'

'She'd like to see you, too,' said Byron, grabbing my shoulder and pulling me in front of him. He pressed his gun to the small of my back. 'Be respectful when you see her this time. We're watching.'

He pushed me forward, and I acted as if I had stumbled, drawing laughter from the stooges. I looked back at them quickly. Byron favored his left side; I didn't know if that was helpful or not, but it might slow him down in a foot race.

We stopped in front of a wooden door with a chest-high frosted glass window. The light was on inside, but I couldn't hear anyone speaking. Tony nudged me forward with his gun, so I went through first. It was a corner office, maybe fifteen feet on a side, with empty floor-to-ceiling bookshelves and a behemoth of a desk in the center. There were two large windows with the shades drawn. Karen leaned against the desk while Hannah sat near her in a metal folding chair with her wrists zip tied in front of her. Her breathing was shallow and quick, and her lower lip quivered when she saw me. My fingernails bit into my palms.

'Where's Megan?' I asked.

Karen slid off her desk and walked over to me. She smelled like Dove soap again.

'She's asleep in the room next door,' she said. 'We let your wife read her a story. Believe it or not, we're not animals.'

I looked at Hannah, and she nodded almost imperceptibly, never taking her gaze from Karen's back.

'I'm here now, and I'll do whatever you want,' I said. 'Why don't you let them go?'

'Soon,' said Karen, putting her hand on my chest. My wife stirred, but made no move towards us. Karen looked at her henchmen, but kept her hand flat on my chest. 'Were there any problems?'

Tony held up my Beretta.

'He was carrying this, but we neutered him.'

The two of them snickered.

'Tsk, tsk, Ash. Bringing a gun to a friendly meeting,' Karen said. 'How do you expect me to trust someone like that?'

I reached into my pocket for the Swiss Army knife I had used in the parking lot.

'Your guards missed this when they frisked me,' I said, pulling it out and glancing at Karen's thugs. They grimaced simultaneously. 'They're also loud when they walk, Tony doesn't know how to disengage the safety on that firearm, and Byron limps on his left knee. If I wanted them dead, they would be. That's why I expect you to trust me.'

Karen looked at her goons and made a disapproving clucking sound with her tongue.

'It's hard to get good help these days, isn't it?' she asked, turning back towards me.

Especially if you're an evil bitch.

'I've shown you goodwill,' I said. 'Now show me some. Let my wife and daughter go.'

Karen smiled.

'I will,' she said, taking a seat behind the desk and gesturing towards an upholstered chair in front. 'Have a seat. We've got a few things to discuss about your trip.'

I looked at Hannah. With Karen behind the desk, she and Hannah were about a meter apart. My wife was a fierce woman, but Karen was armed with a knife. Hannah didn't stand much of a chance if I started a fight. I sat down and glanced at my watch as I did. My heart was starting to beat faster. It was ten after eleven, which meant Bowers and his crew would be there any moment. I was supposed to have my family safe by then, but I didn't know if that was possible.

'Relax,' said Karen. She held the knife in the palm of one of her hands. 'Consider this as a chat between friends.'

'Since we're friends, what's special about Hong Kong?' I asked. 'They have a lot of slayers there? Or am I visiting a new vampire coven?'

Karen laughed, and the thugs behind me snickered.

'Do you really think a tenured professor of molecular genetics would believe in vampires?'

I shrugged. 'You dress in black lingerie and spend your weekends at a vampire bar in the middle of nowhere.'

'Vampires were a means to an end,' she said. 'My nephew and I needed money for research, so we gave social misfits something to believe in. In return, they did whatever we needed.'

371

'If you're not interested in vampires, what's in China?'

Karen smiled and leaned forward, dropping the Swiss Army knife beside her elbow on the desk blotter.

'A billion Chinese people.'

'Besides that, Captain Obvious,' I said.

She laughed but didn't say anything.

'What did you really inject me with?' I asked.

As soon the words left my lips, the building went dark and the hum of the air conditioner ceased. For a moment, time held its breath and stopped. The room was so quiet that I could hear crickets outside. I don't know who broke that silence first, me or Karen, but I screamed for Hannah to get down while Karen ordered her men to open fire.

I thrust my hips back and dropped my left shoulder to the ground while simultaneously bringing my knees to my chest. Tony and Byron raised their weapons while I grabbed my revolver and pulled it from my ankle holster. Bullets thwacked against the desk behind me and ricocheted against the concrete floor. Splinters struck me in the back and side, and something hot skimmed my right shoulder, rocking me back as I raised my revolver. The blood roared so loud in my ears that I couldn't hear a thing.

I squeezed the trigger four times, putting two center of mass shots in each man. The first hit Byron in the shoulder, spinning him, while the second hit him in the neck.

Robbie's revolver wasn't accurate, but it did the trick. I had better luck with Tony. Both shots hit him in the chest, and he fell backwards. Adrenaline rocketed through my body. With those two down, I jumped up, my ears ringing and the room stinking like sulfur. I ran around the desk, holding the revolver in front of me and breathing heavily.

Karen was on the ground unmoving while Hannah leaned against the desk, a dented folding chair between her and the wood. Despite the shield, her shoulder bled, and there was a deep cut on her cheek. She waved her arms and screamed, but my ears rang so hard I couldn't hear. I shouted that I was deaf, so she slowed down, mouthing one word over and over.

Megan.

My stomach dropped, and any pain I felt in my shoulder disappeared as I sprinted out of the office and into the hallway. Their voices sounded hollow, but I heard Mike's men shout 'clear' as they searched offices in another part of the building. I ran in the opposite direction and crashed into the only room I could find. It was a narrow storage room with shelving made from elbow brackets and plywood. There was an empty Winnie the Pooh sleeping bag on the ground and a broken window on the far wall.

I dove through the window without thinking, catching my shirt and jacket on shards of glass still protruding from the frame. I escaped major lacerations and rolled onto a patch of gravel outside. Glass crunched against my back, but I hardly felt it. I put my hands on my knees to catch my breath. I was alone on the far side of the warehouse facing the tree line. I spotted movement in the woods ahead of me. I sprinted, my lungs burning and my arms pumping against my sides. I only had two shots left. I should have grabbed another gun before running out.

The woods were thicker than they looked, and I crashed into them at full speed, tripping on roots. Thorns and twigs bit into my hands and face as I fell. I ignored the abrasions and pushed off. I could hear leaves crunching and twigs breaking ahead of me, and I thought I heard my daughter crying.

'I'm coming.'

I screamed it as loud and as clear as I could, but it sounded more like an animal's snarl than my voice. It gave my quarry pause as he looked over his shoulder. I was almost close enough to make out his features in the moonlight. Megan kicked in his arms. My feet pounded against uneven ground. The soil was loose and light, so it felt almost as if I were running on snow. Tree branches whipped me in the face.

I chased him for another dozen yards, tripping twice, but never slowing down. The terrain rose in front of me, and the figure I was chasing slowed to a stop at the foot of the hill. It was Azrael. My daughter squirmed and cried as he held a knife to her throat.

I raised my firearm, my hand shaking.

'Stop moving, Megan,' I said between breaths. Sweat dripped into my eyes, down my nose, and across my brow. My chest and shoulders rose with each breath. 'It's okay, honey. I'm here.'

'Back off,' said Azrael. He pulled my daughter's chin up to expose her throat. 'I'll kill her.'

'It's over,' I said. My heart pounded from the exertion, but it was slowing. 'Let her go.'

'No.'

I took a step forward, and he jerked my daughter back. I put my hand up again, hoping to calm him.

'She's four years old. Her name is Megan. She likes to do mazes. She draws pictures of her family and sings songs she makes up with her mom. She's a child. Let her go.'

I inched forward, but Azrael didn't move. I didn't trust my firearm, and as tired as I was, I didn't think I could hold my arm steady enough to shoot him without hitting my daughter. My breath came out in quick spurts.

'Her best friend's name is Sarah. They go swimming.'

Azrael looked down, and I saw him shift his grip on the knife as I took another step forward.

'She wants to be a nurse like her mom. Her favorite food is guacamole. Come on. Let her go. She's a kid.'

Azrael shifted again, and I saw him swallow.

'Back off, man,' he said. 'I know what—'

He didn't finish speaking.

I heard the crack of a firearm and saw a cloud of blood before Azrael collapsed. Mike Bowers stood about ten yards to my right, a tactical rifle in his hands.

'Get your daughter.'

Chapter 27

The paramedics treated us as well as they could at the crime scene. I probably would have been fine going home, but since Hannah was pregnant, they wanted a physician to check her out before releasing her. The nurses in the ER patched up my minor cuts fairly well and a second-year intern was able to get some practice with stitches on my arm. Judging by the placement of bandages on my wife, we'd have matching shoulder scars. It was almost romantic. Megan didn't have a scratch on her, and with luck, she'd forget the whole thing eventually.

After we got patched up, the nurses wheeled Hannah into a private room for observation. Megan wouldn't leave her side, and the nurses didn't have the heart to pry her away. Me, on the other hand, they had no problem prying away. I stayed in a waiting room on an upholstered wooden chair and had what was probably the best night's sleep of my life.

We went home the next day, but not before I saw a newspaper in the lobby. Our bust made the front page. The Chief of Police, who had absolutely nothing to do with the events at Karen's warehouse, got most of the credit, but he did mention me. He claimed I was an invaluable undercover member of Mike Bowers' elite anticorruption task force investigating a potential law-enforcement connection with narcotics trafficking. It was nice to hear that I was invaluable. There was no mention of my wife and daughter or Karen Rea; apparently they weren't convenient for the department's narrative.

We took a cab home. I expected a detective or two to be on our front porch waiting for us, but it was empty. Hannah and I unloaded the munchkin and put her on the swing set in the backyard and started the long, arduous task of cleaning our house. Unfortunately, we didn't get very far because someone pounded on the plywood sheet that was our front door about ten minutes after we arrived.

It was Mike Bowers.

I came out of the kitchen and met him on the front porch. He wore black jeans and a navy blue shirt with a police shield on the chest, the same thing he had been wearing the night before. He half-smiled, half-grunted when he saw me.

'What can I do for you?' I asked.

'We need you to come in.'

I looked over my shoulder. I couldn't see it, but I heard the swing set creak as my daughter played on it.

'I've got a lot of stuff to do today. Maybe later.'

'I let you go last night so you could spend some time with your family,' he said. 'Please don't make me regret that.'

'Wow,' I said. 'I didn't expect a guilt trip. You seem like more of the browbeat type.'

Bowers crossed his arms.

'I've got a teenage daughter. I do what works. Now come on, I did you a favor. Please do me one.'

It's hard to say no to something like that.

'Give me five minutes to change.'

Bowers gave me a quick once-over. I was wearing a white T-shirt and the same jeans I had worn the night before. Both had blood stains. He shook his head.

'Keep the clothes on. They'll help.'

I wasn't sure what that meant, but I acquiesced and told my wife I'd be back as soon as I could. Bowers drove us to the station like an expectant father driving his wife to the hospital to give birth. He blasted through stoplights, disobeyed every posted speed limit, and tailed other motorists as if he were in the Indy 500.

'Are we in a hurry?' I asked, grabbing the handle on the door and squeezing.

'We need to get to her before the Feds do.'

That was cryptic enough to pique my interest.

We parked in a handicapped spot outside the station downtown and ran inside to the interrogation rooms. A crowd had formed outside of one. I recognized a couple of the spectators, including my former boss, Susan Mercer. I got a couple of pats on the back and congratulations when I walked up, but Susan didn't move. Her arms were across her chest as she stared at a computer monitor. Karen Rea was alone in an interrogation room. She wore an orange inmate's jumpsuit, and her hair was pulled back into a ponytail. There was a bruise on her cheek where something had hit her.

'Morning, Susan,' I said, stopping beside her. She looked at me and nodded. 'Surprised Jack Whittler isn't here.'

'That's complicated,' she said, not batting an eye. 'Ms Rea isn't talking. Lieutenant Bowers thought you might be able to convince her to speak.'

I looked at Bowers. He shrugged.

'I appreciate the vote of confidence,' I said. 'But I'm not law enforcement any more. I sent my resignation to Jack a few days ago.'

Susan smiled, but there was no levity in her eyes.

'Jack was arrested last night at an illegal poker game organized by a gangster. Because of that, he's no longer an employee of the City of Indianapolis, and as acting Prosecutor, I refuse your resignation. The US Attorney's office is picking Ms Rea up in half an hour, but I'd like to get what we can out of her first. This is your case, so get in there and talk to her.'

I didn't know if Susan could actually refuse my resignation, but I wasn't complaining. I rather liked being employed.

'How long has she been in there?' I asked.

'All night,' said Bowers. 'Hasn't said a thing other than to request food and water.'

'And she hasn't asked for an attorney?'

Susan glared at me. 'If she had, you wouldn't be here.'

I looked back at Bowers.

'Have you guys searched her house yet?' I asked.

'Didn't find much, but yeah,' he said.

'She had a picture of an Asian family on her desk. See if you can find it.'

Bowers motioned to one of the detectives I didn't recognize, and the younger man jogged down the hall, leaving us alone for a moment. Susan went back to staring at the computer monitor, and I went to find a coffee machine I thought I saw on my way in. Bowers followed along.

'You guys find out where Azrael lived yet?' I asked.

'He the guy who took your daughter?'

I nodded.

'Real name was Feng Rui,' said Bowers. 'Guy was a doctor, if you could believe that.'

'PhD or MD?'

'MD,' said Bowers.

'Did you find anything in his house?' I asked, finding my way to a commercial, steel coffee maker beside the detective bullpen's watercooler. I poured a cup and offered it to Bowers. He declined.

'About a hundred vials of blood in his refrigerator and a couple dozen of some other substance we're still analyzing.'

'Did you find any climbing gear?' I asked, taking a sip of the coffee and wincing. It was scorched and weak. I was tempted to pour it back in the carafe.

Bowers raised his eyebrows.

'What do you know?' he asked.

I shrugged.

'Whoever killed Rolando Diaz might have climbed through his window. Figured Azrael was good for it.'

Bowers' eyes glazed over for a moment.

'Yeah. We found nylon rope and some sort of harness in one of his closets. We assumed he was into kinky sex.'

'Might want to rethink that one.'

I took another sip of my coffee. It was as bad as the first; I could see why Bowers declined. When we got back to the interrogation room, it looked like Susan hadn't moved. I offered her my cup of coffee, but she smartly said no. We waited for another five minutes for the evidence guy to come back with the picture, and when he did, it had already been bagged and tagged. Hopefully it'd work.

'Wish me luck,' I said, taking the picture and holding it up. Susan's eyes bored into me. Tough crowd.

I walked into the interrogation room, and Karen immediately looked away.

'I have nothing to say to you, Detective.'

I put the picture and my coffee on the table and slid both to her.

'I got you some coffee,' I said.

She took a sip and made an ugly face before spitting it back.

'You can keep it,' she said, pushing the coffee towards me and pulling the photograph to herself.

'I'm guessing the baby is your nephew Feng,' I said. 'Are those two his parents?'

Karen nodded.

'Where are they now?' I asked.

She looked up. 'Dead.'

I waited for her to say something else, but she didn't.

'Why did you want me to go to Hong Kong?'

She didn't answer immediately, so I pulled out the chair opposite her and sat down to show that I was willing to wait as long as it took. Her eyes were black and hate-filled when she looked up, but I didn't think they were directed towards me. Not solely, at least. I softened my voice.

'Your nephew is dead, Karen, and my guess is that he died for a reason,' I said. 'Don't let him take it to his grave. What were you trying to do?'

Karen didn't answer. I waited a few minutes before glancing at the camera and shaking my head to let them know we needed to try another approach. She started speaking when I pushed my chair back.

'They killed them two months after this picture was taken.'

'Who?' I asked, settling back into the chair.

'Soldiers. They were kids,' she said, scrunching up her face as if she didn't understand. 'Twenty years old, and they executed them for publishing a newsletter about democracy.'

'This was in China?' I asked.

Karen nodded.

'So you wanted revenge,' I said.

Karen shook her head vehemently.

'I wanted to make sure they couldn't do the same thing to anyone else,' she said. 'You should understand that. You have a family.'

I nodded as if I had stepped off the bus at Crazytown, too.

'But things went wrong and Rachel Haddad died,' I said, leaning forward. I glanced at the camera in the hopes that they were recording the session.

'Miss Haddad was an accident,' said Karen. 'My

nephew was experimenting with alternative shipping methods, and some of our products were mixed together. We sold irradiated blood to encourage kids to join us. That blood got mixed with a shipment, and Rachel died after drinking it. It was a mistake.'

Somehow I didn't think that would comfort her family.

'What about Robbie Cutting?'

Karen sat up straighter.

'He walked in while some of our people searched his room. Another regrettable mistake.'

'There seem to be a lot of those going around,' I said. 'So vampires were just theatrics?'

'People will do anything for you if you give them something to believe in.'

I glanced at the camera suspended from the ceiling in the corner of the room.

'Why'd you pick Indianapolis?' I asked.

Karen shrugged. 'Same reason Fedex and UPS build hubs here. Half the country's population is within a six-hour drive.'

That made sense.

'So what were you trying to do?' I asked. 'I know you weren't after money.'

She stared at me intently.

'I wanted them to feel the same pain I felt.'

'You wanted who to feel what?'

She looked straight at me.

'I wanted everyone in the Chinese government to feel the pain my nephew and I feel every day. I wanted them to suffer as we did.'

Our eyes stayed locked, but Karen didn't say anything else for a moment.

'And you thought you could develop a virus that would do that for you?'

Karen looked down at her hands, a wistful smile on her face.

'I didn't think, Mr Rashid. I did. Now I need someone to deliver it.'

As soon as Karen finished speaking, the room's only door flew open and the two FBI agents I had seen with Bowers burst in.

I stood quickly, but Karen hardly moved. Susan walked in shortly after, her cheeks flushed and her lips compressed to a thin line. She held up her hand, stopping me from speaking.

'Dr Rea, you are to go with these gentlemen,' she said, before turning to me. 'Detective Rashid, you are to sit there and shut up.'

At least Susan was direct. I waited to speak until the FBI agents and Karen were out of the room. I stood up. Susan cut me off as soon as I started to speak.

'I appreciate the work you've done on this, Ash, but we don't have the resources to handle this case.'

'You're kidding. Karen was confessing. What more do we need?'

Susan looked at the officers outside.

'Shut the door and turn off the camera,' she said. Someone complied, at least about the door. I sat on the edge of the table, putting Susan and me at the same height. She leaned into me despite the room's privacy. 'We seized more than eight million dollars in cash from Karen's warehouse last night in a joint operation with the local FBI field office. We're announcing that later today. What we're not announcing is that we also found a very sophisticated lab. We're not announcing that because I got an offer from a Deputy Director of the FBI. The federal government gets the case, we get the money. All we have to do is shut up about everything.'

'They found something,' I said.

Susan nodded.

'And it scared them enough to give up a multimillion dollar seizure to make it disappear,' she said.

I mulled the situation over.

'I don't suppose I get any of that money.'

Susan didn't blink for about a minute and a half, but then she burst into a full-blown laugh. A simple no would have sufficed. She left the room a moment later, still chuckling intermittently. I got a ride home after that from Mike Bowers. Neither of us said anything until he pulled up to my mailbox. Hannah was on the front porch, waving at us, while Megan drew something on the front walkway with chalk.

'That's a good-looking family,' said Bowers, nodding. 'You're a lucky man.'

I nodded and stayed in the car. I rubbed the back of my neck, trying to formulate the question in my mind.

'I got an email a few days ago before all this went down,' I said. 'Are you "a friend"?'

Bowers chuckled.

'Don't look too much into that,' he said. 'Olivia Rhodes had been under investigation for months, but the Prosecutor's Office had been dragging their heels about an indictment. We suspected she was fucking Jack Whittler.'

'So you used me to get her?'

Bowers shrugged. 'You use the tools at your disposal,' he said. 'I read your file. I knew you wouldn't quit. I didn't expect this, but it worked out in the end.'

'Then why'd you arrest me and beat down my door?'

He tilted his head to the side and stuck out his lower lip.

'I never really liked you,' he said. 'And I didn't trust you until Rea took your kids.'

I wanted to punch him, but instead I climbed out of the car and shut the door behind me. Bowers drove off as soon as I got out. Megan ran towards me, her arms outstretched.

'I drew the sun,' she said. I picked her up and examined her artwork on the sidewalk. It looked more like a soccer ball than the sun, but I wasn't going to correct her. I put her down near her drawing where she promptly started drawing stick figures that I presumed would later be flaming astronauts due to their proximity to a star.

'The mail came, and there's a letter for you from the law school,' said Hannah. 'How was your meeting?'

'It was interesting,' I said, already walking toward the kitchen door. 'I'll tell you more in a minute.'

As Hannah said, the mail had arrived, and I did have a letter from the law school. It was about as well written as the fine print that accompanied my credit card statement, so I had to read through it three times to understand it. Since the Dean hadn't been able to get in touch with me following my outburst in Professor Ruiz's class, the Judiciary Board met to decide my fate without me. Apparently they knew Ruiz was a dick because they decided not to kick me out of school. Instead, they dropped me from the class and requested I avoid taking it from him that winter. That was one request I could accommodate.

I walked back outside and met Hannah on the front

porch. I didn't know if I wanted to go back to school or even if I wanted to go back to work. All I knew was that my family was safe and that's all I cared about. I sat beside Hannah on the front porch and put my hand on her knee.

'Anything interesting?' she asked.

'Nothing life changing,' I said.

Hannah slipped her hand over mine, and we watched Megan draw for a few minutes. She had been crying in my arms twelve hours earlier, and now she was playing without a care in the world. I wished everything was so easily fixed.

'Did you call your sister yet?'

Hannah nodded. 'She and Jack are fine. A little surprised we weren't home when they came back yesterday, but fine.'

I breathed out and leaned back.

'Good,' I said. 'I was thinking of taking some time off. Maybe we can go on vacation.'

Hannah squeezed my hand. 'I'd like that.'

I didn't have a drink that night; I didn't need to. I knew that eventually I'd have the dreams again. It might be a week or even a month, but eventually they'd come back. Probably the next time I tell someone that they've lost the person they hold most dear in the world. I'd see their faces and share in pain so profound and all-encompassing that there is no escape. It's my penance for the mistakes I've made. But I didn't have to face it right away. For a brief while, I had been granted a peace I couldn't earn myself.